The Interface Man

THE INTERFACE MAN

A Colin Thane, Scottish Crime Squad Case

Bill Knox

Century

LONDON SYDNEY AUCKLAND JOHANNESBURG

This edition first published in Great Britain by
Century, an imprint of Century Hutchinson Ltd,
Brookmount House, 62–65 Chandos Place,
London WC2N 4NW

Century Hutchinson Australia Pty Ltd,
P O Box 89–91 Albion Street, Surry Hills, NSW 2010

Century Hutchinson New Zealand Ltd
P O Box 40–086, Glenfield, Auckland 10, New Zealand

Century Hutchinson South Africa (Pty) Ltd
P O Box 337, Berglvei, 2012 South Africa

British Library Cataloguing in Publication Data

Knox, Bill, 1928–
    The interface man.
    I. Title
    823′.914[F]

ISBN 0 7126 1913 5

Typeset by Deltatype Ellesmere Port
Printed and bound in Great Britain by
Mackays of Chatham PLC, Chatham, Kent

For Holly and Kerry

As before, this story varies in some aspects of detail from the real-life Scottish Crime Squad's operational methods. They prefer it that way. I have been told why.

B. K., Glasgow 1989

Prelude

The high Cumbrian hill country seemed still and empty under the pale September moonlight. There was no wind and the sky that formed such a soft blue background was free of cloud. A dog fox barked harshly in the night and the sound carried, causing a nervous stirring among a flock of blackface ewes in one of the fenced-off lower grazings.

Then there was another sound, at first a gentle vibration coming from a distance but building in the still air. It came from the railway line that glinted in the moonlight, rails carving their own route through the high country with only a lone hill-shepherd's cottage to overlook them.

The sound grew then became an approaching roar of pulsing, rushing high-speed power. The blackface ewes ignored it, didn't even bother to look round, as the brightly lit British Rail Intercity express and its long line of passenger coaches thundered past, heading north towards Carlisle, scheduled on from there and over the English border into Scotland.

The Royal Scot service on the west coast route from London to Glasgow was part of the scenery as far as the sheep were concerned. The dog fox on the hill was much more important.

The train racing past had the standard make-up of twelve passenger coaches behind its big electric locomotive, with the restaurant car located third from the front. A round-faced, slightly bald man in his thirties looked out from one window seat, watching the moonlit scenery as it passed outside. He was alone at his table, in fact the

1

restaurant car was almost empty. The staff had even had time to stop and gossip with him between servings.

But it was September, always a quiet month for London–Glasgow travel, and it was Thursday evening. That was always the quietest evening of any week. The whole train had only a thin scatter of passengers along its length.

The round-faced man's name was Robert Haston. He had enjoyed his meal, he had finished his coffee, and he nursed what remained of an after-dinner brandy. For a moment he considered his own reflection in the window glass with a mild satisfaction. It had been a good two-day trip south, now he was on his way home. His time in London had been long enough to sort out that contract problem. Someone had been trying to alter the agreed terms, had obviously hoped it wouldn't be noticed. Except that when it came to buying, selling or creating electronic control systems, Robert Haston was an expert. He'd made that plain, in a mild, amiable way, and the problem had suddenly ceased to exist.

He took another glance outside, roughly recognizing the countryside, knowing he was already more than two thirds of the way home to Glasgow.

The train lurched round a curve, the brandy left in his glass almost danced. That didn't trouble him. Whatever happened, he wasn't in an aircraft. Robert Haston was terrified of flying, even the thought of boarding one of the Boeing jets on the London–Glasgow shuttle route could leave him white-knuckled with fear. He had tried hypnotism to overcome that fear, it hadn't helped. Alcohol as a remedy only made things worse.

Regular travel to London was involved in the way Robert Haston earned a living. But it was rail travel. The Intercity service did the journey in around five hours, reaching speeds of up to one hundred and ten miles an hour. That, as far as he was concerned, was fast enough.

He sighed and glanced at his wristwatch. When the train reached Glasgow his wife would be at the station with the car. Haston smiled a little. They had been married for just over a year, and life was good. He even liked his job – it could be dull, his earnings were modest, but he could sleep at night.

What had happened in his past was behind him and was going to stay that way.

An approach had been made, the way he'd known it might come some day. He had been frightened, then tempted. But he had turned it down. To hell with the past.

Robert Haston swallowed the last few drops of brandy in his glass. He had already paid the bill. Rising, matching his movements to the sway of the train, he left the restaurant car and started back along the coaches. His reserved seat was near the rear of the train. That was where he had left his briefcase and his small suitcase, and he was halfway through reading a paperback war adventure story he'd picked up at a Euston bookstall on his way to board the Intercity.

Each passenger coach had sliding internal doors front and rear, each hissed open automatically as Haston reached it then closed again with another hiss as he passed through. The end-spaces where each coach joined the next held toilet compartments, baggage racks, and a standing area beside the main external doors. They were where the other noises of the speeding train were loudest.

Robert Haston passed through three almost empty coaches in turn. As he left the third coach he heard the partition begin to close behind him, suddenly jerk open for a moment, then close again.

Someone was coming behind him. It hardly registered with Haston. His way towards the sliding door into the fourth coach was being blocked by a large fat man wearing a dark coat. The fat man was carrying a large portable radio-cassette player which was blasting out some pop number. He had bad teeth, and they showed in a strange grin as he gave a small nod which seemed directed somewhere behind Haston. At the same time he took a step forward.

Robert Haston felt a sudden panic. Before he could do anything the fat man took another half-step nearer with that radio still playing. But it was the second man, a mere glimpse of a figure to the rear, who attacked first. An arm went round Haston's face, a coat sleeve jammed hard against his mouth. At the same moment Haston felt a paralysing blow strike low in his back.

It was the fat man's turn. He drove a knee viciously into Haston's stomach. The edge of his free hand chopped their victim hard on the side of the head. Then, before Haston could even realize what was happening, he was being bundled towards the nearest of those swaying outer doors.

The door opened in a fierce rush of air. Then Haston had gone, tumbling into the night, and the door slammed shut again.

It had taken six seconds from start to finish.

Saying nothing, the two attackers separated. The fat man switched off the tape player and headed forward towards the restaurant car. He hadn't eaten since London. His companion, who was tall and thin, continued on his way towards the rear of the train.

There had been no witness. No one missed Robert Haston until the Intercity reached journey's end at Glasgow's Central Station and a puzzled Joan Haston finally came looking for her husband along the emptied train.

She found his briefcase, his suitcase, even the opened paperback he'd been reading. Twice more she checked the length of the train then spent several more and more worried minutes searching the station concourse area. Then, at last, she went to the glass-fronted office where a sign said British Transport Police.

Twelve hours later, midway through the Friday morning, Robert Haston's body was found close to the track in one of those folds in the Cumbrian hills.

The shepherd who found him had been out with a dog and a shotgun, looking for the fox that had killed yet another two ewes during the night. Whistling in his dog, fighting down an urge to vomit, the shepherd cursed. But he had seen worse sights when he'd been a corporal in Two Para in the Falklands.

He looked again. There were signs that the body had been hit by more than one train.

Shrugging, the shepherd tucked his shotgun under one elbow and set off on the long trudge towards the nearest telephone. This wasn't his problem.

1

It was another Thursday, four weeks later and into October.

The day had been pleasant, warm and dry at Glasgow Airport. Now, just twenty minutes before midnight, a chill breeze had sprung up from the north east. The breeze came in gusts strong enough to swirl clouds of fine grit and rubbish across the lines of vehicles still patterning the airport's well-lit parking areas. Anyone moving out there was glad to reach shelter again.

But it was warm and bright and busy inside the main terminal building, particularly in the International Arrivals area. A British Airways Boeing 737 had landed after a scheduled flight from Malaga in Spain and had unloaded about one hundred and thirty passengers. Most of them were returning tourists who clutched plastic bags filled with duty-free allowances or souvenirs. They queued to pass the immigration desk at Passport Control, dribbling on from there down the long corridor which led to baggage reclaim and Customs.

The new arrivals had an audience they didn't know about, three men positioned behind a one-way observation window in the duty immigration supervisor's office. One was the duty supervisor, a small and slightly worried figure.

'Number two desk, Superintendent,' he said suddenly. 'We have someone.'

The immigration officer at number two desk had just paused, taken out a folded white handkerchief and used it to mop his brow. It was the agreed signal. He put the handkerchief away and took an apparently uninterested flick through the pages of the passport in front of him.

'Well?' The supervisor was impatient as much as anxious.

'He matches.' Detective Superintendent Colin Thane took another glance at the Records head-and-shoulders photograph he held cupped in one hand then looked again through the one-way observation window. The passenger standing at desk two was in his mid-forties, tall, tanned and whipcord thin. He had sharp features with high cheekbones and short, fair, receding hair. He wore a knitted white cardigan over a sports shirt and plaid trousers. The man's name was John William Gort but a telex from Spanish police at Malaga reported that his ticket had been booked in the name of John Williams and he had travelled on a passport which used the same name. Thane saw the supervisor's continued concern and nodded. 'He's our man.'

'Good.' The supervisor made it a sigh of relief. Outside the one-way window the tanned, sharp-featured man had had his passport returned and was past the immigration desks. 'What happens now?'

'Not a lot – we hope.' Thane looked past the duty supervisor to the thin, younger man standing behind him. 'Francey, he's yours. Low-key.'

'Like we don't exist.' Detective Sergeant Francey Dunbar grinned a little.

They were a contrasting pair. Thane was tall and in his early forties. He had grey eyes, thick and slightly unruly dark hair, and wore a lightweight lovat suit with a grey shirt and a lightly patterned brown tie. He had an athletic build without looking heavy. His sergeant was in his twenties and was also dark-haired, but with a thin droop of a bandit moustache. He wore a creased leather blouson jacket over a grey tee-shirt and tan trousers. A thick silver identity bracelet, the disc deliberately blank, clinked gently on his left wrist when he moved.

'You know where I'll be,' said Thane.

'I know.' Dunbar crossed to the rear door of the supervisor's office. It led out into a corridor which wasn't a passenger area. Dunbar left that way, closing the door behind him.

The supervisor drew a deep breath and turned to Thane again.

'Do I get to be told what this is about?'

'Maybe later.' Thane was vague.

'Don't count on it?' The supervisor's voice was wry.

Colin Thane gave a sympathetic grimace. It was something he couldn't properly answer. But Immigration were co-operating, HM Customs were co-operating, airport management were co-operating.

The important thing about the whole operation wasn't just John William Gort but who – if anyone – was waiting to meet him when he left the airport. That had been the priority for weeks now, ever since the first hint that Gort might be flying in.

'This Gort or whatever his name – ' the duty supervisor tried again ' – is he important?'

'He might be.'

John William Gort was a skilled professional criminal. Even three years away from the scene, three years spent owning and running a beach bar on the Costa del Sol in apparent semi-retirement, couldn't alter the fact that he still had almost consultant status when it came to carving a way through electronic security systems or defeating computers.

He had a nickname, the Interface Man. The label had come from a robbery squad detective and was awarded with a reluctant respect.

Gort had been able to choose where and when he worked. His last two jobs before heading for Spain were believed to have been a bullion robbery at London's Gatwick Airport and an even more spectacular break-in at a bank vault in Frankfurt. But there was no proof.

'I'd like more than a "might be",' grumbled the supervisor.

'You're not alone,' said Thane.

Even though he was joint deputy commander of the elite Scottish Crime Squad, it was only that evening when Thane had suddenly found himself thrown in at the deep end of the John Gort investigation. Right up until then it had belonged exclusively to the Squad's commander, Detective Chief Superintendent Hart.

Thane had been two hundred miles to the north, where his evidence had helped to convict two drug smugglers. Their trial had finished at a late sitting of Inverness High Court, still held in historic old Inverness Castle.

He had been waiting for the pair to be sentenced when Jack Hart's first frantic telephone call reached him.

Hart's wife Gloria had been hurt in an accident at home and had been taken to the specialized head injury unit at the Southern General. But Hart had also just been told that John Gort had started out for Malaga airport, and Hart's other deputy, Tom Maxwell, was on annual leave visiting relatives in Canada.

'I need you here.' Hart had said it without frills. 'Cover tonight's situation, any way you can.'

Getting back to Glasgow had meant two and a quarter hours of driving down the A9 as if the Devil was chasing his tail. Thane had radioed ahead as soon as he neared the city, and had gone straight to the airport. Francey Dunbar met him there, bringing a scribble of notes including one left by Jack Hart. They didn't make happy reading. For once, Hart and some other people had been caught wrong-footed. Gort hadn't been expected to leave Spain for at least another week.

9

Thane had taken time off to make a brief telephone call home, to tell his wife Mary that his plans had been altered. Hart's secretary had already called her.

From there, it came down to rushing through half-made arrangements. It meant bringing in cops who knew little or nothing about what was going on. Things didn't so much slot into place as somehow fall that way.

Thane's thoughts had strayed. But at least the duty supervisor had given up probing. Thanking the man, he left the office by that rear door. A narrow internal stairway took him down behind one of the flight check-in areas. From there it was a moment's walk to the nearest exit.

Outside, a new gust of wind cut through Thane's lightweight suit as he set off along the front of the terminal building. He passed a scatter of parked vehicles then reached the one he wanted. A grey Fiat from the Scottish Crime Squad pool, it had been parked there for almost an hour. The position gave a clear view of the exits likely to be used by any passenger arriving on an international flight.

He had been seen. The figure in the Fiat's front passenger seat reached back and a rear door swung open. Thane got aboard. Up front, two faces turned towards him as he closed the door and sank back into the broad rear seat.

'We're in business,' he assured them. 'Francey is bird-dogging our Mr Gort.'

'So we can go home, sir?' Detective Constable Sandra Craig, who was in her twenties, slim and red-haired, gave a cheerfully malicious grin. She was eating a cheese sandwich and she pointed what was left of it in the general direction of their driver. 'What do you think, Joe?'

'I keep telling you, girl, I'm not paid to think.' Detective Constable Joe Felix was a plump, middle-aged

Crime Squad veteran with a round, mild-looking face and a nature to match. Like Francey Dunbar, these two were part of Thane's regular team and worked well together. For the moment Felix was being suitably patient. 'Anyway, Francey isn't exactly on his own.'

Joe Felix was one of the few people alive who could call Sandra 'girl' in that kind of way and remain intact. But Felix was right. Francey Dunbar had two other Crime Squad men with him inside the terminal and an additional plain-clothes back-up from the airport's resident police unit. They were all needed. Any airport had a layout like a rabbit warren, riddled with potential escape routes.

'What about out here?' asked Thane.

'Everything peaceful so far.' Felix answered him then paused with minimal interest as a motorcycle muttered past. He sighed. 'Someone's courier rider. We saw him arrive.'

'Ten minutes ago.' Sandra took another bite at her cheese sandwich. 'I suppose there are worse jobs, if you like bikes.'

Francey Dunbar liked bikes – wrong word, decided Thane. Dunbar owned and cherished a big red BMW motorcycle and always seemed to have a different girl on the pillion.

He gave another casual glance as the motorcycle headed on for the airport exit road. It looked like one of the Japanese makes and wherever it had been that day had left it filthy with mud and road dirt. The registration plates were unreadable. The rider wore stained black leathers, black lace-up boots and a black crash helmet with a full-length spaceman-style face visor. A canvas delivery haversack was slung across youthfully thin shoulders.

'More action behind us,' said Joe Felix laconically. 'What have we got now?'

11

Thane forgot about the motorcycle. A new set of headlights had appeared in the Fiat's rear-view mirror.

It was only an airline courtesy coach. It stopped and the driver climbed out, lit a cigarette, then headed into the terminal. As he vanished the Fiat's radio came to life.

'Sandra or Joe. Is the boss with you?' Francey Dunbar's voice came over as a hoarse whisper against a background mush of airport static. He was using a small handset and an earpiece.

Thane took the Fiat's microphone from Sandra. 'Here, Francey.'

'A small delay,' reported Dunbar. 'The flight baggage is just arriving.'

'At least it got there.' Thane had once lost a holiday suitcase that didn't. 'How do things look beyond the Customs barrier?'

'The usual.' Dunbar didn't sound enthusiastic. 'We've a few hundred friends and relatives waiting to collect people and get them home.' He paused then grunted. 'There's more baggage arriving now. I'll get back to you, sir.'

The static returned to an empty hiss.

'Who'd want to be a sergeant?' asked Joe Felix with a mock solemnity. 'The worries, the responsibility – '

'Give it a rest, Joe,' said Sandra bleakly.

'I didn't mean to annoy anyone.' Felix's plump face showed innocent concern, then he turned to Thane. 'Uh – did you know that Sandra is planning to sit the sergeants' test, sir?'

'No.' It meant a lot of off-duty study time, with police regulations and the legal codes becoming more complex every day. It had stopped being enough just to be good at nailing villains. 'When?'

'They'll let me know, sir.' Sandra glared at Joe Felix. 'Some people don't approve.'

'I'm neutral,' said Felix mildly. 'Nobody can make me

12

– try to be a sergeant, I mean.' He thumbed in the direction of the terminal building. 'Show me your average sergeant and I reckon I'd have more in common with this Gort character.'

Thane grinned. Joe Felix was the Squad's unofficial electrical expert. His desk was usually a cluttered pile of everything from broken toasters to faulty video recorders, each brought in by someone for repair.

'Go on,' encouraged Thane. A couple of airline staff appeared at one of the terminal doors then went back in after looking around. 'What's the rest of it, Joe?'

'I'd call it basic.' Felix ignored the way Sandra was bristling in the darkness beside him. 'The way I see it, sir, most people are troops by nature and most people like being troops. A lot fewer people are bosses – some are born that way, others get lucky. Troops matter, bosses matter. But sergeants?' He gave a slow shake of his head. 'Sergeants aren't one thing or another. Half the sergeants I know seem to be queuing to be issued with nervous breakdowns. Who wants that kind of life?'

'Some people have ambitions,' snapped Sandra.

'If you've ambitions you shouldn't be a cop.' Joe Felix was in one of his occasional trouble-stirring moods. 'You want to be out with a sample case and wearing a dress that shows plenty of everything. Go knocking on doors and selling things – '

He stopped. The radio was muttering again.

'Gort has his luggage, one suitcase,' reported Dunbar softly. 'He has passed through Customs, heading out. I'm following.' They heard a sudden muttered curse. 'Every damned passenger seems to have a fan club waiting out there. Who else has Gort? Come in.'

'I have him.' Another voice, one of the airport's plain-clothes officers, cut in on the same frequency. 'He's still heading out, but with a woman from out of the crowd. Blonde hair, white coat, knee-length boots.'

13

'Got them now.' There was tension in Dunbar's voice. 'They're almost clear of the crush. Only the woman with him so far – no sign of anyone else.'

'I'm looking down on them.' It was another new voice, but one Thane recognized. Bert Halley, one of the Crime Squad detail, had been placed at a balcony viewpoint. 'The woman is mid-thirties, shading towards plump, smallish – maybe around five foot two.' Halley paused. 'You can add a small scar or maybe a deep dimple on the left side of her chin, enough gold chains around her neck like she buys them wholesale.'

In the Fiat, Sandra and Joe Felix exchanged a quick, puzzled glance. Their small war was forgotten.

'Do you know her, sir?' Sandra asked.

'Maybe.' Thane clicked the microphone he still held. 'Francey, there's still no one else involved?'

'No one.'

'Right.' One of the scribbled notes sent him by Jack Hart was a brief list of some of Gort's past known associates – half a dozen or so names, each with a sentence or two of background. 'Forget the hair colour. She's our one.'

'No change in what we're doing?' asked Dunbar.

'No change.'

'They're on their way to the exit doors,' warned Dunbar. 'No interest in the bus stance or the taxi rank, so he must have a car. We'll get back to you.'

The radio noise died. Thane handed the microphone back to Sandra Craig, then realized he still hadn't really answered her.

'Our blonde used to be a brunette, and that mark on her chin is a scar – no dimple,' he told her tersely. 'Her name is Janey Peters and she used to be Gort's live-in personal assistant. People thought they split up a few months before he got out to Spain.'

'Tricky things, women,' grimaced Felix.

14

'True.' Sandra Craig gave a dispassionate shrug. 'Some even want to be sergeants.'

The first passengers from the Malaga flight began emerging from the terminal's brightly lit exits. The difference in temperature compared with that on the Costa had to be cruel when felt through a light cotton top, and some were shivering. One girl, parading her tan in minuscule shorts, suddenly began using a man's jacket as an extra skirt.

'There.' Joe Felix pointed.

John Gort and Janey Peters had just appeared from the building. A tan-coloured suitcase in one hand, Gort had his free arm draped across the blonde woman's shoulders. Wasting no time, yet without appearing to hurry, they weaved a way through the general bustle of people and vehicles then struck away, across towards the general parking area.

For Thane it was another waiting time as he lost sight of the couple again. He knew Francey Dunbar and the other men were out there somewhere. He would hear soon enough. The airport's main parking area usually had two separate exit points, each pay-and-leave style, operator controlled, and with a ticket system. But there was nothing unusual about an exit being temporarily closed for maintenance work.

One had closed a full hour before the Spanish flight was due in and had stayed that way. The remaining exit was brightly lit and clearly visible from the Fiat. Some vehicles were already leaving through it.

The rest would be a familiar-enough Crime Squad routine. Once Janey Peters' car was located the Fiat would be the first to tail it when it left the airport. Thane would stay aboard with Felix and Sandra. A second Crime Squad car would collect Francey Dunbar and some of the others, then follow. Between them, switching position one with another every now and again to reduce

15

any suspicion, they could keep Gort and the woman sewn up.

Night made it easier.

'Sir.' Joe Felix might have been reading his mind, but for a different reason. 'You're still leaving your own car here?'

'Till later.' Thane nodded.

'This place has had its share of late-night thieving.' Detective Constable Felix was at his helpful best. 'Last I heard, Criminal Intelligence reckon there are at least two new pro teams working around Glasgow. Anything they steal gets dismantled, stripped down.'

'Like they had a shopping list?' Sandra Craig showed an interest.

'With cash customers waiting.' Felix fiddled a moment with the Fiat's rear-view mirror. 'The usual wheels and batteries are incidentals to these people. There's a TV executive who had the front passenger door stolen from his Mercedes, someone else who lost the seats from a new Jaguar – '

'I could use new seats,' mused Thane. His current vehicle from the Crime Squad fleet was a hard-used Ford with some visible scars. 'Any time.'

'Seriously – ' began Felix again, then saw he had lost his audience, sighed, and gave up.

Thane's thoughts were back with Gort and the woman.

Things wouldn't, couldn't stop with them. The Inter-face Man had always operated as skill for hire. Other people came up with the basic plan, other people always took the real risks. John Gort arrived as a well-paid mercenary, a very expensive specialist.

Something very big had to be moving. There was no other way Gort could have been persuaded back from the Spanish beach bar.

The radio was muttering again, even sooner than Thane had expected.

16

'We have the car,' reported Sergeant Francey Dunbar in a calm, unhurried voice. 'It's a white Volkswagen hatchback, the woman driving. Gort and his luggage are aboard and they're about ready to roll.'

Thane used the Fiat's radio. Joe Felix already had the car started.

'Where are you now?' demanded Thane.

'Back with our own wheels.' Dunbar paused a moment. 'They're moving, heading out. We'll hang back then do the same.'

It was only twenty seconds later when they saw the white Volkswagen as it coasted up to join the line at the exit gate. Within moments other cars were waiting behind it. Cold engines pushed out thick jets of white exhaust to be whipped away by the wind.

'Sandra.' Thane tossed her the microphone. 'Ask Francey if he is getting a PNC check on the Volkswagen.'

As the redhead called the other Crime Squad car, Thane allowed himself a slight grin. Dunbar would snarl to himself at such a basic reminder, but it was something which could easily be forgotten.

Feed the English-based Police National Computer a vehicle registration number and within eleven seconds it should advise if the vehicle was on any British force's 'reported stolen' list. Move on from there, key an additional instruction, give it a little longer, and it would produce details of the registered owner. Any delays were because of the human links involved.

Meanwhile, the Volkswagen was going to be next for the exit. Thane caught Joe Felix's glance in the rear-view mirror and nodded.

'In your own time, Joe. But don't scare them.'

The Volkswagen emerged, blending into the pace of a light flow of traffic heading away from the airport. Humming under his breath, Joe Felix let two other cars and an aggressively driven taxi get between before he set the Fiat moving in the same direction. The plump, round-faced driver was still humming. The tune sounded off-key but vaguely familiar.

'Must you?' asked Sandra wearily.

'Sorry.' Felix stopped humming but beamed. 'That was Bach, girl – culture. If you want to be a sergeant you need culture.'

'Thank you, Joe.' Her teeth showed in a smile like a quick slash to the jugular, then she turned to Thane. 'Francey says he has passed on a PNC request. As soon as he hears, we'll know.'

'Good – ' Thane stopped short then shaped a soft curse.

On ahead where the road became a T junction, with the main route prominently signposted to the right, the Volkswagen had made a last-moment turn to the left. Everything else was swinging to the right. Suddenly, the whole safety pad of vehicles that had separated them ceased to exist.

Surprised and flustered, Felix put the Fiat into a similar left turn. The Volkswagen's tail lights were now a bare three hundred yards ahead, the car almost loitering along a narrow ribbon of otherwise empty road.

'Warn Francey,' ordered Thane.

He heard Sandra call Dunbar's car, somewhere out of sight behind them, while Joe Felix concentrated on trying to keep the gap between them and the Volkswagen.

Thane knew this road. It was a local short-cut, a snaking minor road which ran near the airport's eastern perimeter fence. The Fiat's headlights were catching warehouse buildings and huts, the shapes of fuel storage tanks and the silhouettes of a line of small private aircraft, left for the night like lifeless bats outside a flying club.

Suddenly Sandra Craig yelped a warning. Then Joe

18

Felix was braking and wrenching at his steering wheel while a big, tall-sided delivery van without lights came lurching out of the shadows of a warehouse building. It stopped at a right angle across the road, impossible to avoid.

'Hold on – ' Felix made it a shout, still trying, still braking, the Fiat's tyres screaming.

Thane had a moment to register the van's fancy striped paintwork and the words 'Magic Bakerman' in large lettering. Then the Crime Squad car hit the van, spinning clear in a tearing of metal and smashing of glass. He was thrown hard across the rear seat. They had stopped, the Fiat's engine had stalled, one of their headlights still lit the scene but pointed skywards.

He pulled himself upright. The two in front were moving, Sandra nursing her head and dazed, Felix beginning to struggle to open the driver's door. Thane was first out, caught a brief glimpse of the Volkswagen's tail lights disappearing ahead, then turned towards the Magic Bakerman van.

Before he had taken two steps the van's cab door flew open and the driver sprang out and began running. He was short and he was stocky, and he had a knitted ski-cap mask, complete with eye-holes, pulled down over his face.

The masked man wasn't alone. As he ran down the road and Thane started after him, a motorcycle engine rasped to life then the machine appeared from another patch of shadow just ahead, to stop on the road. Still in black leathers and a black helmet, the rider even had the same canvas delivery satchel slung over those thin shoulders that Thane had noticed back at the airport.

The van driver ran faster. Without a word the motorcyclist reached into the satchel and brought out the unmistakable shape of a sawn-off shotgun. The short twin muzzles swung in a tight arc to point directly at Thane.

19

The warning was clear – and Colin Thane stopped where he was. As the van driver leapt on the pillion seat, the rider returned the weapon to the satchel. Then the machine snarled to full life and raced away in the same direction the Volkswagen had taken.

Thane was still standing, still staring, when Sandra Craig reached him. Blood was making a thin trickle down her face from a cut somewhere above her hairline. Joe Felix, limping painfully, was not far behind.

'I saw it,' said the redhead. She scowled. 'For a horrible moment I thought you wanted to be a hero.'

'Always be polite to a sawn-off shotgun,' said Thane. 'It's good manners.' The motorcycle had gone. He winced at the blood on Sandra's head. 'What happened to you?'

'I bounced off the windscreen.' She considered the damaged delivery van. 'I'd say the Magic Bakerman is going to need a magic repair shop before he gets back on the road.'

Joe Felix arrived. He had slammed his knee against the Fiat's steering column, his limp showed how much it hurt, but nothing seemed actually broken.

'They had us spotted, I suppose – right back at the airport,' he said in a resigned voice.

'That doesn't win you a prize.' Thane nodded towards the Fiat, which looked as crumpled as the van. 'What about our radio?'

'It died,' said Felix sadly.

Another car had arrived behind the Fiat. A large, smartly dressed woman, a stranger, had climbed out and was coming towards him.

'Anyone hurt?' she demanded in a loud, brusque voice.

Thane shook his head. He could see two other sets of headlights approaching, both beginning to slow.

'Cuts and bruises, nothing more.'

'Good.' The large woman sniffed at the crashed vehicles. 'You'll need to clear the road.' Pausing, she frowned. 'I didn't see what happened, but shouldn't someone call the police?'

The other vehicles were stopping. One was the second Crime Squad car and Francey Dunbar was the first figure to emerge. Thane recognized his sergeant's mop of dark hair and battered leather jacket, then saw him start to hurry over.

'I think we should get the police,' said the large woman for a second time.

'We're here,' said Thane sadly and showed his warrant card.

'Reassuring, isn't it?' The woman was coldly sarcastic. 'Well, I presume you'll still start by clearing this road – then I can get home.'

She marched back to her car. As she left, a bewildered Dunbar arrived and stared around.

'What happened?' he asked. 'What – ?'

'Everything,' snarled Thane, cutting him short. 'Don't ask – listen.'

He told the brief story. For once Francey Dunbar had sense enough to keep his young, hawk-like face totally blank.

'Bad luck.' Dunbar sucked an edge of his thin straggle of moustache. 'All I know is that Sandra was on the radio one moment, then she wasn't.'

'They're well clear.' Thane got rid of some of his disgust by kicking a small stone. It hit the side of the Magic Bakerman van and he felt better. 'We've no chance with the motorcycle – not now. What about the Volkswagen?'

'Not stolen.' Regretfully, Dunbar shook his head. 'Not according to the PNC listings, sir. The read-out has the registered owner as a doctor over in Edinburgh.'

'Then we check – like is he still the owner? Then I

21

want anything known about Janey Peters.' Thane winced as the large woman impatiently sounded her car horn. 'But we'll sort out this mess first – before that damned female really gets going!'

The next two hours were not happy for anyone. Particularly not happy for Francey Dunbar as he coped with some of the immediate mopping up and accepted that other things could sensibly wait until morning. The only time he lost his temper was when a local traffic patrol car arrived and its uniformed crew of two constables ambled over, notebooks ready, wanting to ask questions.

A minute of vintage Dunbar, with Thane silent in the background, and the traffic crew fled.

The road was cleared and the vehicles now waiting on both sides began to move again. The damaged Crime Squad car was hauled away by a tow-truck. Another Crime Squad car arrived and Sandra Craig and Joe Felix, both still shaken, their protests ignored, were dispatched to their homes.

A second tow-truck removed the Magic Bakerman delivery van. Its regular driver lived only a mile away and had left his vehicle parked near his home as usual, for the night. The first he knew of what had happened was when a local beat cop knocked on his door and got him out of bed. It didn't make the Magic Bakerman happy to be told that his van now looked like it had been attacked by a giant tin-opener and that there was no way he could have it back until a fingerprint team had finished.

About fifty miles away, on the east side of Edinburgh, someone else was roused out of bed. The Volkswagen's registered owner – a doctor of divinity, not a medical man – didn't show much in the way of Christian understanding when local police followed up a telexed Crime Squad request and quizzed him about his car.

It had stopped being his car about two weeks before, when he had traded it in against a newer model. That was all he knew, the car sales firm was one of Edinburgh's biggest Volkswagen distributors and the salesman had said they'd take care of the ownership paperwork. Now could he go back to bed?

By then Thane had moved back to the airport terminal and was using a borrowed desk and telephone in a corner of the airport police office as a temporary base. He had talked to the Boeing's cabin staff, he had even found one air hostess who remembered Gort as a passenger, but nothing more. Another failure was the total blank from a general police radio request for any sighting of the Volkswagen.

For the moment they'd lost John Gort and they'd lost Janey Peters. They'd lost the motorcyclist with the sawn-off shotgun and his ski-masked companion – whatever way they fitted into the general jigsaw. The only good news had been passed on to him from Inverness. The two drugs dealers up there had each been given a twelve-year sentence. By now, he supposed, other contenders were moving in to take over the vacant territory.

He sat back in his borrowed chair, stifled a yawn and looked across at Francey Dunbar. His sergeant was drinking a mug of airport coffee with minimal enjoyment.

'You said you had an address for Janey Peters.'

'A last-known address,' qualified Dunbar. The duty-shift inspector at Scottish Crime Squad headquarters had done some extra digging when asked. 'Our Ms Peters rents a place out at Williamfield – in the Rawley Farm area, middle-budget territory. But she doesn't seem to use it very often. Commander Hart had it checked a few times.'

'We'd still better take a look.' Thane shoved back his

chair and rose. It might be unlikely but it still wasn't impossible that Gort and the blonde had gone there. 'We're finished around the airport. We'll use my car, go over to Williamfield, then stop for what's left of the night before anything more goes wrong.'

'This whole thing was thrown at you, boss.' For once Dunbar tried to be sympathetic. 'Things came unstuck, that's all.'

'Can I quote you?' asked Thane solemnly.

'Any time.' Dunbar grinned. 'But who'd care?'

They left the terminal, had to stop to let a trio of airline service trucks rumble past, then crossed to where Thane's blue Ford was parked. It was still intact, despite Joe Felix's dire warnings.

Williamfield was a village north of the River Clyde, a village that had now almost disappeared under new housing developments which made it just another dormitory area for its giant neighbour, Glasgow. It was only a dozen or so miles from the airport, a distance that began with a brief motorway journey then crossed the Clyde on the high span of the Erskine Bridge with the river a broad glint far below.

A few miles later they were in Williamfield and had located the Rawley Farm area where Janey Peters sometimes lived.

There had once been a real Rawley Farm. Now it was mainly covered in concrete and the name was used for a closely packed mix of assorted housing which ranged from small bungalows to sprawling apartment blocks. The streets were lined with parked cars, most of them probably on their second or third owner. Shops were few and had their windows protected by steel shutters. Rawley Farm was one of those places which didn't know whether it was going up or down or just getting ready to explode.

They wanted Rawley Drive. When they found it, a local divisional police car seemed to appear out of nowhere and drew in behind Thane's Ford as he parked.

The sergeant who got out and came over was overweight and obviously nearing retirement. His driver was a fair-haired policewoman young enough to have been his daughter.

Thane stepped out and met a leer that was meant to be a welcoming smile.

'Superintendent Thane?' The forced smile widened as Thane nodded. 'Sergeant Merreday, sir. Your people said you might be over this way tonight.' Merreday thumbed at the young policewoman. 'Like I told Wilma, it never does any harm to make sure visitors don't get lost.'

'I appreciate the thought.' Thane's voice was dry. Someone, somewhere, had a loose mouth. 'You know our interest?'

'This Peters woman, like before?' Merreday thumbed across the road, towards a long two-storey apartment block. It had a flat roof, no lights showed at the windows and each house had its numbered, individual street-level door. 'Ground floor right, the end house – nobody has seen her for about three weeks.' He anticipated Thane's next question. 'Her place still seems empty.'

'How about neighbours?' queried Dunbar with minimal hope. 'Do they know anything?'

'Most of them don't even know her name, don't care.' Merreday shrugged. 'They're too busy doing their own thing – or worrying about it. We had to break down a door here, early summer – midway along, upper floor. There was an old man in his bed. He'd been dead for a month, nobody missed him.' He shaped a grimace. 'And nobody cared. One hell of a way to go, I say.'

'Janey Peters,' reminded Thane firmly.

'She goes away a lot.' Merreday shoved his hat further

back on his balding head and frowned at the young policewoman as if seeking inspiration. 'Do we know why, Wilma?'

'Business,' said the girl vaguely. 'It seems to vary.'

'It does.' Francey Dunbar gave her a helpful nod. 'Our file says she works as a holiday time-share sales negotiator part of the year, then picks up casual jobs as an in-store cosmetics demonstrator the rest of the time. She travels around.'

The girl gave him a grateful glance. Her sergeant had switched his attention back to Thane.

'This Peters woman, sir – is she getting important?'

'It seems that way,' said Thane.

'Yet your people haven't tried for a search warrant?'

'We hadn't enough reason until tonight. We still might have some problems.'

'I see.' The overweight sergeant gave a grunt. He had two medal ribbons on his tunic. One, blue and white, was the 'never been caught' police Long Service and Good Conduct medal. The other, red and blue and very faded, was a bravery medal from somewhere in the past. 'So you could be back, sir.' He made a noisy, sucking sound with his lips. 'Wilma – '

'Sergeant?' She was close beside them under the dim street lighting.

'You heard the Superintendent. It means we'll need to keep a special eye on that apartment, right?' He nodded at her. 'So be a good wee police officer and check the security, right now. Take a torch and watch your feet – the dogs around here plant land-mines.'

The girl nodded, went back to their car and brought out a heavy, rubber-covered electric torch.

'I'll go with her,' volunteered Dunbar.

'No need.' Merreday shaped a fractional scowl at the notion.

Dunbar shrugged, stuffed his hands into his pockets

26

and stayed where he was while the girl walked over to the apartment block. She disappeared from sight behind the building, and Merreday gave a confident grunt.

'That one knows her job, Superintendent,' he assured Thane. 'She only joined the force about eighteen months ago, but few people would guess it. She learns fast.'

'And you do the teaching?' asked Thane, knowing the question was expected.

'I try, sir.' The overweight veteran was suitably modest. 'I try.' He gave Francey Dunbar a frowning glance. 'One thing I teach is that she has to know what needs doing – then get on with it. That's the only way I know.'

They waited in the night chill, the only real sounds an occasional, cooling crackle from the cars' exhausts and the faint, distant barking of a dog. Then, suddenly, muffled but distinctive, they heard the crack of breaking glass. The local sergeant shuffled his feet a little but showed no other reaction. Thane glanced at Dunbar and kept him silent with a slight shake of his head.

In a few moments the young policewoman appeared again from behind the building and walked back towards them.

'Everything all right, Wilma?' asked Merreday mildly.

'There's a small problem, Sergeant,' she said calmly. 'One of the rear windows has been broken. The window catch behind it has been freed.' The torch gestured vaguely. 'A prowler, maybe.'

'But he was scared off, eh?' Merreday scraped a thumb along his chin and eyed Thane blandly. 'I suppose someone should check inside, Superintendent. It's always best to make sure.'

'Something else you teach, Sergeant?' Thane's voice was icy and he didn't wait for an answer. 'You stay, we'll do it. Francey, bring that torch.'

27

They set off. Thane was under no illusions about what had happened and Francey Dunbar's uncharacteristic silence showed he didn't need or want anything spelled out. But Merreday's young policewoman had acted without a word being said to her. How often had something similar happened before?

The apartment block was still in darkness, the occupants had slept on. Going round to the rear of the building, they reached the broken ground-floor window. Shattered glass still clung to its frame and Dunbar shone the torch at the exposed and freed catch, then raised an eyebrow.

Thane nodded. The window opened with a mild squeak of hinges, more of the broken glass fell to the soft ground below, then they climbed through into a bedroom. Using the torch again, they closed every curtain in the apartment then switched on the lights.

'Not bad,' mused Dunbar appreciatively. 'My size of place.'

Janey Peters' home was compact, neat and tastefully furnished. It had a small hallway, a fully fitted kitchen and an ivory-tiled bathroom. The one bedroom had a large and luxuriously quilted double bed and there was also a large living room with a dining area.

'Do we look for anything special?' asked Dunbar.

'Whatever we get.' Thane laid a hand on his arm. When Francey Dunbar searched he could give a fair imitation of a bulldozer having passed through. 'No demolition job, Francey. Everything stays tidy, the way we found it.'

They started in the kitchen where the cupboards were almost empty apart from a few dishes and pots. The refrigerator contained only a couple of cartons of fruit juice, a tub of salad cream and a thin slab of mouldy cheese. On a worktop, one canister held instant coffee powder and another was filled with tea bags. In the bathroom a medicine cabinet offered a small, empty glass bottle with a gummed-on label which said it had held sleeping pills as prescribed for Janey Peters.

'Bedroom next?' Dunbar sounded slightly bored.

'Bedroom.' Thane nodded and let Dunbar stride ahead while he took a moment to think.

He was beginning to doubt their chances of finding anything that might matter. The apartment had a general air of being seldom used. There were no photographs on display, few ornaments, no books, no magazines or newspapers – it had almost the same lack of personality as an unoccupied hotel room.

But they still had to try. He followed his sergeant into the bedroom. Dunbar was over beside a white dressing table, the mirror reflecting the mild hope on his face as he reached out to examine a carved wooden jewellery box which was lying central on the top. The box was teak, with the glint of elaborate brass hinges, and Thane's memory clicked in sudden horror as he realized he had seen one like it before.

'No, Francey!' He dived forward as Dunbar's thin, strong fingers began to open the hinged lid. 'No! Leave it!'

Startled, Dunbar hesitated. An instant later Thane punched the box out of his hands and simultaneously shouldered Dunbar clear. Flying through the air, the box crashed down on the carpet and the lid burst open. As it did, the box seemed to take on a separate life of its own. The lid flapped outwards, the sides quivered, and there was a harsh metallic click from inside. The box jumped then lay still.

The colour drained from Dunbar's face as he stared down at the way the bedroom light now glinted on the fine coiled steel of something resembling an oversized mousetrap. But this particular mousetrap was tipped by a sharp and narrow knife-blade. The strength of the

29

freed spring had buried that sharp edge into a strip of wood positioned below.

'Bloody hell.' Moistening his lips, Dunbar knelt down, took a ballpoint pen from his leather jacket, prodded briefly at the exposed trap, then looked up at Thane with something close to awe. 'If that thing had come down on my fingers, that would have been bad news.'

'Enough to keep your mind off other things,' mused Thane. 'That's the general idea. If you'd been a genuine prowler you'd just want to get out then find a hospital with a casualty doctor who didn't ask too many questions.'

'I'll believe it.' Gingerly, Dunbar lifted the remains of the jewellery box. The carving on the lid showed a stylized viper, ready to strike. He grimaced. 'All right, I'll ask it. How did you know?'

'Two winters ago my wife hauled me out for a week's sunshine in the Canary Islands.' Thane smiled a little at the memory. 'We stayed at Puerto de la Cruze, in Tenerife. You're not too far off the North African coast, there's a big Arab marketplace – and that's where I saw them. They're made in Morocco, they've all got some kind of snake carving on the lid.' He nodded at the box Dunbar was holding. 'The real owner doesn't want to keep losing fingertips, so there's a securing catch on the side to make it harmless the rest of the time.'

'But if you're an uninvited visitor, you get zapped.' Carefully, Dunbar poked at the box again. 'And the damned thing is empty anyway. So she left it there as bait, for anyone who came?'

'But cops are supposed to know better,' said Thane dryly.

'Some cops.' Dunbar drew a deep breath. 'The Canary Islands belong to Spain. Could these things turn up in mainland Spain – like on the Costa del Sol?'

30

'Probably.'

'Our Janey has a nice choice in souvenirs.' Dunbar scowled. 'Damn her.'

There was still a job to do, and they got on with it.

Janey Peters had left some of her wardrobe of clothes hanging up in a large fitted cupboard. But there were some items of men's clothing among the skirts and dresses, and it was the same when the two detectives looked in some of the built-in drawer space to one side. Everything looked as though it would have fitted a man of John Gort's size and build.

They checked through pockets, they checked through blouses and underwear. Thane paused, frowning at the bedside telephone. It was a push-button model, one of the newer types with a Last Number Redial facility button.

'I want that saved,' he told Dunbar. 'The telephone hasn't been unplugged, the last number she called should still be stored in the memory. Get a telephone engineer out in the morning – one who knows what he's doing.'

Dunbar nodded and they started through to the living room. On the way, going through the apartment's tiny lobby, they collected the handful of mail which had accumulated behind the letter-box flap in the front door. Most of it was junk advertising mail, but three items looked more genuine.

'We haven't that search warrant,' reminded Dunbar unemotionally.

'We're here,' said Thane. 'Just don't ask me to thank Sergeant Merreday when we leave.'

Thane opened all three. One, only a couple of days old from the postmark, was Janey Peters' quarterly bank statement. The deposits and withdrawals seemed modest and ordinary, the amount in credit didn't reach four figures. The next, the oldest, from a local plumber,

31

was an estimate to supply and fit a new waste-disposal unit in her kitchen. A hand-written postscript apologized for a delay of almost two months in sending the estimate. The plumber had been ill.

But the third letter was very different. He read it a second time then gave a soft whistle through his teeth.

'Got something?' Francey Dunbar paused from working his way down one side of the living room.

'Something maybe useful.' Thane waited until Dunbar came over. 'This last one.'

Dunbar took all three from him, glanced briefly at the first two, then concentrated on the third.

'Clearing her decks,' he suggested.

Thane nodded. The third was from the London office of Worldfriend Timeshares International. It thanked Janey Peters for advising them she was no longer available for temporary sales work. The final paragraph offered best wishes in her 'proposed new business venture in Spain'.

'With Gort as partner.' Dunbar gave a sardonic grin. 'Does that make her Interface Mate?'

'If she's getting out, then she decided it not too long ago.' Thane indicated the plumber's estimate for the waste-disposal unit. 'You don't think of spending money that way when you're planning to disappear.'

Dunbar went back to searching. Barely a minute later he gave a quick, hopeful grunt.

'What about this?' he asked.

Thane went over. Francey Dunbar's searching had reached an expensive, teak-framed combined TV and video-recorder unit with a storage cabinet below. The cabinet held some video tapes and instruction booklets. But something different and brightly coloured had slipped down behind the tapes, partly hidden until Dunbar pulled it out.

It was a glossy, slim and specialized sales catalogue

for computer and word-processor equipment and accessories. The firm named in large lettering on the front cover, Computer Cabin, were equally specialized with a warehouse-showroom at the low rental end of Argyle Street.

'Let me see that,' said Thane with a sharp interest.

Where Dunbar had found it, the catalogue could have been overlooked or forgotten when Janey Peters moved out. But anything that involved computer equipment had to matter when the Interface Man could be involved.

Dunbar handed him the catalogue. As he did, a single sheet of very light blue notepaper slipped out from between the pages and fell on the carpet. Dunbar swore softly, squatted down beside it, and picked it up.

'Anything?' asked Thane as Dunbar smoothed out the heavily creased sheet.

'Yes.' Dunbar grimaced. 'Looks like her shopping list – coffee, bacon, and a couple of other things. How about the catalogue?'

Thane shrugged. A glance at the few pages baffled him with technical data and startled him in terms of price tags. One page, with the heading 'Modems', had been circled, then two items beneath it ticked. He felt in the wrong league.

'A modem?' Dunbar was peering over his shoulder. 'That's some kind of signal convertor, isn't it?'

Thane nodded. That much he did know. He swopped the catalogue for Dunbar's sheet of notepaper, scowled at the small shopping list which had been neatly written in ink, then considered the paper itself. Good quality, it was roughly the width and breadth of a man's hand. A rough edge along the top looked as if some kind of printed letterhead had been torn away.

But it hadn't been creased, originally it had been folded in a definite pattern. Some creases ran vertically, others crossed horizontally in a deliberate pattern. He fingered along the fold lines and suddenly he was looking at a small, oblong envelope shape that could have been a container.

'Drugs?' suggested Dunbar, but doubtfully. He sucked on his teeth. 'Maybe too big?'

'Give it to Forensic,' said Thane. 'Let them do some worrying.'

They finished checking the rest of the room, put out the apartment lights again, re-opened the curtains and left by the same rear window. Thane glanced at his watch. They had taken just over seven minutes.

Sergeant Merreday was still standing across the street where they had left him. Hands clasped across his paunch, he gave a sly but wary grin as they walked over.

'Any luck, Superintendent?' he asked in a hoarse whisper.

Thane shrugged. The young policewoman was back in the divisional car, sitting demurely behind the wheel.

'Like I tell young Wilma, sometimes cops have to make their own luck, eh?' Merreday had become uneasy. 'I'll do something about getting that window fixed and – uh – keep an eye on the place. You'll be back?'

'Someone will,' said Thane curtly, then nodded to Dunbar.

They left the local sergeant and went back to Thane's car. They were driving away before Dunbar spoke.

'I'm not squeaky-clean – never have been.' Dunbar scowled back to where Merreday stood under one of the street lights. 'But I do my own dirty tricks. I don't use kids in brand-new uniforms.'

'He'd call it helping us,' said Thane grimly. 'We accepted.'

But something would have to be done about Sergeant Merreday, and quickly.

He sighed. Even so, Merreday had saved them a few

hours. Thane now had a list of things on his mind, things he wanted done as soon as people came back on duty again. He talked as he drove in towards the city, and Dunbar's face grew longer as he listened.

Francey Dunbar had moved house that summer, to what had been part of the attic of a one-time dockside warehouse, now converted and fashionable as Glasgow tried hard for a new Merchant City image. Once Dunbar had been delivered there, Thane set the Ford moving again and headed south, through the city and across the river.

It was an area where the streets were old, dark, empty and yet familiar enough to be friendly. Here and there a late-night worker was walking or driving home. Neon signs flashed silently above shadowed shop windows, and an occasional uniformed beat constable plodded along, checking doors and padlocks while he planned where he'd hide to have his next illicit cigarette.

Like most cities, Glasgow always looked her best in the time between midnight and dawn. In some special way, buildings and people were both neutralized and equalized until daylight and reality came round again. Colin Thane had lived most of his life with that, had come to accept it.

Nearly home, reaching the start of the South Side's maze of suburban streets, he felt himself relax, then treated himself to what was another late-night indulgence. He let the Ford drift to a halt where the view was from a low hill, back towards the city.

All the way to the horizon was a twinkle of lights except for a solitary dark ribbon near the middle which was the River Clyde. He could pick out the bright slash of the Kingston Bridge where it crossed that ribbon. Further out, one particular patch of bunching lights was Glasgow University. That patch lower down was a hospital, that tiny caterpillar of lights crawling below was a train, further to the west was his old territory of Millside Division.

Another car was coming towards him. It had a Police sign on the roof and Thane raised a hand in a greeting as it went past, seeing one of the patrol car's crew returning the greeting.

Releasing the handbreak, he set the Ford moving again and took a brief sideways glance at the city's lights.

He smiled to himself. Glasgow had a reputation which might be outdated but was still hard to discard. It was like the old story of the little Edinburgh boy saying his prayers, and finishing, 'Goodbye God, we're moving to Glasgow so I'm sorry, but we won't see you again.'

Glasgow could still be rough, could still be tough – but it was his city.

It had been that way since he had started as a young cop, the first steps in a police career which had been shaped and tempered in everything from gangland thieving to dockside brawls, on his way to becoming the youngest divisonal CID chief in the city.

He had run his Millside Division with a reputation for mixing logic with hunches and usually winning. Then, unexpectedly, promotion had come again. This time to the rank of detective superintendent with an immediate secondment to the elite and independent Scottish Crime Squad as joint deputy commander.

Nothing could have suited him better. The Crime Squad was real, sharp-end policing, his kind. It didn't answer to local politicians, its funds came direct from central government. If that sometimes meant knowing how to fight street-wise, that was back to the first lessons he'd learned.

But not the kind being taught by Sergeant Merreday out at Williamfield.

36

It was late. He pushed Merreday from his mind as he finally turned the car into a short avenue lined with small, sleeping bungalows. Each had its tiny garden and looked identical to its neighbours.

Thane's house was midway along. He parked the Ford outside, switched off, and closed the driver's door gently when he got out.

Leaving the car he stopped in the garden to consider his one solitary rosebush and appreciate its one surviving September bloom. Then he moved on again. To be caught even thinking garden thoughts at three a.m. would have confirmed his resident teenagers' worst suspicions about their father.

Tommy and Kate were still at school. Tommy had dark hair and adolescent pimples. Kate was a couple of years younger and starting to grow into a woman, already showing every promise of being almost as good-looking as her mother.

When Tommy and Kate slept it could take a bomb to waken them. But as Thane used his key, opened the front door, and stepped in, he heard a soft, querulous bark from the kitchen.

'It's me, you idiot,' he answered in a low voice. 'Shut up.'

He entered the kitchen, switched on a light, and a large boxer dog named Clyde watched the next familiar routine. Mary had left a glass of milk and a cheese sandwich on top of the refrigerator. Thane drank the milk, shared the sandwich with the dog, then put out the light, closed the kitchen door and went upstairs.

Past the closed silence of Tommy's and Kate's bedrooms, he went into the main bedroom. A vague shape stirred under the blankets.

'You're late.' Mary Thane made it a sleepy murmur as he got into bed beside her. 'What time is it?'

'Three a.m.'

37

'Never heard of it.' She yawned. 'How did the airport thing go?'

'It was a foul-up.' He hauled an edge of blankets back to his side of the bed. 'Any news of Hart's wife?'

'The last time I phoned, the hospital said she was comfortable – whatever that means.' Mary sighed and yawned again. 'Goodnight, whoever you are.'

Her lips brushed Thane's mouth then she turned away, burrowing down. In another moment her faint, regular breathing told him she was asleep again.

'Goodnight,' said Thane softly.

He lay on his back for a spell, hearing the house's small night sounds, fighting off sleep for a few minutes more, thinking.

John Gort had been the name of a top British army general in World War Two. He couldn't exactly remember what that illustrious soldier had done and didn't particularly care. The only Gort who mattered now was the Interface Man.

He had the smell of real trouble.

2

Early October can be a time of good weather in Scotland, the days bright with sunlight, the sky staying a clear, almost high-country blue – a last bonus of a barricade holding back winter.

It was that kind of morning when Colin Thane wakened. The sun was pouring in through his bedroom window and the alarm clock beside him, already silenced, showed it was after eight a.m. Mary was up and dressed and he could hear her moving around downstairs. Tommy and Kate were making their own kind of noise, preparing for school, and Clyde the dog had already draped his smooth-haired bulk across the foot of the bed.

Thane moved, ignored a grumble from the dog, shoved Clyde back where he belonged on the floor, and yawned his way through to the bathroom. He showered, shaved, dressed in a fresh white shirt and a knitted blue tie to go with his Donegal-weave suit, pulled on his shoes, then went downstairs.

Tommy and Kate were leaving. He rated a quick grin of a good morning from Kate and a reasonably cheerful grunt of a greeting from his son.

'Tell him.' Kate elbowed her brother. 'Try it.'

'Now?'

'Somebody has to think it funny,' declared Kate. 'But get the timing right.'

'Dad – did you hear about the two fleas going shopping?' asked his son.

'Go on,' Thane surrendered.

'One flea says to the other flea, "Shall we walk or shall

39

we take the dog?" ' Tommy paused hopefully. 'Well, what do you think?'

'Desperate.' Thane grinned. He had heard the same story earlier in the week, from a mortuary attendant who collected tired jokes. 'But they come worse.'

'I call it pathetic,' said Kate coldly. She shoved her brother and a moment later they had gone, the front door slamming in a way that threatened its hinges.

Wincing, Thane went through to the kitchen. Mary paused from clearing used crockery into the dishwasher, and he gave her a goodmorning-style kiss. She looked at him, sighed and wrinkled her nose.

'Never let anyone tell you that you're any kind of sleeping beauty,' she declared. 'You were still snoring when I woke, and that's nasty on its own. I would have hit you with something if I hadn't felt charitable.'

Thane grinned and poured himself a mug of coffee from the pot on the stove. Mary Thane was a slim, attractive, dark-haired woman and it still seemed ridiculous that she could be the mother of two teenagers. Friday was one of the days she worked part time as a receptionist at the local medical centre and she was wearing one of her work outfits, a brown two-piece with a white blouse.

'Were you told about the two fleas?' he asked.

'I suffered. Better leave some coffee in the pot.' She indicated the telephone on the wall. 'Jack Hart rang while you were in the shower. You've to wait here, he's coming over.'

'Here?' Thane raised a surprised eyebrow while he helped himself to some toast. The Squad commander didn't usually make morning visits. 'Did he say why?'

'No. So I didn't ask.' Mary made it a stubborn rule.

'How about his wife?'

'Gloria seems out of any kind of danger.' She made a sympathetic noise to herself. 'But he still sounds worried – he's going back to the hospital again from here.'

40

He nodded and drank more of the coffee. But he was still puzzled. 'It could be about last night, at the airport. Things went sour.'

'I got that notion when you arrived back at three a.m. or whenever,' she said dryly. Her handbag was lying on a countertop near the table. She lifted it and checked her purse and keys were inside. Then she gave him a quick grimace. 'You said things went sour. How bad is sour?'

He told her, briefly. When he had finished she came round and laid her hands on his shoulders.

'It sounds like these people are willing to play rough,' she said quietly.

He nodded.

'Remember that part for me, will you? Please?' She deliberately switched her mood. 'I suppose that damned dog will be back up on our bed again by now?'

'Where else?' Thane gave a mock yelp as she lightly clipped his ear. 'But why take it out on me?'

'You encourage the brute.' She glanced at her wristwatch. 'I'll move him, and tidy up there.'

Her lips brushed the top of his head then she headed upstairs. Seconds later, Clyde suddenly appeared in the kitchen. The dog glared around, then settled under the table.

Soon Thane heard his wife leave the house, then the sound of her car starting. Mary had recently traded up to a three-year-old Datsun coupé, bright red in colour, with only two previous owners. Listening to the car drive away, he sighed to himself then absently munched at another piece of toast.

So Jack Hart was coming. That meant he wanted something, and Colin Thane had a good idea what it might be.

It was another fifteen minutes before Commander Hart's car arrived. It was a large black BMW – the

41

acknowledged flagship of the Crime Squad car pool and a vehicle openly envied by some highly paid chief constables who were held down by local police committees with more sedate ideas. Hart's usual driver, a young detective constable who always looked newly laundered, was behind the wheel and stayed there as Hart stepped out.

The BMW had grimy paintwork, but her driver wasn't to blame. Crime Squad cars, even Hart's, were seldom washed. A dirty-looking car blended better into most backgrounds. It was common sense. The Squad operated several rules in that hard-earned category. Now Jack Hart seemed to have learned another.

'Never be damned fool enough to allow your wife to land in hospital,' he advised as soon as he was in the house and had settled in a kitchen chair. He nodded his thanks as Thane handed him a mug of coffee. 'We've been married more than twenty years. I'll tell you this much – last night I even missed her shouting at me!'

Thane smiled at the libel, and translated.

'Meaning she's improving, like you told Mary.'

Hart nodded, his relief plain. He was a thin, usually sad-eyed man with greying hair and a lined face. He dressed like a bank manager. But Thane had seen Hart go into more than one back-street fight leading his men from the front – and he also knew Gloria Hart. She was a quiet, easy-going woman who could twist her husband round her little finger any time she wanted.

'Here's what happened.' Hart took a gulp of coffee first. 'She was painting our kitchen ceiling – the usual story, I meant to do it but I couldn't find time. So the ladder slipped and she went over backwards.' He sucked his lips. 'She could have been killed, and it would have been my fault.'

'But that didn't happen.' Thane sensed the intensity of feeling behind Hart's words. 'She's improving.'

42

'Yes. The medics say Gloria's broken leg is no problem. It should heal like new. There's no sign of any skull fracture. But they've got her sedated. They're still worrying about possible concussion.'

'So they're being careful. They know what they're doing,' soothed Thane. The city's Southern General Hospital had the established reputation of being one of the best head-injury units in Europe. Glasgow's regular outbreaks of violence gave students plenty of learning material. 'Trust them.'

'I do,' said Hart. 'But the medics say they can't be sure for at least another forty-eight hours. It could be more before she's totally clear.'

Thane nodded, knowing what he meant. Any head injury could leave a danger of haemorrhage, bruising or laceration. Under the table, he saw Clyde had inched close to Hart's feet.

'Don't look for me at my desk for the next few days.' Hart paused, looking at Thane but absently scratching Clyde behind one ear. 'I want to be at the hospital. If we were talking about Mary instead of Gloria, you'd do the same – right?'

'Yes,' said Thane quietly.

'Good.' Hart took another swallow of coffee. 'So now let's talk about you and last night.'

'The shambles,' said Thane.

'That's the way I heard it.' Hart scowled. 'And I set most of it up, agreed?'

Thane didn't answer, but was glad Hart remembered.

The Squad commander wasn't finished. 'These people need John Gort, need him badly. That was spelled out clearly enough last night – and they're careful, they believe in insurance. That trick roadblock with the bakery van would take time to organize. It must have been ready even before we were spotted.'

Yet things could still have been worse. Into Thane's

43

mind came some of the horrific possibilities if they'd tried to grab the Interface Man in the airport's crowded arrivals lobby. Had there been more 'insurance' hidden there?

'Any more of this coffee?' asked Hart, draining his mug. He accepted a refill. 'Right, let's get to why I'm here. As of this moment, I want you to take over the Gort case – all of it. Will you?'

'If that's what you want.' It was what Thane had seen coming all along. But he still had to have things crystal clear. 'In total?'

'In total. No interference from me – or anyone else,' emphasized Hart. 'Your current caseload we can spread around or put on ice. Gort has total priority.' He drew a deep breath. 'Confession time, Colin. My real mistake with Gort so far has been to treat him like personal property, the desk-bound warrior goes thief-catching again. Gloria's accident has shaken that nonsense out of me. You understand?'

Silently, Thane gave a nod.

'There's one thing you don't know,' said Hart grimly. 'It looks like I'm not just handing you Gort. I may be handing you a murder that goes with him.'

'I see.' Thane didn't, and stared at Hart. Under the table Clyde had become bored. Ambling across the kitchen, he collapsed in his favourite corner. Thane felt like joining him. 'Does this maybe murder have a body?'

'Yes. Someone who was killed exactly a month ago.' Carefully, Hart traced a pattern on the kitchen table with his fingertip. 'Look, I was finally thrown out of the hospital last night, told to go home and get some sleep. I tried that, I couldn't – I ended up back at my office. It was around five a.m. People were keeping out of my way. I needed something to do – I hid in a corner reading through some of the overnight telex traffic.'

'That should win you a prize.' Thane smiled a little.

Overnight telex traffic was low priority, a torrent of usually routine messages being circulated round the various police forces. Most of them, once sifted, were shredded and dumped. He saw Hart's expression hadn't changed. 'You mean – '

'I found this.' Hart reached inside his jacket, brought out a folded telex message, then flattened it out. 'Read it.'

Thane took the telex. It was a general circulation, originated by British Transport Police.

18864 90 1735. REFERENCE EARLIER CIRCULATIONS FOLLOWING DEATH OF ROBERT HASTON, AGED 37 NATIVE OF GLW, HIS BODY DISCOVERED BESIDE RAIL TRACK, MAIN LONDON–GLW LINE SOUTH OF CARLISLE, HASTON LATER ESTABLISHED AS PASSENGER ON INTERCITY LONDON–GLW TRAIN. BTP INQUIRIES CONCLUDED, NO FURTHER ASSISTANCE REQUIRED. FORMAL REPORT TO BE SUBMITTED. ENDS BTP (S).

Puzzled, Thane read the telex again then returned it to Hart.

'It almost says suicide,' he remarked bluntly.

'It does. But people could be wrong.' Hart tucked the telex away. 'I told them that around dawn this morning, as soon as I'd checked it was the same Haston. I missed the original messages about his death, they just didn't reach me the way this one did. Robert Haston – ' he shook his head ' – no, I don't believe in that kind of coincidence.'

'Should I know him?' asked Thane.

'No.' Hart shook his head again. 'Not you, not the railway cops – they checked, of course, but he didn't have any kind of criminal record. At least John Gort has one previous conviction, but not Haston – and any hassle the Squad had with either of them was before you joined us.'

45

'What kind of hassle was Haston?' Thane was on full alert now. His mouth felt slightly dry again, and he managed to squeeze a last half-mug of coffee from the pot. 'Did he matter?'

'Then? I was ready to bet on it.' Hart almost spat the words. 'It was three years ago, John Gort had slithered off to Spain, and we were investigating a new string of smaller hi-tech raids. They happened here, they happened there – electronic security systems left sick, every time a break-in involving some kind of theft.' He scowled at the memory. 'We knew we were chasing someone who wasn't as smooth an operator as Gort – but he was almost as good. I found Haston, an over-age electronics yuppie. He worked for a computer maintenance firm that had done business with every firm where there had been a break-in.'

Jack Hart fell silent. For a few moments the only sounds in the kitchen were the soft tick of a clock and a low, groaning wheeze which meant the dog was sleeping.

'But you couldn't nail him?' Thane spoke first.

'We couldn't.' Hart's thin, leathery face shaped a scowl. 'I gave him three separate grillings. But I had to let him go. We made no other arrests for any of the raids. Later, I heard Haston had quit his computer job. Later still, that he was running a legitimate one-man security consultancy business from his home.'

'And no more hi-tech raids?'

'None with his style.'

'So the suggestion is that first Haston falls off a train and quietly dies. Then we're tipped that John Gort is coming back to Scotland?'

'We're tipped just days later.' Hart nodded and showed an unusual embarrassment. 'We can put that together now.'

'I'm still catching up, sir.' Thane allowed himself a dry edge of sarcasm. 'Who tipped us about Gort?'

Sadly, Jack Hart shook his head. 'What we got was a typed anonymous letter – Spanish postage stamps and a Malaga postmark.'

'In English?'

Hart nodded. 'I've left the original on your desk. Very short, very basic, from someone who knows Gort – and even our damned postal address. There's a hint that Gort was being pressured to come back.'

'And he came.' Thane pursed his lips. 'So there was a lot of pressure – or a lot of money?'

'Or both.' Hart abandoned his coffee mug on the table and took a quick glance at his watch. 'That's what I'm dumping in your lap. I started off wanting to use Gort to lead us to the people who maybe mattered even more. I still think I'm right.'

'I'd go along with that.' Thane meant it.

'Good.' Hart suddenly pushed back his chair and stood up. 'One final thing I've done is fix for you to meet with a Transport Police detective inspector named Pat Emslie. He handled their inquiry into Robert Haston's death. Emslie is out, but he's being contacted right now. I gave them your home telephone number, you should get a call any moment.' The Squad commander took another glance at his watch. 'Whatever you do, I'll back it – that's a promise.'

Then Jack Hart was on his way out of the house. In another few seconds he was back in the BMW and being driven away.

He was going to get to that hospital on time.

Three minutes later Colin Thane was adding his breakfast dishes to the load waiting in the dishwasher when the telephone rang. He answered it on the kitchen extension.

'Sergeant Gorman, sir. Transport Police,' said a man's voice, the accent heavily Liverpool-Irish. 'I'm

47

passing on a message from Detective Inspector Emslie. He says you know what it's about.'

'Go on,' agreed Thane.

'He's busy thief-catching right now, sir.' The Liverpool-Irish voice was cheerful. 'Rattling handcuffs – the usual kind of thing, and it won't take long. He sends his apologies. Any chance you could be at Polmadie railway yard inside the next half hour? It would save some time.'

'His time or mine?' asked Thane dryly. He didn't wait for an answer. 'Tell him I'll be there.'

He replaced the receiver, started the dishwasher going, and fed Clyde some bonus biscuits. He had a few minutes to spare, and two telephone calls of his own to make. Lifting the receiver, he tapped out the first number.

The switchboard at Strathclyde Police Headquarters was having one of its better days and answered straight away. He gave the extension number he wanted, there was a brief pause, then a familiar dry voice came on the line.

'Moss.'

'Having a good start to your day?' asked Thane mildly.

He heard a surprised chuckle. Detective Inspector Phil Moss had been the CID second-in-command when Thane had Millside Division. Soon after Thane had moved, Moss had been transferred to a new job as liaison officer to the Strathclyde force's Assistant Chief Constable (Crime). Moss didn't like being part of the Headquarters scene. One day, he promised everyone, he'd escape.

'I've been reading about you,' said Moss with an acid amusement. 'Our people out at Glasgow Airport have sent in a report about last night. Had fun, didn't you?'

'Go to hell,' said Thane stonily. 'Phil, I need a favour.'

48

'What kind?'

'There's a sergeant named Merreday out at William-field. Can you sneak a look at his file? I want him moved.'

'Hold on.' Moss broke off and Thane heard him talking to someone. Then Moss was back on the line. 'Sorry. That was my boss passing through for another day. You want this Merreday moved. Where?'

'Somewhere far away, Phil. Where he stays lost.'

Moss gave an interested murmur. 'Like that? What's the alternative?'

'Discipline Branch.'

'Consider him lost,' promised Moss. 'I know a couple of people in Personnel. They both owe me one. When will you be in?'

'Maybe today. Tomorrow at the latest,' said Thane.

He thanked Moss, said goodbye and hung up. Then he made another call. The number rang a few times, then a man's voice answered.

'Harry Duke, Electrics.'

'Harry, it's Colin Thane.' Their sons were in the same class at school. 'Remember I ordered some new light fittings last time I was in?'

'Uh-huh.' Duke was cautious. 'Changed your mind about them?'

'No.' They were for the upstairs rooms, long-promised replacements. 'I said I'd fit them myself. Maybe you'd better do it, like you suggested.'

'Not me – your wife did.' The electrician chuckled. 'Otherwise, she reckoned she'd be the one who ended up doing the job, right?'

'Something like that,' agreed Thane vaguely. 'Any-way, put the job in your book for some time next week, will you?'

He heard Duke make a confirming noise. Then he hung up, grinned sheepishly at Clyde, and left the house.

49

*

Polmadie is a major railway yard located not far from Glasgow's old, notorious and now mostly demolished Gorbals slumland. Some parts of the Gorbals now boast grass and young trees. But the only real romance about Polmadie is in its name – a story that goes back over the centuries to Mary, Queen of Scots. It was a turbulent reign. At one point Mary's troops fought a battle in open country near the village which was then Glasgow. They lost. In the retreat, her favourite horse named Paul was fatally wounded and collapsed.

Legend claims that Mary decided, 'Paul may die, but I must flee.'

Which, over the years, became Polmadie. Mary escaped. Years later her cousin, Elizabeth of England, imprisoned her then had her executed.

Today's Polmadie is a large area protected by walls, barbed wire, lights and security cameras. It stays busy by day and by night. Railway rolling stock was being shunted everywhere when Thane arrived and checked in at the main gate, to be directed on by a security guard. From there he drove through part of the yard to where some vehicles with British Transport Police badges were already parked. They were empty, standing close to where a shabby diesel locomotive sat on a loop of track. The locomotive was pulsing a steady plume of exhaust and was hitched to three dilapidated metal-roofed goods wagons and what looked like a track repair van.

But the repair van's door was open. A thin, grey-haired figure in Transport Police uniform looked out then smiled a greeting as Thane came over.

'I'm Sergeant Gorman, sir.' The smile widened. 'I'll give you a hand aboard.'

Thane clambered up then looked around as the door

50

closed behind him. About a dozen men in Transport Police uniform were seated in the van and he could hear a radio receiver crackling from a screened-off compartment at the rear. He saw the way the van's windows were protected by iron grilles and wire mesh.

'Inspector Emslie will join us directly, sir,' promised Sergeant Gorman easily. He grinned as the locomotive up front gave a brief hoot of its siren. 'Here we go.'

Thane gripped a stanchion for support as the little train of wagons jerked then began moving, gradually gaining speed. The wheels squealed over crossing rails; the squad of transport police gave him a few curious glances then ignored him.

'You've been on a Q train before, sir?' asked Gorman.

Thane shook his head. 'But I've heard about them.'

Q trains always looked innocent and ordinary. But they could carry everything from their radios to searchlights and riot gear. They had space for prisoners and basic living facilities for the teams of officers who might have to wait in them for hours on end. The locomotive pulling a Q train also had its cab windows protected. No locomotive driver liked having his windows smashed in.

A Q train, in short, was a railway answer to many crime problems. It could appear out of nowhere and strike. Or it could wait, apparently innocent and empty, where trouble was anticipated. When it would erupt to life.

'This time, it's all because of a woman,' explained Sergeant Gorman. 'Her husband came home drunk and beat her up last night.' He shrugged. 'She didn't like it. So she managed to phone and tell us what her man should be doing just about now. He'll be with a rat's nest of thieves who expect a trainload of malt whisky to come their way.'

'But?' Thane raised an eyebrow.

51

'They're in for a disappointment, sir,' said Gorman solemnly, and winked.

The Q train travelled on for about two miles, the world outside mainly railway embankments or glimpses of the backs of factory yards or houses. Then, brakes squealing, it halted. Sergeant Gorman opened the 'repair van' door.

The man who clambered aboard was in his mid-thirties. He had a boyish face, his fair hair was cut as close as corn stubble, and he was short and stocky. He was wearing a dark green wool shirt with a quilted red waistcoat, serge trousers and heavy workboots. Seeing Thane, he came over.

'Detective Inspector Emslie,' murmured Gorman.

'Pat Emslie, sir.' Emslie made his own introduction and they shook hands. The van's door had closed again and the train was already under way. Emslie looked at Thane with what could have been a glint of caution in his shrewd grey eyes. 'Sorry about this, Superintendent. But we already had everything set up, so – '

'So you didn't want to waste time,' said Thane dryly. 'All right, I'll come along for the ride. But then we talk.'

'Yes, sir.' Emslie looked almost relieved, and turned to his sergeant. 'They're there and waiting, Harry. Get everybody ready.'

Gorman nodded and crossed the moving van to talk to their men.

'It's a simple enough one, Superintendent,' said Emslie, turning to Thane again. 'There are about twenty of them – more than usual on a daylight caper, but whisky brings them out. There's a small shunting yard at Cassidy Wood, where the whisky wagons were due to link up with the rest of a long-distance train being put together. The Cassidy Wood yard is too public for them.' Emslie grinned with his teeth. 'They're lying ready to hit us on the Up gradient before it.'

'That's where you've been?'

Emslie nodded. 'They'll hit us while we're moving.'

'How?' Thane broke off to curse and grab his stanchion again as the train lurched.

'Most shunting locomotives have a struggle on that gradient. They slow down. We know most of this gang – they're not beginners. They've a lookout posted. The moment he signals we're coming, the rest of them do a fast job brushing lubricating oil on the rails. They slop it on thick.' Emslie balanced on his feet through another lurch. 'Think of steel locomotive wheels trying to grip oiled metal rails, with no advance warning – no chance for a driver to use a sand box or anything else. The train stops moving, the gang are swarming aboard like ants. It's almost a routine.'

'You make it sound that way.' Thane saw the other men around him stirring. 'How did they know the whisky was scheduled for today?'

'How do they ever know, sir?' asked Emslie unemotionally. He took another glance from the van window, half-turned, and raised his voice. 'Everybody ready?'

The little train was starting on an upward gradient, the diesel locomotive struggling, their pace beginning to slow. Suddenly, everything changed. Thane heard a scream of sliding steel wheels and a brief, tortured bellow from the diesel as it began racing. Another moment, and the driver had the engine shut down to prevent damage. The train stopped.

For a second or two there was silence outside. Then they heard shouts.

'Now!' called Emslie. 'Let's get them!'

The van door flew open. As Emslie and his men poured out, Thane caught a glimpse of another rushing wave of figures heading towards the train. Some had reached the wagons. One was using a sledgehammer on a door, another was swinging an axe at a padlock.

53

Then police whistles blew. For a moment every thief seemed to freeze. Another moment, and the whole scene erupted. Jumping down to the track, joining the Transport Police squad, Thane saw other police he hadn't known about as they emerged from the leading wagon. The length of track beside the stopped train became struggling, shouting, cursing confusion. A massive constable appeared near Thane, holding two thieves by their necks in his huge hands, monotonously banging their heads together. A few feet away another uniformed figure was down on his knees moaning and clutching his middle.

'Look out – ' the yell came from somewhere near, then a snarling, unshaven figure in a torn jersey jumped in front of Thane and swung an iron bar.

Thane dodged, the bar brushed his shoulder, and he clasped both fists together and used them to piston a single blow into the man's middle. As the man started to fold, Thane turned and stuck out a foot, tripping a younger, scurrying thief and leaving him sprawled dazed across the rails. He could hear Emslie shouting orders. Sergeant Gorman was waving a pick-axe handle he'd acquired from somewhere, using it like a club.

As suddenly as it had begun, it ended. Everywhere, thieves seemed to be giving up, to be queuing for handcuffs. Others were running away. A few people on both sides were bleeding or limping.

'Thanks for your help, Superintendent.' Emslie came pushing through the settling confusion and gestured around. 'We've got most of them.' He paused to nod an amused greeting to one prisoner, the thin, pimple-faced teenager Thane had tripped. 'You again, Peter boy? You backed a loser this time.'

The prisoners were being loaded into one of the wagons, the last of the runners had disappeared from sight, the locomotive driver had his diesel muttering again and was spreading sand on the rails. Sergeant Gorman came over to join Thane and Emslie.

'How many do you count, Harry?' asked Emslie.

'Eleven prisoners, sir.' Gorman beamed. 'One or two need a hospital stitch or two, one may have broken his wrist. One of ours got nicked with a knife – nothing serious.' He turned to Thane and gave an approving nod. 'I saw the big fellow you took, sir. Very neat – I liked it.'

'We know most of the others who ran. We'll collect them later.' Emslie was confident. He glanced at his sergeant. 'Take over, Harry. I've to talk with Superintendent Thane.'

'Now,' agreed Thane.

Emslie led the way back into the big, shabby 'repair van' then down into a rear compartment. It had a table with a radio. Two large armchairs looked comfortable enough to have strayed from some railway hotel.

'This is the office.' Emslie gestured an invitation towards the nearest chair but remained standing as Thane sat. 'About that juvenile you brought down, sir. Would you worry if I lost him, no charges?'

'Not if you told me why,' said Thane.

'His father touts for us sometimes. It always helps if they owe us.' Emslie looked relieved. 'Some coffee, sir?'

Thane nodded. Emslie opened a cupboard marked First Aid and his visitor had a brief glimpse of a bottle and glasses. But the Transport Police inspector brought out a coffee flask and two large mugs. The coffee poured black and hot.

'You want to know about Haston, sir.' Emslie perched himself on the arm of the other chair then paused for a moment as a quick warning hoot from the locomotive was followed by a squeal of wheels and the little train got under way again. 'I've been told to help any way I can.'

'You know why it matters?'

'Someone found that Haston had criminal connec-
tions.' Emslie gave a sardonic shrug. 'The same someone
thinks he has found a murder and wants to know what
we've been doing.'

'Correct.' Thane sipped his coffee, feeling the Q train
gathering speed. 'I'm here to listen.'

'We gave Haston's death a fair go, sir.' Emslie's grey
eyes didn't waver. 'Your average railway doesn't
approve of passengers disappearing from trains – it's
bad for our image. It was a London to Glasgow train, he
lived up here, so Glasgow handled the case.'

Thane took another sip of coffee. It had a definite
flavour of rum, but that wouldn't have been polite to
mention.

'No problem identifying Haston?'

'We didn't let his wife see him.' Emslie grimaced.
'When anyone is hit by a train the result is nasty. But we
had his briefcase and luggage from the train, we
recovered his wallet and an ID bracelet from the body.
We confirmed with his dental records.'

'Anything missing?'

'Missing or stolen?' Emslie shook his head. 'His wife
couldn't think of anything.'

'Forget the reports you've written,' invited Thane.
'We'll talk – that way there's a better chance I'll
understand. Begin at the absolute beginning. Tell me
about the train.'

'In basics, sir?' Emslie scratched his close-cropped
fair hair, puzzled. 'Well, she was your normal Intercity
express in Royal Scot configuration – that means a set of
twelve Intercity coaches pulled by a Type Eighty-seven
electric locomotive – '

'Fast?'

Emslie nodded. 'A Type Eighty-seven can give five
thousand horsepower and weighs eighty tons on her
own. On the London–Glasgow run she clocks a lot of the

distance at an average of a hundred and ten miles an hour.'

'How about crew?'

'These days, just two – a driver and a ticket-collector guard. Then a catering team of six, for the restaurant car and buffet bar.'

'Passengers?'

'The evening Haston was killed?' Emslie was patient. 'Thursdays are quiet, Superintendent. We reckon there were no more than two hundred aboard.' He saw Thane raise an eyebrow. 'Remember, an Intercity makes an occasional scheduled stop along the way. There are always a few passengers joining and leaving on any Royal Scot run.'

'You seem to know your trains.' Thane made it a mild compliment.

'I should.' Emslie smiled. 'I was raised in a railway family. My grandfather was a passed fireman in the old coal-fired days, my father spent most of his life as an engine-driver. Hell, I was even born in a signal box on the West Highland line – but that's another story.'

'For another time.' Thane felt the Q train rattle over points. 'Back to your Royal Scot. You talked with the crew, with passengers?'

'The crew – and any passengers we could trace.' Emslie scowled. 'When you travel by train, your name doesn't usually go on a passenger list – you usually just buy a ticket. We located some people because they had made named advance bookings. We found a few more through a newspaper appeal. None of them could help.' A new, defensive edge had crept into his voice. 'We tried interviewing station staff at halts along the way. That was another damned waste of time.'

'Do you think this is a waste of time?' asked Thane.

'That's for you to decide, sir.' Emslie's face became impassive. He put down his coffee mug. 'I feel we did everything we could.'

'I'm sure you feel you did,' mused Thane. 'But tell me what "everything" means, Inspector.'

'The post mortem on Haston's body, the usual forensic tests, those passenger and crew statements.' Angrily, Emslie began ticking a list on his fingers. 'The entire damned train was taken out of service for three days for examination. We interviewed Haston's wife, his friends, the people he did business with – some of them around London. He glared at Thane. I've a good team.'

'I don't doubt that.' Suddenly, Thane understood.

The Transport Police were unique in some ways yet often ignored or overlooked by other cops. Their numbers weren't large, their units were scattered through Britain, they seldom made headlines. Their basic role was to police the railways and railway properties, some ferry ships and seaports. They didn't always get their share of credits. Sometimes they rightly complained they were treated like second-class citizens although they had to meet the same standards and pass the same training. But it wasn't the moment for anyone to go on a crusade.

'Pat.' Thane used Emslie's first name then waited until he had the man's full attention. 'You say you were born in a signal box. I don't care if you were conceived on a footplate. We do the same job. So no more guided-tour nonsense. You're a cop, I'm a cop. Do you understand?'

Emslie hesitated for a moment, then gave a wry nod. 'Yes, sir. I'm sorry.'

'I decide when you're sorry, Inspector.' Thane took any sting out of it with a smile, and saw Emslie look happier. 'You say you examined that Intercity. How?'

'The coaches, sir.' Emslie was back on familiar territory and confident again. 'The way they're constructed, the only way Haston could have got out was by using a door. All the door locks were as normal, no catches were broken or damaged. So then we brought in the railway research people – '

'Research?' Thane blinked. 'Why do that?'

'The aerodynamics side. For a reconstruction. They have a wind tunnel, we needed it.' Emslie was suitably patient. 'First, we knew the speed of an Intercity train on the section of track where Haston's body was found. The average is around eighty miles an hour.'

'So?'

'Intercity coaches are built to a standard front and rear door layout. The front door is hinged on its leading edge, the rear door is hinged in the reverse way, on the trailing edge.'

'Front. Rear.' Thane tried it with his hands and decided he understood. 'Go on. Keep it simple.'

'They used a wind tunnel, sir. Open an Intercity's rear door at sixty-five miles an hour or over, and that door gets thrown back with enough force to break the safety straps – it hadn't happened. With a leading-edge door, you've the opposite. You're pushing against that wind. But an adult could open one of those leading-edge front doors – could, if he's no weakling – at around eighty-five miles an hour. Haston could have done it, could have jumped.'

'And the door would slam shut again, no damage?' Thane anticipated the inevitable.

Emslie nodded.

'Do you think it happened that way?"

'I don't know, Superintendent.' The fair-haired young inspector was wary. 'The only label I could use is "unexplained death". It can be easier on relatives – '

'Easier than murder?'

'I didn't know the real background.' Emslie didn't make it an apology. 'Maybe I was sorry for his wife. Haston's death was south the border, meaning English law, not Scottish. The Coroner's Court sat, agreed to continue the case till later, and we released the body. Haston was cremated. We were going for an open verdict.'

There was a rushing roar of sound outside as a main-line train raced past them. Thane winced. Whatever way that front door had opened, the sound of it slamming shut again probably wouldn't have been noticed in the general background noise.

'How do you feel about it now?' he asked.

'I could have looked at a few things differently.' Emslie chewed his lower lip for a moment. 'Everything we got about Haston's marriage and his business seemed – well, there was nothing major. Most people have problems.'

'True.' Thane paused, looking at him closely. Emslie's eyes were worried in a way he hadn't seen before. 'Or people remember something. You'd better tell me about it.'

'Two passengers on the Intercity who looked like a married couple began quarrelling, shouting at each other. The other passengers didn't know why. Then it ended, and the couple left the train next stop, at Carlisle.' Emslie swore under his breath. 'We heard about it, it didn't seem to matter.' He drew a deep breath. 'It's not in our report.'

'Where and when?' asked Thane quietly.

'About four coaches back from the restaurant car.' Emslie looked at him and nodded. 'Around the time Haston died. We couldn't trace them.'

'Descriptions?'

'Mid-thirties, ordinary.' Emslie looked more unhappy than ever. 'People couldn't even remember when they boarded. The train was half empty, they just suddenly began making a noise – '

Thane sighed and nodded. No matter how good a diversion, it didn't have to be linked. Descriptions

60

hardly mattered. One way or another, they were usually wildly wrong.

'Get it on paper.' He left it at that.

'Sir.' Emslie looked grateful. 'I was told to work with you, any way that helped.'

'Have another look at every statement you took. If anything else seems odd, check it again.' Thane knew it would be a drab, time-consuming task. But necessary now. 'If you come up against the names John Gort or Janey Peters, that's total priority. Get straight to me.'

The Q train was beginning to slow. Thane saw they were almost back at the Polmadie yard. He could see his car where he'd left it. A black police van was waiting for the prisoners to be unloaded.

'I'll have to talk with Haston's widow.'

Emslie nodded.

'What did you think of her?'

'She was shattered. Vague about some things.' Emslie gave a small gesture with his hands. 'They hadn't been married long. I felt sorry for her.'

The little train came to a halt in a squeal of brakes. Emslie went with Thane to the repair van's door and watched him leave. Thane looked up from the track.

'See me tomorrow, Pat,' he suggested.

The train was beginning to unload. Thane walked to his car, started it, and bottomed the suspension a few times as he drove out along the pot-holed track. The Ford's low-band radio was muttering, but the message was for another Crime Squad car.

He was glad. He wanted time to think.

Commander Jack Hart's hunches had an unpleasant habit of paying off. The evidence might not be worth much. But Robert Haston had been murdered – by arrangement.

A few minutes took the Ford to one of the feeder lanes for

the west-bound side of the M8 motorway. Colin Thane joined the main flow of traffic near where the motorway ran close to the River Clyde, and saw a large cargo ship had docked overnight at one of the docks. Ships that size didn't arrive too often any more. The river was dying in maritime terms, the new Glasgow depended on a rapidly growing number of new hi-tech industries.

The newcomers were international in origin. They were welcome. Particularly if they offered new jobs and if any key workers brought in from overseas could decide basics like which football team they intended to support.

He left the motorway again at the third exit ramp along. Then the Ford travelled a tree-lined road until it reached a gate in a high boundary fence. A sign said Police Training Area and the gate had a guard.

The gate opened and Thane drove in. A long stretch of parkland was hidden behind the trees, parkland used for training by both the city's mounted police and its dog-branch handlers. The long, low building behind that was where the Scottish Crime Squad was based.

It didn't have many visitors. The Crime Squad preferred to go out to do business. Witnesses were usually interviewed somewhere else. It was a head-quarters which didn't possess a single overnight holding cell for prisoners.

The Crime Squad worked that way.

In terms of psychological warfare, it helped.

The main parking lot was in front of the building. Thane parked his car, got out, glanced from sheer habit at the nearest of the surveillance cameras which covered the area, then walked over.

When he went in by the glass doors, a smartly dressed middle-aged woman was standing talking to a young constable at the front desk. The constable greeted Thane with a polite nod of recognition then turned away to glance at the bank of TV monitor screens beside him. Two showed Thane's Ford, from different angles.

'Good morning, Colin.' The middle-aged woman came over. She was well groomed, her name was Maggie Fyffe, and she was Commander Hart's personal secretary. She was also a cop's widow. She reached Thane, shook her head and chuckled. 'I heard about last night. Better luck next time.'

'I've had happier moments,' said Thane dryly. He grimaced. 'You saw Jack Hart?'

'This morning?' She nodded. 'His file on John Gort is on your desk. I opened another for Robert Haston, and a Transport Police messenger brought a copy of their report on his death. Except for two, your caseload has been shuffled and dealt around. The Commander thought you could keep the antiques fraud and the Triad blackmails, that they'd hold for later.'

'That's the two I'd most like to lose.' Thane made it a joke, but it was near to the truth. The antiques fraud was a tangle he was still trying to understand. The Triad case was a confusion that led all the way back to Hong Kong, with more complications than anyone could calculate.

A click of approaching high heels made him glance round. A slim woman with short, jet-black hair smiled a greeting as she went past, heading out. Her name was Tina Redder, she was a detective chief inspector, and her speciality was embezzlements.

'Stop looking at her legs,' said Maggie Fyffe with a mild irritation. 'At her age, she should have varicose veins.' She watched Tina Redder go out and the doors swing shut again. 'The Commander said any paperwork that comes in can wait until he gets back.'

'Keep it that way, Maggie.' He made it a plea.

'But if it looks urgent – '

'Use your own judgement. Right?'

She nodded, a slight twinkle in her eyes. 'Will you use his office?'

'No need.' Hastily, he shook his head. Jack Hart made a virtue out of running a neat, tidy desk. Colin Thane's reputation ran in the opposite direction. 'Keep the enemy from my door and that's all I ask.'

He left Maggie Fyffe and went along a short corridor to his own office. The door lay wide open. It was a modest-sized room, plainly furnished, although as a detective superintendent he now rated the carpet on the floor and a detective superintendent also rated a desk with a couple of extra drawers, and a swivel chair with padded arms. The chair was occupied. Thane made a throat-clearing noise and Sergeant Francey Dunbar looked up, showed surprise, then abandoned the bundle of telex messages he'd been reading.

'I didn't know when you'd get here, sir.' His sergeant almost made it a complaint as he rose from the chair. He wore blue corduroy trousers and an open-necked yellow-and-blue-patterned sports shirt with the sleeves rolled up. 'The boss left a note you'd gone off to see a Transport cop.'

'Did he say why?'

'I got that from Maggie Fyffe,' admitted Dunbar. 'Does the Haston thing stand up?'

'As murder?' Thane took off his jacket, hung it on a peg behind the door, then dropped into the vacated chair. 'It has that kind of smell. We're low on proof.'

Overnight, his desk had sprouted a new crop of papers, from the telexes to scribbled messages. Two plastic folders lay central to it all, one headed John Gort, the other Robert Haston. There was also a large brown envelope with the British Transport Police crest. It was addressed to him, but it had been opened.

'Read everything?' he asked Dunbar.

'Just to pass the time,' murmured Dunbar. He had

propped himself against a filing cabinet near the only window in the room. The view was out across the parking lot towards the trees, with glimpses of distant motorway. 'I understand a few things now – I think.'

Thane nodded. 'What's new and overnight?'

'Not a lot,' admitted Dunbar. 'We're getting our search warrant for Janey Peters' apartment. After the airport, that's no problem. As soon as we have it Joe Felix will head out there with Scenes of Crime and a telephone engineer.' His thin moustache twitched. 'Do I ask about Sergeant Merreday?'

'No.' The overweight sergeant was an unpleasant memory Thane could do without. 'I'm organizing something. You don't want to know about it.'

'Forget I asked.' Dunbar was satisfied. 'Sandra has a couple of men helping her work through some of the rest of your list from last night.' He paused and gave an attempt at an innocent grin. 'I heaved Jock Dawson and his livestock out for a daylight check around where you met the Magic Bakerman last night. They'll look in at the aiport while he's there. Maybe someone will fly them off as cargo.'

Thane kept a straight face. Jock Dawson was a dog-handler on temporary attachment to the Squad, Dunbar was wary of dogs, and Dawson's pair of four-legged friends seemed to have known it from the first moment they met. But when any kind of search was involved then the lanky, lazy-eyed Dawson was the obvious choice.

'Anything from Forensic?'

'This early?' Dunbar glanced at his watch. 'This is still coffee time.'

'That's how the quality people live, Francey.' Thane was used to the libel. He gestured at his desk. 'I'll get down to this lot. You can give things another stir.'

Dunbar nodded, left the room and closed the door behind him. On his own, Thane shook his head at the collection of waiting reports. But he had to begin somewhere.

The thing he wanted to see most was at the front of the John Gort folder when he opened it. The anonymous letter which had begun everything else amounted to a single sheet of typed, cheap air-mail paper. Like its envelope, it was in a plastic evidence bag. Just as Jack Hart had said, the envelope had Spanish postage stamps and a Malaga postmark. It had been addressed to the Officer in Charge, Scottish Crime Squad – and even the postal code was correct.

The letter was short and direct:

Do you remember John Gort, the Interface Man who made it to Spain? He is coming back, short-stay, to do a job. Someone twisted his arm, and the money is good. He was out of the game till this turned up.

He knows you still can't arrest him. Be patient and you'll maybe hear from me. Codeword Pony. Go in heavy and you can forget it.

There was no signature, no spelling or typing errors. A laboratory report had been attached. It had yielded nothing that could help. It was the first and only time they'd heard from Codeword Pony.

Colin Thane sat back, rubbed a hand across his forehead and wished again that his wife hadn't won her campaign to make him give up cigarettes. He took another long scowl at the unsigned letter, cursing whoever had written it for the way the hook had been so effectively baited, cursing Jack Hart for the human-enough way the Squad commander had decided to play it, cursing the unpredictable way things had gone wrong.

The first part of the letter had come true, John Gort was back. But what came next?

66

He kept on with the folder.

First came a condensed version of John Gort's history. The Interface Man had been a Clydeside engineering apprentice, then had become hooked on electronics. Night school classes then an Adult Education course had won him a job with the computer-design research department at a Japanese-owned plant in the English Midlands. Five years later he was sentenced to six years' imprisonment, found guilty of being the technical brain behind a safe-deposit robbery, suspected of several more.

It hadn't happened that way again. When he came out of jail he had new friends. They appeared to introduce him to a better, international class of thieving. The nearest thing he had to a home base was back in his native Scotland. But the Interface Man seldom dirtied his own doorstep and only left one trademark behind him after a job – sheer hi-tech skill.

Until at last he had gone to his beach bar in Spain.

Thane frowned at the folder, his thoughts drifting. The people who had summoned the Interface Man had no reason to anticipate trouble when he flew in on his false passport. Yet they had still set up enough trip-wire precautions to leave chaos behind them. Go back from there, and suppose the same people had earlier tried to recruit Robert Haston. It wasn't too wild a possibility. Suppose there had been a reason why Haston had to die, suppose they had first lined up John Gort as their replacement electronics man?

If they operated that way, what might happen to Gort afterwards, when his part was finished?

The telephone on his desk began ringing. The thought ended and he lifted the receiver.

'Thane.'

'Good morrow, Brave Captain.' The voice at the other end of the line was a near bellow. 'How are things?'

'Don't ask,' advised Thane.

That brought a bray of amusement, the kind of bray which, once heard, was impossible to forget. Derry Hull was a detective inspector with the Crime Squad's permanent detail over in Edinburgh. Prematurely bald, habitually loud-voiced, he was regarded as slightly mad. He greeted everyone as Brave Captain. Nobody knew why, nobody wanted to ask.

'Does this help?' roared Hull. 'We've sorted out the Janey Peters car thing. She bought the VW from that Edinburgh dealer's used-car line-up three days ago. I talked with the salesman, the description matches, and she was on her own.'

'He's positive?'

'Positive,' confirmed the foghorn. 'The woman traded in an old clunker of a Chrysler four-door, the ownership documents in Janey Peters' name, then paid the balance in cash. She had a wad of notes in her handbag that would have choked a horse.' Hull saw the question coming. 'Used notes, Brave Captain. He remembers.'

'What happened to the Chrysler?'

'The trade-in?' Hull barely paused. 'Still here, untouched by human hand. They're not the kind of firm who advertise they sell clunkers. The thing is lying in their yard, until they can haul it to some out-of-town vehicle auction and get rid of it. Why?'

'Grab it,' ordered Thane. 'I want it taken direct to the Edinburgh forensic laboratory. Don't let them put this at the back of any queue, Derry. I want them to go over that Chrysler, inside and out, until they can play tunes on it. Janey Peters vanished from her local scene two weeks ago. If that Chrysler was with her, can they tell us anything about where it has been? Ask for anything that might help.'

'You'll get it,' promised Hull in a farewell bellow. 'I'll call you.'

Thane said goodbye, then hung up. It was a thin chance, but one that might pay.

Making a hopeful noise through his teeth, he turned back to the Gort folder. There were a series of telex messages between Jack Hart and Spanish police on the Costa del Sol. The Guardia Civil operated an undercover anti-terrorist unit based on Malaga, with the secondary role of monitoring local foreign resident criminals. There were enough of them to form a prosperous, sociable little colony – and Spanish law was still weak on things like expulsion or extradition unless a foreigner offended locally.

John Gort had never been that kind of fool.

Then one telex from Spain had confirmed that something seemed scheduled. John Gort had told the senior barman at his beach bar that he might have to make a brief business trip to Britain. If that happened, the senior barman would be in charge.

The senior barman sometimes slept with a woman who was a regular Guardia informant. She heard, she reported back, and the Guardia watch began in earnest.

Thane read on, into the ways Jack Hart had had checks made on any Scottish or English contacts known to have been used by the Interface Man. No one had been allowed to suspect it was happening. Hart had done everything possible that way and every other way.

It had all been useless when Janey Peters, with her new car and new blonde hair, turned up at Glasgow Airport.

Thane heard a knock at his office door. It opened and one of the typists brought him in coffee. It was in a cup and saucer instead of his usual mug and, once the girl had gone, Thane raised an eyebrow. The fine bone china with the gold key pattern was normally kept for Jack Hart and his guests. Maggie Fyffe was giving him her own Good Luck gesture – even if he still only rated a cup with a crack down one side.

He sipped the coffee and turned to the folder on Robert Haston and the Transport Police report on his death. But as he started the door burst open and Francey Dunbar looked in.

'We've got our search warrant,' said Dunbar, pleased. 'Joe Felix is on his way to Williamfield.' He shaped a grin, sardonic at the edges. 'I told him about your fat friend Merreday.'

'Good.' Thane sat back for a moment, clasping his hands behind his head. 'Denny Hull has located her last set of wheels, through in Edinburgh. Any word back yet from Jock Dawson at the airport?'

'Nothing.' Dunbar moved a piece of gum he had been nursing in one cheek and made a mild suggestion. 'Maybe his dogs ate him.'

'I like dogs,' reminded Thane wearily. 'Often enough I prefer them to people. What else is happening – in the real world?'

'We're trying.' Dunbar shook his head. 'Mostly, we're running into problems. Like we're hoping for a return call from Worldfriend Timeshares in London. Their sales supervisor is the only one who knows much about how Janey Peters worked for them, and he's out somewhere.'

'The Computer Cabin catalogue, and the equipment that was marked?'

'The modem and bits?' Dunbar shrugged. 'Sandra is chasing that one. They're going back through their sales records. It shouldn't be too difficult – modem units don't exactly sell like cans of beans.'

'At least I understand cans of beans,' growled Thane. Hands still behind his head, he looked up at the ceiling for a moment. 'Tell Sandra I'll want her along with me in about fifteen minutes. I want to try talking to Haston's widow.'

Dunbar raised a hopeful eyebrow. 'I could – '

70

'No.' Thane shook his head. 'I don't know the questions yet – so I want a woman along. We can look in at the Computer Cabin store on the way back.'

Dunbar nodded. 'About Sandra, sir – '

'What about her?' Thane lowered his hands and frowned at his sergeant. 'Francey, if she wants to sit the sergeant's test, good luck to her.'

'That?' Dunbar shrugged. 'No. She'll pass it standing on her head. But she has a notion about last night. She was telling me – '

'Then maybe I can get to hear,' suggested Thane.

'It's different,' warned Dunbar. He rubbed a heel for a moment into the carpet. 'It's about the biker last night – the leathers and sawn-off shotgun. Sandra was there, I wasn't.'

'Well?'

'Sandra reckons he could have been a she – a woman.'

Thane froze. 'Why?'

'She says it can take one to know one.' Dunbar gestured vaguely. 'Something about the way she rode that bike. You know about women – '

'I think so.' Thane was sarcastic. Then he sighed. 'The Transport cops have something about a woman on the train when Haston was killed. So we don't rule it out for last night. Now give me a couple of minutes' thinking time, and tell Sandra I'll collect her.'

Dunbar nodded, started to leave, then hesitated.

'Can I disappear for half an hour this afternoon?' he asked. 'It's Federation business.'

'Just don't tell me, then I won't miss you,' suggested Thane.

Dunbar grinned his thanks and closed the door as he went out. Thane sighed again as he reached for the Haston folder. Sometimes he regretted that his sergeant was the Crime Squad's elected delegate to the Police Federation, their nearest thing to a union official.

71

But Francey Dunbar was a mixture. He had his off-duty passion for motorcycles, he seemed to effortlessly collect young women who were glamorous beyond belief. But show him an obscure cause, from contemplating on a clifftop onward, and Francey Dunbar could be there. He might not let it show too often, but he cared about people.

That didn't always help when you were a cop.

The folder still waited. It didn't take long to read, because there wasn't a lot.

Robert Haston had come from a comfortable middle-class background, had drifted his way through school and university, then, still apparently drifting, had obtained a Regular Army short-service commission as a lieutenant in a signals regiment. The army had taught him all he knew about electronics and computer techniques but he had left when his short-service time was up. He had claimed he could make better money as a civilian. The army's memory was different, including some signals equipment going missing then turning up on the black market.

Haston had taken his army-taught electronic skills into industrial security. A few years later, when Jack Hart had been questioning him as a suspect behind at least one major break-in, Hart's memories came down to one pungent paragraph:

'He wouldn't talk. You could almost smell the fear, and I didn't believe him. But there wasn't enough evidence, I couldn't charge him.'

Well, now he was dead. Thane took a quick flick through the separate Transport Police report, saw that it mainly dealt with what he'd been told by Pat Emslie, and made a note of where the dead man had lived.

He dumped the folders and other paperwork in one of his desk drawers and went over to the window. Some

72

police horses were being exercised in the grassland beyond the Squad parking lot.

It must be a reasonable life, being a police horse. Free oats, no forms to fill, and someone to rub you down at the end of the day. Sadly, he remembered the grafitti he'd seen in one of the airport lavatories:

'Join the Police. They don't run away from trouble, they start it.'

Underneath, someone else seemed to agree:

'If Pigs could fly, Scotland Yard would be London's third airport.'

The horses galloped on. He went along the corridor to the Squad's main duty room.

This was one of the quiet times. Only a few of the day shift were still around, mostly working at their desks. The maps around the walls covered all of Scotland and anywhere marked with a pin meant a Crime Squad operation. Yet the Crime Squad wasn't a large unit. It was a modest-sized group, drawn from forces throughout the country. Those men and women went back to their own forces eventually. But while they were Crime Squad, they owed no other loyalty.

Nobody lasted who couldn't take the pressure.

He saw Sandra Craig finish a telephone call and replace her receiver. She saw him at the same time, collected her jacket and handbag, and came over.

'Ready, sir.' She was wearing a pleated tan skirt and a white and green hooped sweater and could have been some young college student. Her jacket was a tan waterproof nylon. 'Francey warned me.'

'Did he say where we were going?'

'He said we'll be talking to a widow. I'm the statutory sympathetic female.' Her voice was tart. 'We want to check if she's doing enough weeping.'

Thane winced but nodded. 'That's part of what it's about.'

73

He heard his name shouted. A detective constable at one of the desks beckoned, holding a telephone receiver high. Thane went over.

'For you, sir.' The detective constable had slapped a hand over the telephone mouthpiece. 'A woman. She keeps saying she has to talk to whoever is in charge of the Interface Man case.'

Thane nodded and took the receiver. Anyone who knew Gort's tradename could matter.

'My name is Thane,' he said quietly. 'I'm a detective superintendent.'

'Tell me this, Mister Detective Superintendent.' The woman's voice was curt and brittle, educated enough to be wiped free of any accent. 'Did you lead that herd of clowns I saw at the airport last night – the clowns trying to shadow John Gort?'

'Were we?' countered Thane. He knew it would be a waste of time to try to trace the call. 'Have you a name?'

'You know it. Pony.' The woman's voice tightened. 'Be stupid again like last night, and people could be killed.'

'Where is he, Pony?' asked Thane. 'You know, don't you?'

'I thought I did.' There was a bitter laugh. 'You've got till next Tuesday. You need help – so does John Gort.'

Then there was only a buzz on the line. The woman had hung up.

He cursed, then handed the receiver back to the detective constable.

'If she calls again, she matters,' he told the man. 'Whatever she says, tell her we'll listen. Make sure Francey Dunbar knows.'

Somehow, he had been expecting that kind of a call. But now he knew he only had four days – and Pony was frightened. For Gort's safety as much as her own.

Sandra Craig was waiting, puzzled. He beckoned, and they left the duty room.

3

Friday is not a happy day for your average cop. Friday morning is a peak time of the week for armed robberies, Friday afternoon is when the professional shoplifting teams work any decent-sized department store, and Friday night is something else. In Glasgow's darklands, it produces the 'Hey you, Jimmy' stabbings.

A 'Hey you, Jimmy' is usually the end product of a drunken argument that becomes a quarrel. It is the kind of knifing which can end with blood and slurred apologies. Even if it becomes a murder, the aggressor is seldom identified to the police – particularly if he is close family to the victim. He becomes a vague stranger. After all, if apologies aren't good enough then things can be sorted out later.

The day was cool and bright and Friday was well into its usual pattern as Thane drove his Ford out of the Crime Squad's tree-fringed base. Sandra Craig was beside him in the front passenger seat. She had the volume of their radio turned low; messages about some of the day's crop of guns-and-masks hold-ups coming in over the general police channel were reduced to barely a mutter.

She had offered to drive. She was one of the safest as well as one of the fastest drivers in the Squad. But driving usually helped Thane, allowed the things in his mind to fall into some kind of shape with some kind of priority attached.

Usually. As he watched the road and coped with the traffic, one of the few things that came through to him was the latest addition to his list, the woman who called herself Pony. It hadn't come as any surprise that Pony was a woman. But why was she involved, what was her motive?

He had until Tuesday. That wasn't long by any standard.

'Sandra.' He spared his red-haired passenger a sideways glance, and saw that she was demolishing a half-eaten chocolate bar. 'You say you think our motorcycle friend last night was a woman. Would you put money on it?'

'That's the way I woke up feeling this morning, sir.' She squeezed the chocolate bar's wrappings into a small, messy pellet and jammed it into the Ford's ashtray. 'I knew there was something wrong. That was the answer.'

'We're building a list,' he said bleakly.

'Sir?'

'Janey Peters, Haston's widow, the Pony woman – add your bike woman. Then maybe another woman on Haston's train. She started what sounds like a diversion just when it mattered.'

'I hadn't heard.' Sandra Craig grimaced. 'A female takeover?'

'Keep that kind of funny for your sergeant's examination.' Grimly Thane squeezed the Ford past a wandering delivery truck in a way that brought a startled blast from the other vehicle. He swore under his breath, then shaped a half-apology to his passenger. 'I'm not having a happy day.'

She nodded. 'How do we play things with Haston's widow, sir?'

'Gently.' Thane checked his rear-view mirror and was glad they'd lost the delivery truck. 'Unless we decide differently. I want to know the way things were before her husband died – and how she feels now. Reasonable?'

'Yes.' Absently, Detective Constable Craig rummaged in her handbag and produced a comb. 'Sir, can

77

you warn me when you're thinking of passing another truck like that last one?'

'Why?' He was suspicious.

She grinned. 'So I get time to use the ejector seat.'

Robert Haston's home and office had been in a small Victorian terrace at Crathes Street in Kelvinbridge, on the north side of Glasgow. Crathes Street was built of red sandstone, respectable without being expensive, and each house had its own small strip of private garden and its own front door.

Haston's house, halfway along, had a small red Datsun parked outside. The Ford stopped behind the Datsun and Thane got out, closely followed by Sandra Craig as he crossed a short path of concrete slabs to the Haston front door. There were a bellpush and a plastic name-plate to one side of the door and someone was at home. They could hear the muffled theme tune of one of the lunch-hour soap operas coming from inside.

The music ended when Thane rang the doorbell. But almost another minute passed before the door clicked, then opened a modest gap. The woman who looked out at them was in her early thirties, plump to the point of being overweight.

'Mrs Joan Haston?' asked Thane.

She nodded. Joan Haston was medium height. She had a fat face and sad, spaniel-like brown eyes and her straight black hair had been cut in schoolboy-short style. She was wearing a dark grey wool jacket and skirt with a slightly grubby white blouse, but she didn't have shoes.

'Police, Mrs Haston.' Thane made it an apology and showed his warrant card. 'I'm Detective Superintendent Thane.'

'A superintendent this time.' She ignored the warrant card, looking at Sandra. 'What about her?'

'Detective Constable Craig.'

'In case I go peculiar and shout rape?' Joan Haston's expression didn't change. She had the look of someone who had decided never to be surprised again. 'I thought you people were finished with me.'

'We need some extra help, Mrs Haston.' Thane paused, seeing the bitterness in the depths of those spaniel eyes. 'It shouldn't take long.'

'Am I supposed to believe that?' She had a naturally high-pitched voice and the tight sarcasm behind her words didn't help. But she opened the door wider. 'All right. Come in.'

Thane and Sandra Craig went past her into a small, dull hallway. There was an alcove for coats and a glass door ahead gave them a view of a kitchen. The hallway's only decoration was a framed print of a Degas ballet painting, hung between two room doors. Behind them, Joan Haston closed her street door then led the way to a living room at the rear. A TV set still flickered silently in one corner and she glanced at the screen action for a moment before switching it off.

'Sit down.' She nodded towards a pair of armchairs and a couch, all covered in dark green nylon fabric. 'There's not much left for anyone to ask about.'

Her two visitors settled in the chairs. They could see she had been using the couch – her shoes were still lying on it, beside an open newspaper. With a slight shrug, Joan Haston returned to sitting on the couch again, her clasped hands resting on the lap of her grey skirt. Apart from her wedding ring, her only jewellery was a small silver and diamante brooch on one lapel of her jacket.

'Where's Inspector Emslie?' she asked. 'He promised me he had everything he needed.'

'Pat Emslie is Transport Police, we do a different job,' said Thane. He saw Sandra Craig's notebook and pen were already out of her handbag. But she wouldn't use them unless it was necessary. Only a known, working tape recorder rated as a worse distraction than a notebook. 'When did you see him last?'

'Inspector Emslie?' She frowned. 'About two weeks ago, just after the Carlisle coroner released Robert's body. He brought some papers I had to sign.'

'You know that the Transport Police can still only say that your husband died from injuries?'

'They'll settle for anything that doesn't suggest there was a fault in their damned train.' Her plump face flushed under that black skull-cap of hair. 'I know they wanted to call it suicide. My lawyer says I can't prove one way, they can't prove the other. That's how it stays.'

'But what's your opinion, Mrs Haston? How do you think it happened?'

She pursed her lips. 'I only know he didn't jump from that train. He didn't have any reason, Superintendent. I know they examined the doors and the windows and found nothing – but things can happen, can't they?'

'And none of this makes it easier for you,' said Thane quietly.

Joan Haston looked down at her hands. 'I had a marriage that lasted just over a year.' Pausing, she looked across at Sandra as if hoping for a better understanding. 'We maybe weren't the greatest love story of all time. But we – well – '

'Got along?' suggested Sandra with a slight, sympathetic smile.

'We got along.' Joan Haston nodded agreement. 'No real worries – and that included the business. I've been asked that often enough.'

'No problems of any kind?' asked Thane.

'Everyone has problems, now and again. There was never anything we couldn't handle.'

'How long had you known him before you married?'

'Three months. Would you like to hear how we met?' She kept a tight control of her voice. 'I was a secretary,

80

he arrived after we had a break-in at the office, and he tried to sell my boss a new security system. He didn't get the order, but he bought me dinner.' Again she paused. 'What else?'

'Tell me about family,' suggested Thane. 'Your family, his family.'

The question surprised her, but was simple enough to answer. Joan Haston's parents lived out of town and she had a brother and two sisters. Robert Haston's parents had been dead a few years, killed in a car crash. His only relative was a cousin, a woman who had been about the same age. She was married and lived in New Zealand.

'Have you met?' asked Sandra.

Joan Haston shook her head. 'But I telephoned to let her know. She cabled flowers for his funeral.'

Thane sighed. It all fitted very easily into what he'd expected. He sat silent for a moment, looking around the modestly furnished room. If there had ever been photographs, wedding or any other kind, they had been put away. There were different ways of mourning.

'Mrs Haston, do you know very much about your husband's life before you met?'

The plump young widow stared at him, bewildered. 'Why?'

'Do you?' persisted Thane.

'He never really talked about it.' She moistened her lips. 'He'd been in the army, of course, but – '

'Do you know any of his friends from then?'

'No.' Her bewilderment was still growing. 'But we didn't go out much. We were too busy trying to build up his business.'

Softly, Sandra Craig cleared her throat. Thane gave her a sideways glance which meant she could take over.

'I don't know too much about what he did, Mrs Haston,' she said apologetically.

'He designed special security systems for special

81

needs. Then he'd put the system together and install it.'

'He always worked from home?'

Joan Haston nodded. 'Our front room was the office, he used our spare bedroom upstairs as a workshop.' She gave a faint smile. 'I was secretary and general dogs-body.'

Thane left it to Sandra Craig to take things from there. The redhead didn't waste time, yet didn't rush the other woman. Haston's business had amounted to locating a prospective customer, interesting him, then selling him the idea of a new system of security hardware which had been designed to match his problems. Assembly and installation, with Haston always supervising, was the only stage where he would hire outside help for a few days.

'No one else?'

'Never.' Joan Haston shook her head. 'We were selling on price as much as quality. That meant no overheads we could do without.'

'I'd like to see where he worked,' said Thane.

'His office? All right.' She got to her feet but then her mouth firmed and she didn't move. 'Tell me I'm right. You're not any kind of Transport Police, are you?'

'No.' Thane shook his head. 'We're Crime Squad officers, Mrs Haston.'

'Crime Squad.' She moistened her lips. 'Are you trying to tell me that my husband was some kind of crook?'

'I'm not, Mrs Haston.' Thane tried to leave it at that.

'Don't ever try, or you'll regret it.' Joan Haston glared defiance at him. 'You want to see his office – I'll show you it. There's nothing to hide.'

Still without her shoes, she led the way and they followed her back out into the lobby. She opened another door, gestured, and Thane went in first.

The front room of the little terrace house still showed

traces of when it had been a lounge. It had fancy light shades, an empty, blocked-off fireplace with a tiled surround, and a small built-in display cabinet in one corner which had a stained-glass front.

But that had been in the past. Now it was a mix between office and storeroom. Metal rack shelving climbed the walls and was filled with assorted cartons, reels of thin, plastic-coated wire and items of electronic equipment. At floor level a line of plastic bread bins had been used as filing cabinets. In the centre of the room a full computer work station sat with its VDU on a swivel-arm turntable. Beside it was a printer on a trolley stand. A second, smaller desk was occupied by a word processor. The fourth main item, a designer's easel-board, was near the word processor, positioned to catch the best of the natural light from the window.

'This is where it all happened – if he wasn't out getting an order or installing somewhere.' Joan Haston was standing behind Thane. 'Everything here was bought second hand, then he'd just take it to bits and rebuild it.' There was pride in the memory. 'He worked hard. We both did.'

Thane nodded his understanding. There was a framed photograph of the couple on a shelf beside the word processor. They were both smiling broadly, the camera capturing a happy moment. He turned to face the window.

'There are two names, Mrs Haston – a man named John Gort, a woman Janey Peters. They may be people from before you married, or they may have contacted him not long before he died. Do you know them?'

'No. But I can check.' Frowning, she went over to the computer, touched a couple of switches, and let the VDU screen come to life. Then, standing over the keyboard, she tapped a brief code and fed in both names. They appeared on the VDU, she tapped another couple

83

of keys, then shook her head as the words 'Not Listed' appeared beside each name. 'Sorry. If he knew them and they had mattered, their names would have been stored. Robert made it a golden rule.'

'For everything?' Thane raised an eyebrow.

'For even our Christmas cards list, down to names and addresses.' Her high-pitched voice frosted at the edges. 'Before you ask, Superintendent, I'm no computer expert. But I'd know if there were any murky corners on that thing that I couldn't access.'

'Does it work with firms, Mrs Haston?' asked Sandra Craig mildly and unexpectedly. She had been making a slow tour round the room, but she had stopped at the metal shelving, beside one of the cartons. She ran a finger across a label on the side. 'This is from Computer Cabin. Did your husband do much business there?'

'Not a lot, but we had an account with them. They carry a good stock of electronics software, things he sometimes needed quickly.'

'So they'll be listed?'

'Yes.' Joan Haston tapped the computer's keys again and the VDU screen wiped, then changed. The Computer Cabin data which appeared ran to several lines. 'This shows our account and order details.' She paused, studying the display for a moment. 'The last time we bought from them was about four months ago.'

At the bottom of the screen were two names and telephone extension numbers.

'People you know?' asked Thane.

'People who matter – or they did. David Mark is their sales manager, Louise Croft is their credit controller.'

'And the same detail is on file for other firms, other people?'

She nodded.

'Can you tell if your husband recently placed an order with anyone for a modem convertor?'

'That's into computer ware. What kind of modem convertor?'

'Any kind.'

She asked the keyboard. The screen gave a negative.

'But you'd heard him talk about them?'

'Like he'd talk about a lot of things. Maybe for a special job – I don't know.' She stopped, then the question she had been nursing burst out. 'Superintendent, tell me the truth. There's only one possible way I can make sense out of the kind of questions you're asking. Do you think Robert could have been murdered?'

'There's that possibility,' said Thane carefully.

'Thank you.' She meant it. 'Thank you for telling me.' For a moment her hands pressed for support on the computer desk. But she shook her head as Sandra made to go over. 'No, I'm all right. I – I almost feel better. Maybe I've been waiting for someone to say it. There's no other way, is there?'

'You could help us find out,' said Thane.

She stared. 'How?'

'A way you know better than anyone else.' He indicated the computer. 'I could get some fancy expert to work on that. But you know how your husband stored information, you know the best ways to retrieve it.'

'Retrieve what?' She fingered her wedding ring, her face pale but eager.

'You'd be looking for something small, something that maybe didn't matter to him when he fed it in. Something you'll maybe spot, because now it doesn't look right.'

'And if I can't find it?'

'You tried,' he said simply.

'I'll do it.' She nodded.

'But if you find anything, then you call us – no one else,' warned Thane.

'I understand.' She switched off the computer, drew a

deep breath, and looked across at Sandra. 'You'll keep in touch?'

'Yes.' Sandra nodded. 'It works both ways.' She wrote the Crime Squad number on a sheet from her notebook and handed it over. 'Call me at any time.'

They were ready to go. Joan Haston saw them out into the lobby again and opened the front door.

'I'm selling the house – and what's left of the business.' She made it a flat statement. 'One of my sisters runs a baby-clothes boutique. She could use some help.'

She said a quiet goodbye, and the door closed. They went back to Thane's Ford and got aboard. He started the car, but let it idle for a moment.

'I believed her,' said Sandra Craig. She sighed. 'At least, I think she was telling us what she believed.'

'Her husband still got himself killed,' said Thane brutally. 'What you mean is she doesn't know why.'

The redhead refused to be ruffled. 'How many wives go through life not knowing their husband has something nasty hidden in a cupboard?'

'I'd get hell if I even tried it,' said Thane dryly. 'But keep her looking in that computer. Visit her, phone her – encourage her to call you.' Joan Haston was going to need that kind of support. Going through a dead husband's files would be a daunting task for anyone. 'Don't rush her – but keep pushing.'

'I will.' She fastened her seat belt. 'What about the way Computer Cabin surfaced? Just a coincidence?'

'The kind to be marked Handle with Care.' It was a tenuous wisp of a link between the vanished John Gort and the dead Haston. But Thane couldn't discard anything outright unless something better came along. 'I don't like coincidences.'

'Are they still next on our list?'

'No.' Thane stopped her as she squirrelled yet another

chocolate bar from her handbag. It was after two in the afternoon, he was feeling hungry. 'We'll eat first.'

Detective Constable Sandra Craig smiled. Inwardly, she said a little prayer of thanks to anyone listening.

Thane put the Ford into gear. As they began moving, Sandra took a routine flick through the radio's emergency channels.

Yes, Friday afternoon had arrived. A patrol van had to collect two assorted trawls of shoplifters arrested in the Buchanan Street shops. Among them was a six-foot-tall male, now handcuffed, who had tried to walk out of a store with a mink coat stuffed under his jacket. Among the women, at least one looked pregnant and another had been caught with a stolen compact-disc player tucked beneath her baby in its pram.

'Different,' said Thane mildly.

'Doesn't beat a microwave,' said Sandra Craig.

He nodded. Someone had tried that the previous Friday, lowering it out of a fourth floor ladies' room on the end of a rope. The rope had broken and the microwave had fallen thirty feet, hitting a parked car like a bomb.

Other shoplifters were still being arrested, other patrol vans wanted, as Thane stopped the Ford at a small bar-lunch restaurant only about half a mile from Crathes Street.

The restaurant wasn't much to look at. It had flaked pink paintwork and faded pink plastic tablecovers. But it was on the police grapevine listing of 'hot food, cheap prices' and it was also reported that the kitchen looked clean. It was called Ecstasy, which no one took literally.

By the time the Ecstasy's two new customers arrived, the normal lunch trade had gone back to work. Only one other table was occupied, used by two middle-aged men who were nursing the dregs of a carafe of white wine and marking their way through the evening's dog racing card.

They took a table and a waitress appeared, producing a menu. Sandra wanted a steak sandwich with salad, Thane settled for the Ecstasy's lamb stew, and Sandra asked for a serving of apple pie and cream to follow.

The waitress left, Sandra departed for the ladies' room, and Thane went over to the restaurant's public pay-phone, which was half hidden behind a pink bamboo screen. He fed the coin-box some change, then dialled the Crime Squad number. In another couple of moments he had Francey Dunbar on the line.

'Half the world is looking for you.' For once, his sergeant seemed relieved to hear his voice. 'All of them say it's urgent.'

'I'll believe you,' said Thane dryly. 'Any kind of sighting on Gort or the Peters woman?'

'Nothing,' complained Dunbar. 'It's like they found a hole, got in and closed the lid.'

'And no more calls from Pony?'

'None.' Dunbar didn't hide his curiosity. 'How was it with Haston's widow?'

'Not enjoyable, not spectacular.' Thane paused to let the two middle-aged men go past, on their way out. 'Stay with the things that matter, Francey. What have we got? How about at the airport?'

'Jock Dawson.' Dunbar sighed at the inevitable. 'One of his four-footed friends located where that motorcycle had waited before you were jumped last night. We've a heel mark from a boot and patch of soft soil with a good, clean tyre tread.'

'Enough for a make?'

'Better than enough,' declared Dunbar. 'That machine was a Yamaha trials bike – probably a three-fifty c.c. They're expensive and they don't grow on trees. Not too many women could handle one.'

'Then we're back among the quality,' suggested Thane acidly. Sandra had returned to the table, the waitress was bringing their orders. 'What about Joe Felix and his search warrant at Williamfield?'

'Janey Peters? Well – uh – ' Dunbar's voice hesitated at his end of the line, there was a brief mumble of conversation, then he returned, a note of near awe in his voice. 'I'm in your office. Would you believe a girl just brought in coffee in a cup and saucer, looking for you?'

'Enjoy it.' Thane was patient. 'Williamfield, Francey. Or I go for your throat.'

'All they've got is that Last Number Redial memory from her telephone. But it's certainly different – '

'Your throat, Francey,' warned Thane.

'It's an unlisted number,' said Dunbar. 'Out of town, over on the east coast – at St Andrews.' He paused as a warning. 'It happens to be located in the members' bar at the Royal and Ancient Golf Club – you know, the Old Course?'

'I know.'

Anyone anywhere who had ever swung a golf club at a ball knew it. The Royal and Ancient Club at St Andrews was the world's acknowledged, almost sacred home of golf. Thane grimaced at the telephone mouthpiece. What did he mean 'almost'? To any golfer, St Andrews was the Promised Land. So how did Janey Peters, who had run off with a hardened hi-tech criminal like the Interface Man, have any link with the Royal and Ancient's members' bar – the Holy of Holies?

'Still there, sir?' asked Dunbar. He cleared his throat. 'You play golf – I don't. Do they let common policemen see round over there?'

'On public holidays,' said Thane viciously. 'No chance of a mistake, Francey?'

'No.'

'Do we know when she tried it?'

'No chance. They don't have computerized numbers

89

account billing out at Williamfield,' said Dunbar. 'Hell, we don't even know if she got through.'

'Great.' Thane saw that Sandra Craig was somehow managing to eat, watch him and lip-read his end of the conversation all at the same time. 'Is that the lot?'

'Until some of the other things come together.'

'When do you have to leave for your Federation meeting?' asked Thane.

'We're too short-handed.' Dunbar said it flatly. 'I can dump it, sir.'

'And set back the cause of democracy in the police for another generation?' asked Thane sarcastically. 'Go. That's an order. I'll send Sandra back, and I'll come in later. Just remember the generosity, Sergeant.'

'The lower orders thank you, sir,' said Dunbar meekly. He knew Thane's annoyance at the fact that a superintendent or above had to leave Federation membership. Superintendents had their own association. Then he stopped play-acting. 'I'll be back as soon as I can make it.'

'Don't worry. You can owe me,' suggested Thane.

He hung up then stayed in the telephone booth for a moment, thinking. He was back again with Janey Peters and the Royal and Ancient. They didn't mix. Add John Gort, and it didn't help at all.

He went back to their table, where Sandra had finished off her steak sandwich and salad. Thane told her what he'd arranged, and for a moment she scowled at her apple pie. Then she shrugged.

'There's a new pay claim coming up.' She began eating again, then added, 'Federation only.'

When they were ready to leave, the waitress brought them separate bills without being asked. They left her separate tips, then went out to the car and Thane handed over the keys. Once the Ford was moving he settled back in the passenger seat and studied his notebook.

90

'Those names on Haston's computer – David Mark, Louise Croft. Who is helping us at Computer Cabin?'

'David Mark, sir.' She kept her eyes on the road. 'He made helpful-enough noises.'

'Don't they all?' Thane scowled at the passing traffic. 'When you get back, check with Maggie Fyffe that someone sent flowers to Jack Hart's wife from the Squad. Then find out who paid for them.'

'Like Maggie herself?' She gave a slight nod and a smile. 'It's usually that way, isn't it?'

He grunted. But she happened to be right.

Six minutes later Colin Thane was dropped outside the Computer Cabin building in Argyle Street. As the Crime Squad car drove away he stood for a moment in afternoon sunlight and looked up at the four-storey building. It came straight out of the shoebox school of architecture. Originally built as a cinema, it had been occupied since by a health centre, a firm who had thought they could make money out of an indoor ski-slope, then an insurance company followed by a power-boat agency.

Now, as a temple to the microchip world, it had big, spotlit display windows, bright neon signs, and an advertising budget which kept Computer Cabin as a name most people knew about.

It also had security. As Thane went in through the store's main door a closed-circuit TV lens picked him up and showed him on a display row of TV screens. He spotted two other security cameras backed by infra-red sensors, and he knew there would be more. The store was busy with customers, most of them – though not all – in their late teens or twenties. Around them, stands offered computer decks and information systems while VDUs shifted data pages or played game programmes to admiring audiences.

Thane made his way to an information desk at the rear of the department. He gave his name and showed his warrant card to the middle-aged salesman on duty, then waited while the man used an internal phone. After a moment he was led over to an elevator.

'Top floor, Superintendent. They're expecting you.'

Thane rode the elevator up. When the cage stopped he was facing a closed door and a small TV camera. Then a relay switch clicked, the door slid open and he stepped out into Computer Cabin's office area. Smoothly the door closed again behind him.

'Superintendent Thane?' A well-dressed young woman came over from a reception desk. 'Mr Mark would like you to come straight through.'

He followed her across a busy open-plan accounts and general office area then into a private corridor which had office doors on both sides. They stopped at one which said Sales Manager, the receptionist tapped a button on the doorpost, and a green light winked an answer. Smiling at Thane, the woman opened the door and ushered him in.

'Good to see you, Superintendent,' greeted one of the two men in the room, coming over. He nodded at the receptionist, who left and closed the door behind her. 'I'm David Mark.'

'And he was hoping for someone better looking,' said the other man with a chuckle. 'She made the phone calls. She was a policewoman and she said her name was Sandra.'

'She'll be disappointed too,' said Thane dryly. 'Sorry.'

It was a big room, thickly carpeted, mainly furnished in a rich-grained rosewood. But the two men dominated their surroundings. Both were tall and in their mid-thirties, both were well built and they were alike enough in several ways to have to be related.

'You've guessed it.' David Mark had been watching

92

Thane, and indicated his companion. 'You know the saying. Everybody gets to choose their friends, nobody gets to choose their relatives. This is my brother Jon.'

'Known as Jon the Good-looking One,' agreed Jon Mark easily.

They shook hands with Thane. David Mark had shaggy, mousy-coloured hair and a thin face with a long, broad nose. He was lanky and wore thick-rimmed spectacles, a dark blue business suit, a blue and white striped shirt and a dark blue tie patterned with tiny stripes. His expression was bland, his attitude towards his brother seeming mostly a resigned tolerance.

'Jon is what we call a publicity executive,' he explained, indicating his grinning brother. 'For him, work amounts to wining and dining clients.'

'Hard work,' said Jon Mark solemnly. 'The women are the worst.'

Jon Mark was perhaps a couple of years younger than David. He had the same thin face and prominent, not unattractive features. But Jon Mark's nose had been broken at some time and not particularly well straightened. He had short, straight hair the colour and texture of old rope-yarn, and he looked superbly, sun-tanned fit in a way that showed in every move. When he grinned he showed strong white teeth which were spoiled by a small centre gap.

'On your way, little brother,' said David Mark with a controlled impatience. 'Don't let us keep you from the great outdoors. The police wouldn't want that, would they, Superintendent Thane?'

Thane shook his head. It was easy to see Jon Mark was on his way out. He was wearing an open-necked tan shirt with a tan zip-front jacket and expensively cut dark green trousers.

'Unless he knows about modem convertors,' he suggested.

'That's technical, not my department.' Jon Mark dismissed the thought with a grimace, then turned to his brother. 'Dave, I'm running late and I'm still waiting for your answer. If our friend says yes, does he get the discount he wants?'

'He gets it.' David Mark nodded. 'Don't forget his toy, for God's sake.'

'Toy.' Jon Mark scooped a wrapped package off his brother's desk and stuffed it in a pocket. He made an apologetic gap-toothed grimace at Thane. 'Sorry, duty calls. Meaning eighteen holes of damned hard work – what do you do when a customer is a good golfer but cheats?'

'Cheat back,' said his brother impatiently. 'He'll respect you.'

'Right.' Jon Mark headed for the door, opened it and glanced back at Thane. 'If there's another time, Superintendent, send this Sandra female. As a favour.'

He went out and the door closed behind him with a hearty bang. David Mark sighed, gave a half-smile, and led the way over to his rosewood desk. He offered Thane a high-backed chair already placed in front of the desk, saw his guest seated, then lowered his lanky frame into the chair on the other side.

'Don't mind Jon,' he said amiably. 'He'd just looked in before you arrived. What he does, he does well.'

'Including play a lot of golf?' asked Thane mildly. In the last minute a small warning bell had begun ringing in his mind. 'Line of duty style?'

'Yes.' Mark gave a shrug. 'A lot of firms do plenty of business on the golf course. Don't knock it, Superintendent. You know the real trick, the way Jon plays? Never try to lose – just make sure you don't always win.'

'And always have a gift-wrapped toy to hand out?'

'Always.' The Computer Cabin sales manager turned his thick-rimmed spectacles towards a glass display

94

cabinet. 'Today's is the same as that thing like a cigarette case, top left.' He gave Thane a chance to find it. 'That's a new mini-translator – American designed, stores ten thousand words, each word in six languages. Locate your word, touch a button, and you language-hop.'

'Everyone should have one,' said Thane politely.

'You mean it sounds like garbage.' The big, bushy-haired man snorted through his big nose. He sounded acidly amused. 'People like them, people want them. Toys? We've a sensor element that picks up body heat at twenty feet and will switch on a light – a lot of people buy them for home use. Or we've a new solar-powered dictionary that gives a twenty-character display and tells how to spell the one hundred thousand most-used words. Secretaries love them.'

'So would a few cops,' mused Thane. He knew he was being sold something – he had an idea it wasn't just Computer Cabin's sales philosophy.

'People enjoy toys, people want any damned thing that uses a microchip. Go anywhere in this building, see what's on display, what those people are buying. Toys for adults.' David Mark removed his spectacles for a moment, took a paper tissue from a box on his desk and polished the lenses. 'But real money, Thane? That's different. That's when we land a king-sized order from a university department that wants new computer equipment, or get a job supplying the electronic controls for someone's new production line – or one like last week's special, a truckload of bar-code price readers for a new supermarket that still doesn't have a roof.'

'Where you got in first?'

'That's my job.' The spectacles went back on and David Mark flicked an imagined speck of dust on his jacket lapel. 'I've sales targets to meet. If I don't, I've a general manager ready to fire me – if he doesn't, someone will fire him.'

'Do the same rules apply to your brother?'

'Yes.'

'Mainly playing golf?'

'Earning his keep.' Mark frowned and glanced deliberately at his gold wristwatch. 'But you're not earning me anything, Thane – and the same goes for your persistent policewoman from this morning. So can we get to it? You want to know about modem convertor units we've sold in the last three or so months?'

'Any sale, any inquiries.' Thane brought out his notebook, checking the entry. 'One type in particular.'

'Our catalogue number ZB 198 C,' agreed David Mark. 'She told me, we've chased it. I still don't know what's important about it.'

'An inquiry I've been landed with.' That part was true. He tried to show a convincing lack of enthusiasm to go with the follow-on lie. 'A man wanted for armed hold-up was arrested down in Liverpool. He happens to be a Scot, he operates as a quartermaster for some of the Northern Ireland terrorist gangs – '

'Which kind?' David Mark showed a mild interest.

'Either kind. He'll take anyone's money – and they know it.' Thane knew two operators who fitted that bill. 'Our man had a shopping list when we searched him, though he won't say who wants the stuff or why. The ZB modem is on the list, with Computer Cabin's name.'

'It would have to be. We've the exclusive British franchise.' The bushy-haired sales manager frowned through his spectacles. 'The ZB 198 is a West German design, made in Japan. It is probably the best and the most expensive dual digital and analog signal convertor unit on public sale. Have you see one?'

Thane shook his head.

'Be my guest.' David Mark reached down under his desk then, one-handed, lifted out a plastic box about the size of a small portable typewriter. He thumped it in

96

front of him and Thane saw convertor wires and a small row of control keys. The other man tapped it with a finger. 'I had this one brought from stores. We had sixteen in stock until two months ago. Eight went to a Norwegian off-shore oil platform. We've two out on loan to an airline office. That leaves us six – and we've checked we still have them.' He shook his head. 'No other sales or orders, and I had our people check further back than your three months to make sure. You know what they cost, each?'

Thane nodded. 'A lot.'

'If you want Concorde quality, you pay Concorde prices.' David Mark took another glance at his wristwatch. 'You'll get plenty of choice of cheaper single-function units. But anyone who wants a ZB wants the best.'

'To do what?'

'Terrorist style?' David Mark removed his glasses again, frowned at them, then replaced them. 'I wouldn't know. I just try to sell the things – legitimately. Any modem does things like take a signal pulse coming in over a feed wire, then convert it into impulses then into words, figures, and that kind of information.'

'And the ZB unit?'

'Simply does it better, fine-tune.' David Mark got to his feet. 'Thane, I'm sorry. But I've another appointment due – '

'Thanks for your help.' Thane had already risen.

'You people actually did me a favour, Superintendent,' said the man, going with Thane to the office door and opening it. 'Our ZB sales are bad. I'm going to put brother Jon to work unloading them, before anyone else realizes how few we've been moving. Uh – if you need more help, come back.'

Then Thane was outside the door and it had closed. Immediately, a red Engaged light snapped on above it.

He started back towards the general office and the elevator then heard one of the other corridor doors open behind him. Sheer curiosity made him glance back, and he saw a tall, blonde, angular woman with a small, high bust crossing towards David Mark's office. She looked about thirty, she wore a light grey suit with a pastel green shirt and a patterned silk scarf, and her hair was tied back by a short bow of black ribbon. She ignored the red Engaged light, opened David Mark's door, went in and closed the door behind her.

'Not many people can do that,' murmured an amused voice beside him.

He turned. The girl from the reception desk had come over.

'Who is she?' asked Thane.

'Louise Croft, our credit controller.' The receptionist wrinkled her nose. 'That's female for debt collector.'

'I suppose.' It also gave Thane the second name he'd seen on Robert Haston's computer. 'Does she work closely with David Mark?'

'Very.' The girl winked. They went together to the elevator and she pressed the call button. 'Did you meet the other brother, Superintendent?'

'Jon?' He nodded. 'I like what I heard about his job. I could give it a try.'

'Join the queue.' She gave an envious sigh. 'But Jon is nice with it. He also happens to be a top-line golfer. I know people who say he could turn pro if he wanted.'

'Where does he play?'

'Jon?' She shrugged. 'Anywhere that happens to be the best.'

'St Andrews?' He asked it casually.

'Sometimes. Do you play golf, Superintendent?'

'Now and again.' On a little local course which flooded every time it rained. Another twenty years, and he might get to be captain, with that prized reserved car-parking space. He wondered if Jon Mark could have even found the place on a map. If it was on a map.

The elevator arrived. He thanked the girl, got aboard and it took him back to ground level again. Leaving it, he began to thread his way through the display stands and customers towards the exit doors.

A fat man was entering the store. He had dark hair and a greasy complexion, he looked in his late thirties, and he was wearing white trousers and a blue and white sports top over a blue tee-shirt. His feet were in white trainers.

Their eyes met and the fat man seemed to freeze. His small, sulky mouth fell open, showing he had bad teeth. Next instant he turned on his heel and, moving surprisingly quickly for his bulk, was heading out through the doors again.

Colin Thane knew him, although the name was still coming. It was from years back, and the fat man was a ned – the Glasgow label for any low-grade thug. But the fat, greasy face and sulky mouth hadn't changed.

Starting forward, Thane reached the exit doors maybe six feet behind his target. Suddenly, as Thane came out into the street, the fat man acted. He seized a middle-aged woman carrying a shopping bag, spun her round, and literally threw her straight towards his pursuer. The woman screamed, her shopping went flying, then she collided with Thane. He had to grab her to stop her from falling. Another woman screamed.

The tangle lasted seconds. When it ended, the fat man was gone. Argyle Street had only its usual horde of Friday afternoon pedestrians parading along both sides, the usual nose-to-tail lines of buses and cars crawling past in a stink of exhaust fumes.

A friend had appeared and was soothing the middle-aged woman. Someone else was gathering up her shopping.

Colin Thane escaped up a side street and kept walking, glad to get away. He had remembered the fat man's name. He had been christened Frank Slater, but everyone knew him as Beanbag. He had been vicious, small-time, hired muscle with a knife. Usually he had been on the fringe of something nasty.

But why had he been so anxious to escape when he recognized Thane? Why had he been about to visit Computer Cabin – when the Beanbag Thane remembered would probably have failed a test on how to use a video recorder?

It was one more coincidence to mark up against Computer Cabin.

Then, it all depended how you felt about coincidences.

Most of the business heart of Glasgow is built north of the River Clyde on a long hill. The headquarters building for Strathclyde Police is located halfway up that hill and is home for the largest British police authority outside of London.

The Crime Squad's giant sister-force is run from a large, modern complex of a structure which rises tall and also burrows unsuspectedly deep into the ground. It has eaten up an entire block of streets – and it has two problems.

The way the Strathclyde force's need for office space kept growing, it was already too small the day it opened. The second problem is that anywhere around the headquarters area is the worst place in the city to find a parking space. Even senior officers are ready to commit mayhem to win any of the building's underground slots that become vacant. Outside, street-level parking is a nightmare.

It is something worse than a nightmare on Friday afternoons, when cars from every corner of Strathclyde's far-flung police empire arrive to collect dispatches or

100

deliver people to meetings before the administrators lock up for the weekend.

It was the usual turmoil when Thane arrived on foot. He squeezed past a gaggle of traffic wardens who were watching it all with a mild disinterest, then went over to the main door orderly.

'Detective Inspector Moss?' he asked.

'Out, sir.' The orderly, a constable who always wore white gloves and had enough years of service to know how to avoid getting them dirty, shook his head. 'I saw him go. He said not to expect him back till Monday.'

Thane thanked the man. For Phil Moss, life at Headquarters had to be a different kind of world after being a Divisional cop. But in Moss's case he'd earned it.

From the lobby he took the elevator up to the top floor, where Strathclyde's scientific laboratory was located. He emerged behind a line of police who were queuing at a counter to hand in the usual tagged plastic bags containing everything from the inevitable blood-stained clothing to what looked like some dog food, eased past them, then saw the man he wanted weave a way between the busy benches in the main work area. Matthew Amos, a slim and bearded civilian who always sported a dazzling line in bow ties, was the laboratory's assistant director.

'How goes it, Colin?' Amos greeted him with a cynical grin. 'Looking in to disembowel a few more slaves for not working fast enough?'

'It's an idea,' agreed Thane solemnly. Amos was a respected maverick who had earned his assistant director title the hard way. He also took personal charge of most Scottish Crime Squad requests that were passed to the Strathclyde laboratory. 'Spare me a minute?'

'Maybe even two.' Hands stuffed into the pockets of his white laboratory coat, Amos led the way into his

101

private office. He rescued a mug of coffee from a shelf. 'Like some?'

Thane shook his head.

'Wise.' Amos took a swallow of coffee and grimaced. 'The day we analyse this stuff, some of life's mysteries will be solved.' He perched himself on the edge of his desk. 'I know. You've got the Interface Man caper, then Jack Hart tries to tie in a possible murder.' He took another gulp of coffee. 'Is Hart's wife still on the mend?'

'The last time I heard.' Thane looked at the partition wall beside him. Amos collected newspaper cartoons about policemen. The latest additions ranged from the absurd to the might-even-happen. 'I'm looking for help, Matt.'

'We're trying.' Amos set down his coffee mug. 'You know that motorcycle last night was a Yamaha three-fifty?'

'A trail bike.' Thane nodded.

'We got nothing from that Magic Bakerman van, nothing else at the airport.' Amos made a vague noise and scratched at his beard. 'You may get lucky with that car the Peters woman traded in part exchange. The Edinburgh laboratory people say they've got some possibly interesting dust and debris from the passenger area. They've more work than they can handle, they know this one is marked urgent, so I've told them to send the samples through, that we'll cope.' He shrugged aside any thanks. 'We owe them a few. But don't push me – it still takes time.'

'That's my problem.' One of the cartoons caught Thane's eye. It was an old-enough theme. A new recruit lay in chains in a dungeon. He had given his chief constable's wife a ticket for speeding. 'Matt, what about the place out at Williamfield?'

'Janey Peters didn't go blonde until after she left there – any hairs we found were brunette. The sleeping tablets

102

she'd been using were low-strength, we found various smudges of fingerprints.' Amos gave a shrug. 'Eliminate those I'd say were her own, eliminate a few I know belong to a couple of cops I could name, and we've still some left over. But they don't match with anything on record.' He wasn't finished. 'You know about the stored telephone number?'

'St Andrews?'

Amos nodded. 'Don't charge off in the wrong direction, Colin. Somebody made that call, or tried to make it. That doesn't mean she made it.'

'Explain,' said Thane grimly.

'Whoever last used that telephone took the trouble to wipe it afterwards – even the key-pad,' said Amos sadly. 'Would she do that with her own phone?'

'Thanks,' said Thane in a flat voice.

They exchanged a grin and he left. His second stop in the Headquarters building was at Criminal Records, where he asked the duty sergeant to give him any update information they had on Beanbag Frank Slater. Then, while the sergeant checked, Thane borrowed a telephone. He put a call through to the Crime Squad duty room and asked for someone – anyone – to pick him up from the Strathclyde front door.

The Records sergeant was gone about five minutes. He came back with a Records print-out to back up the basic card-and-photograph file on Beanbag Slater.

'I'd have thought he was down-market for Crime Squad,' said the sergeant, passing them over. 'Anything special about him, sir?'

'Not yet, Sergeant.' Thane took them over to a vacant desk and chair.

Beanbag Slater's last conviction had been six years back, a modest eighteen months for a minor part in an armed robbery. Since then, Criminal Intelligence noted that two charges of assault had been dropped for lack of evidence. After the second he'd been found beaten up but couldn't remember how it happened. His more recent history was uneventful, he was thought to be making a modest living as a part-time enforcer for a moneylender.

There was even a last-known address, the Sorcerer, a cheap bed-and-breakfast hotel in the Main Street, Bridgeton, area. The entry was an up-date only a few weeks old. The only other detail that mattered, the name of a known associate, had been deleted. For the last year or so, Beanbag's friend had been locked away in Peterhead Prison. He was serving a five-year sentence for attacking a woman when he broke into her house.

Thane made a note of the bed-and-breakfast hotel, returned the Records sheets to the duty sergeant, then went down to the main door. He talked with the orderly and dodged the first of the flow of assistant chief constables leaving for the weekend, then saw his transport arrive and went out to meet it.

The four-wheel-drive Land-Rover had a light panel truck body, wasn't new, and even by Crime Squad standards needed a wash. That also came close to summing up the man behind the wheel. Jock Dawson, the Squad's dog-handler, hadn't got round to shaving and wore overalls and heavy boots. He hadn't come alone. As Thane climbed in beside him the two dogs in the Land-Rover's rear compartment began to growl and scratch at the metal.

'Shut up, you pair of heathen,' yelled Dawson. They quietened and he turned to Thane. 'Back to the office, sir?'

Thane nodded. He didn't ask about the dogs. Wherever Jock Dawson went, the dogs went. The dog-handler, a tall, thin man with a slow-burn conversational pace, was married to a gamekeeper's daughter who probably fed them all on dog biscuits. Rajah, the largest of the two dogs, was a massive alsatian who had officially retired because of age. Dawson had ignored that decision. The replacement dog, a young golden-haired labrador bitch named Goldie, had more brains than brawn and was drugs and explosives trained.

'Much happening?' asked Thane.

Dawson shrugged, setting the Land-Rover moving again. 'Nothing fresh I know about, sir. People trying here, people trying there – the usual. Wearing out telephones. Nothing for dogs to do.'

By Dawson's standards, it was a speech. Thane smiled.

'They'll be outside again soon,' he promised.

'They could use the exercise.' Taking a bend in the road, Dawson removed one hand from the steering wheel, rubbed a thumbnail along his stubble, and gave Thane a sideways glance. 'Francey went out. Some Transport Police inspector came looking for you – Sandra talked with him.' He paused, his eyes firmly back on the road. 'A pity about Sandra. But she'll get over it soon enough.'

'Get over what?' asked Thane, lost.

'Sailor boy,' said Dawson shortly. 'That Royal Navy lieutenant. You know the one?'

'I've seen him,' said Thane cautiously.

'He dumped her,' said Dawson. 'That's what this sergeant's exam thing is all about – to get him out of her system.'

'She told you?'

'Not me, sir,' said Dawson patiently. 'She told the dogs. But she knew I could hear, right?'

'Right,' said Thane, and gave up.

He waited until the Land-Rover had reached the Crime Squad parking lot. Sandra Craig had left his Ford in its usual place, the keys would be on his desk.

'I've a job for you, Jock.' He looked at the unshaven

dog-handler. 'There's a fat man named Beanbag Slater, last known address the Sorcerer bed-and-breakfast in Bridgeton. I don't want him hassled, but I want to know if he still lives there, what he does, and who he does it with – and go easy, he doesn't like cops.'

'Does he like dogs?' asked Dawson innocently.

'I wouldn't think so,' said Thane mildly.

He got out of the Land-Rover. As he closed the door Dawson put the vehicle back into gear and drove away again. As long as he had his dogs, Jock Dawson didn't worry about back-up.

A few minutes in his office were enough to convince Thane he should have stayed away. Over the next three hours he developed a headache, he borrowed aspirin tablets from Maggie Fyffe, and he gradually managed to file most of the papers on his desk into the wastepaper basket.

Some things mattered. Jack Hart had telephoned from his wife's hospital ward and her progress seemed steady. The Crime Squad flowers had arrived and were appreciated – at least by Hart. His wife was still under sedation.

Other things flowed around and over him. They still hadn't heard again from the woman called Pony. But the London time-share agency which had employed Janey Peters had returned the Crime Squad call. The first news that Janey Peters planned to resign had been a brief letter less than three weeks back. In it, she had told them she planned to marry and that her husband-to-be planned to buy a hotel on the Costa del Sol, where he already had business interests. They would Fax a copy of the letter.

He switched Joe Felix and Sandra to a background scan on the two Mark brothers, including Jon Mark's golfing status. Sandra had already kept her word to Joan

Haston and had been in telephone contact with her.

Pat Emslie returned to the building again. The young British Transport Police detective inspector was trying hard. He had badgered the station staff at Carlisle about the quarrelsome couple who had left the Intercity express train at Carlisle. A porter remembered them for a particular reason. Not so much as a couple, but because a large blue Mercedes had been waiting to pick them up. The woman's handbag was the only thing they'd been carrying, and the Mercedes had driven them away.

'Keep at it,' encouraged Thane. 'I want oddities from that train – any kind of oddities.'

'Sir.' Emslie gave a wry nod and left him. But Thane noticed it was another half hour before his car left the parking lot.

The big blank remained what had happened to Gort and Janey Peters. There was still no sighting of their Volkswagen hatchback – but there were plenty of that model around, and a change of number plates would have been almost enough to lose it for ever.

On the plus side, Matt Amos telephoned from the Strathclyde laboratory. The dust samples from Janey Peters' previous car had arrived. Edinburgh had also sent through a variety of fingerprints found on the car, but Amos was more enthusiastic about the dust.

'Tomorrow,' he promised. 'Give me till tomorrow to work on it, and you could be lucky. Hell, Colin, I'm going to turn out on a Saturday. Can I do more?'

Thane thanked him. A moment later Francey Dunbar walked in, back from his Federation meeting. He was holding a set of telex messages he had collected from the duty room.

'The Spanish are going ape asking what's going on,' he complained, waving the telexes. 'This is from some Guardia captain at Marbella. How much will I tell him?'

107

'Try *manana*,' snarled Thane. His head was beginning to throb again.

'*Manana*.' Dunbar said it woodenly. 'Will do, sir.'

'Francey.' Thane stopped him. 'Tell him we've got problems. Tell him we need any kind of background help he can give us from his end.'

'Do we care how he gets it?' asked Dunbar. His thin face shaped a studious doubt and he stroked an edge of his drooping straggle of a moustache. 'Or do we just not ask?'

He went out without waiting for an answer. Seconds later there was a brief knock on Thane's door and it opened again. Jock Dawson came in. Unusually, both dogs were with him, sticking close and silent at his heel.

'Your fat man Beanbag, sir.' The dog-handler shook his head. 'He packed and did a bolt from his room at the Sorcerer about an hour before I got there. Surprised them – even paid his bill.'

Thane sighed at the inevitable. 'Any hint where he was heading?'

'No.' Rajah had slumped in a patch of sunlight on the office floor, but Goldie was exploring Thane's waste basket. Dawson muttered and the Labrador bitch stopped, looked at him, gave the next best thing to a canine shrug, and sat on her haunches. Dawson sniffed. 'Only thing I got is that he was collected – someone came for him in a blue Mercedes.'

'You're sure?' Thane stiffened, thinking of the blue Mercedes which had met the Intercity at Carlisle.

'Sure that it was a Mercedes – they don't get too many calling for the Sorcerer's kind of customer.' Dawson shrugged. 'Nobody saw who was driving it or remembers anything else.'

'Log it,' said Thane.

'Sir.' Dawson snapped his fingers and his dogs rose to their feet. He grinned at them. 'They're due to be fed –

108

we're doing some extra overtime tonight, to keep the hours up. I've got a couple of jam doughnuts in the duty room for afters.'

'A couple?' asked Thane.

'Maybe three,' admitted Dawson, and the threesome left.

There was a time when things had to slow down. The day-shift team were starting to leave, the night-shift squad had begun taking over where an inquiry was running – and stirring in some of their own problems.

One was a plain-clothes man who had spent two nights pretending to be asleep in a doorway overlooking an abandoned warehouse. He had nearly frozen, he had been bitten by fleas. But two stolen truckloads of pharmaceuticals were hidden in the yard. Who would eventually collect them?

The local police hadn't been informed that the trucks were there or that the warehouse was being watched. They had a beat cop who might be involved.

Thane persuaded the plain-clothes man to put up with the fleas for another night. Then, a sure sign it was really late, Maggie Fyffe looked in before she went home, and made him sign some papers. She was followed by Sandra Craig, who had her coat draped over her shoulders.

'Had enough?' Whenever he could, Thane let his team choose their own hours.

'For now.' She gave him a weary grin. 'I called Joan Haston again – I said I'd maybe take a look in.'

'But nothing new from her?'

'Not yet.' She shook her head. 'And no earth-shattering revelations on the Mark brothers, sir. Except that brother Jon rates good enough to play in any pro-am tournament that comes along. Joe Felix is still working on them.'

Sandra left. Thane gave it another twenty minutes,

then the wall clock reached seven thirty and he decided he had had enough. He pulled on his jacket and went through to the duty room, where Francey Dunbar was sitting with his feet up on a desk and demolishing a carry-out curry supper.

'I'm taking a break,' Thane told his sergeant. 'I'm going home, I'll be there if anyone wants me. You might as well disappear.'

'I will.' Dunbar didn't argue. He reached for the telephone, looking pleased. 'There's an air hostess I can call, someone I met last night, sir.'

'Research,' agreed Thane stonily. He caught a whiff of Dunbar's curry and hoped the girl had no sense of smell. 'Leave a contact number.'

Outside, it had gone from dusk to evening darkness, with a hint of rain in the air. The sky was already heavy with cloud and more seemed to be coming in. He started the Ford's engine and put the heater switch on a notch. Then, as he set the car moving, he made a sweep through the radio channels from sheer habit.

Yes, it was Friday evening. Police and ambulances were out mopping up around the usual quota of stabbings and assaults. Someone had been accidentally shot with a handgun over in Govan. Someone who wanted to be different had run amok with an axe in the city centre and was still on the loose somewhere.

There was nothing spectacular so far. But it was still early.

It was after eight p.m. when Thane arrived home. Mary had heard the car draw up and met him at the front door with a kiss and with a malt whisky already poured. Tommy and Kate had eaten and were out for the evening, Clyde the dog was sleeping on a bed somewhere and didn't put in an appearance.

He took a first swallow of the whisky then went

110

upstairs and washed. When he returned, Mary had his meal ready. She had made a chicken and rice dish, one of his favourites though they both knew the sauce came straight from a packet. She had waited to eat with him, and had poured herself a glass of wine.

He stuck with the malt. While they ate they talked a little, but not a lot. Mary's clinic had been going like a three-ring circus most of the day. Some new mysterious virus was going the rounds. She had telephoned the hospital about Jack Hart's wife and had ended up speaking to Hart, who sounded reasonably happy.

For once, both their children had had no particular crisis to report.

'So.' She looked across the table at Thane. 'How about you? Do I get to hear, or is this into silent time?'

He grinned. 'Plodding.'

He started to tell her. It sounded flat, but she seemed interested. Then, suddenly, Clyde began barking and their doorbell rang.

Mary went through to the door. Clyde's barking continued, and he heard a familiar acid voice. Grinning, Thane got up and went through. Phil Moss was standing in the hallway, rubbing Clyde behind the ears and letting Mary take his coat. A small, thin bachelor with a wrinkled face and sparse, mousy hair, Thane's one-time second-in-command gave his usual impression of having slept in his clothes. He needed a button sewn on his shirt and his tie was like a discarded shoelace.

'You've a husband who should offer me a drink,' Moss told Mary. 'I've been burying a body for him.'

'At Williamfield?' asked Thane.

'Are there others?' Moss winked at Mary. 'I'd settle for a glass of milk.'

Mary brought the milk. Thane watched him sit down and sip at it. It wasn't many months since Moss had been hospitalized for a stomach-ulcer operation which

111

had left him classified as fit for light duties only. But Moss seldom mentioned it.

They talked for a few moments then Mary brought Thane's whisky through from the kitchen and disappeared back in that direction.

'Williamfield, and your Sergeant Merreday,' said Moss at last, sitting back. 'I was out there, I've just left him.' He took another sip of milk. 'He won that bravery medal as a first-year constable, overpowering an armed gunman. He's just a cop who went sour as the years passed by.'

'And?'

'A few people at Williamfield know about him.' Moss sighed. 'Anyway, he moves. On Monday he starts a new job a long way from there – indoors, and they can keep him hidden until pension time.' A slight grin crossed his mouth. 'I saw the girl too. She's being moved as well, but she'll be all right.'

'Thanks for doing it,' said Thane quietly.

'These days, dirty politics is my speciality,' said Moss dryly. He took another gulp at his milk and shuddered. 'So – suppose I risk a suspicion of whisky in this stuff, and then you tell me about the Gort hunt – and this little extra that could be a murder?'

Thane fetched the whisky.

Phil Moss was a good listener, economic when it came to questions when he didn't understand. At last, satisfied, he sat back and gave a modest low-key rumble of a belch, a mere reminder of what he'd once produced.

'Problems,' he agreed. 'One thing, though – this Janey Peters. Your mystery Pony could be a close friend. Have you located anyone who matches?'

'Not yet.' Thane shook his head. 'We're trying.'

'And I'd keep trying – if I wasn't emptying ashtrays along the corridors of power.' Moss glanced at his watch. 'Kids not home yet?'

'Soon.' Thane shrugged. 'This side of midnight, we don't argue.'

The phone was ringing. They heard Mary shout through, asking Thane to answer it. He took the call on the living room extension.

'Duty officer, sir.' He recognized the voice of the Crime Squad night supervisor. 'I'm afraid we've a problem.'

'Go on.' Something in the man's voice made Thane's mouth dry.

'We've one person killed and one of our people injured – ambulance summoned. Message in, twenty-two forty.'

'Time now – ' Thane glanced at his watch, completing the formality ' – twenty-two forty-six. Where and how?'

'An explosion of some kind at a house in Crathes Street, Kelvinbridge. No arrests.'

'Who was injured?'

'Detective Constable Craig, sir,' said the night supervisor.

'I'm on my way,' said Thane.

4

Colin Thane silent behind the wheel and Moss hard-eyed in the passenger seat, the Crime Squad car travelled fast across the city, carving its way through the Friday night traffic. There was a faint drizzle of rain in the air, enough to make the roads gleam in pools of light under the street lamps.

Normally it would have taken close on half an hour to get across the width of Glasgow to Crathes Street. They did it in twenty minutes, headlights glaring and Thane's seldom-used blue emergency light placed out and flashing on the Ford's roof. The car's low-band radio was muttering a steady stream of police messages, from plain ordinary Code Threes – alleged drunk drivers – to a Code Twenty armed hold-up over in the East End. But, ominously, there were only two brief, routine messages about Crathes Street, logging other vehicles' arrivals.

Then, suddenly, they were there. A constable was waving them past a reflective tape barrier. On the other side two fire tenders and two ambulances had about half a dozen police cars as company under the continuing drizzle.

'Damn it to hell,' said Phil Moss softly as their car slowed and they saw the rest.

The Hastons' little Victorian red terrace house had become a shattered husk. Windows and the front door had been blasted out into the street. Part of the roof had gone. A rag of torn curtaining hung wet and limp from what had been one of the upstairs windows. Firemen still had one hoseline rigged, though their task seemed finished. A small huddle of figures had gathered round the open rear door of one of the ambulances. A yellow plastic Fire Service sheet covered something lying on the ground close beside the other ambulance.

'I need a favour, Phil,' said Thane as he stopped the car. 'Whatever happened, I've one set of priorities and your local division will have another. We sort it out later.'

'Keep them off your back?' Moss nodded his understanding. 'No problem. I'm Headquarters staff, remember?' He scowled at the night. 'And don't worry about the media side. We'll do a temporary spray-paint press release that'll keep them happy – '

Then he stopped and swore. Thane was already out of the car, smelling the smoke still in the air, hurrying over to the group beside the ambulance. Somehow it seemed right that Detective Sergeant Francey Dunbar was one of them. His sergeant had seen him and met him halfway.

'She's over there.' Dunbar thumbed towards the ambulance. He wasn't in a mood to explain how he had heard or how he had arrived. 'She's too damned stubborn to let them take her to hospital until you've talked with her. Her story is she pressed the doorbell and the house blew up.'

'How is she?'

'Damned lucky,' said Dunbar unemotionally. 'She'll be all right.'

'Joan Haston?'

Dunbar shook his head and indicated the limp shape under the Fire Service yellow. 'The fire boys hauled her out before they realized she was dead.'

'Very dead.' Two more figures from the group had joined them. One was a Fire Service officer, a smear of soot across his face. The other, who had made the comment, was a small, dapper man wearing a raincoat

115

over a dinner suit. He had removed the black bow tie from his white evening shirt. Doc Williams was a senior police surgeon. When he was called out on a Friday night it was usually from some up-market function. He nodded a greeting to Thane. 'That was before the bang, Colin.'

'How?'

Doc Williams shrugged. 'Official? Wait for the post mortem.'

'But?'

'Murder. Two bullet wounds in her chest, one probably through the heart.' The police surgeon was calmly factual. 'My guess would be something like a thirty-eight handgun. We'll find out when I go in.'

Somehow, it was no surprise. Thane sighed, saw the fire officer ready to add his piece, and quickly shook his head.

'Give me a minute. I'll be back,' he promised.

He went over to the open rear door of the ambulance. The driver and two local uniformed men discreetly faded back and he was left looking at Sandra Craig. His red-haired detective constable was sitting on one of the ambulance beds, a blanket wrapped around her. Her right eye was badly swollen, she had several small cuts on her face, one hand was bandaged, and every breath she took seemed painful.

'Francey says you're being stubborn.' Thane gave her a slight encouraging smile. 'So I'm here. How do you feel?'

'Rough,' she admitted, took too deep a breath, and grimaced at the result. 'Doc Williams reckons I've cracked a couple of ribs.' There was something else, Thane noticed. It wasn't a cold night but sheer shock had left her shivering. Her eyes looked past him. 'I know about Joan Haston, sir. I identified the body.'

'So you tell me your side, then you get a free trip to hospital. Agreed?'

116

She nodded.

'Good.' Out of the corner of his eye Thane saw that Jock Dawson's dog van had just arrived. Dawson was getting out, so was Joe Felix. He'd almost expected that too. 'Just what happened. Formal statements come later.'

'I looked in to see her when I came off duty.' Sandra tried to shrug. 'She was working at that computer, she hadn't found anything, but she was still trying.' Pausing, the redhead took another painful breath. 'She asked if she could have my home phone number in case anything turned up – that she didn't want to speak to some stranger.'

'You gave her it?' Thane sighed as she nodded. That wasn't supposed to happen, but it did all the time. 'Then?'

'I went home, I freshened up, I didn't feel like cooking a meal, so I walked down to the little Italian place at my corner.' She looked at him through her good eye. 'Alone, sir.'

'Somebody's loss.' Thane coaxed a slight twist of a smile from her.

'I ate there, I walked back home, then I checked my phone's answering machine.' Sandra Craig was the only person in Thane's Crime Squad team to own one. He had heard her joke about it being the only thing that held her social life together. Pausing, taking another breath, she recalled the moment. 'Joan Haston was on it, sir. She said she had to see me right away. Whatever time I got back, she wanted me to come straight over. She'd found something on the computer – something she thought mattered.'

'Did she say what it was?'

Slowly, sadly, Sandra shook her head. 'Just that it was something she hadn't known about, something that went back to her husband's army days. Then –' she

117

shook her head again, puzzled ' – all she said was it was about a corporal in Robert Haston's old army unit. Then something about him using some computer file trick, reversing an entry – that she'd show me, that she'd checked and it was true.'

'You didn't phone her back?'

'No sir.'

'You came over on your own, without any kind of back-up?'

'Sir.' Sandra Craig avoided his eyes. 'Anyway, I drove over. She hadn't given any time when she made the call, but there were lights on in the house although the curtains were closed. So I – well, I just rang the doorbell – '

'And?'

'And the house blew up,' she said wearily. 'The next thing I knew, I was out in the street, under the front door – it had been blown off its hinges. The house was on fire, someone appeared – a neighbour – and dragged me out from under the door, someone else called the fire brigade. As soon as I could think sensibly, I made my own call in.' Fingering the blanket, she looked out past him towards the shattered little terrace house. 'That's it, sir. Nothing more – nothing I know about.'

'You cared. You came over.' Thane left it there, but touched her gently on the shoulder. 'Hospital, right?'

'Damned right,' said Francey Dunbar from just beyond the door. He had the ambulance driver with him and gave the man a warning scowl. 'Go easy with her, friend. She's special.'

The ambulance driver raised an eyebrow but nodded.

'Get Joe Felix to ride in with her and make sure she doesn't escape,' said Thane dryly. He gave Dunbar a slight nod. 'I need you here. Ask around, don't stand on the local division's toes.'

Dunbar didn't argue. He was already beckoning to Felix.

Some Scenes of Crime men were moving round the front of the terrace house and a police photographer was busy. Thane returned to where the fire officer was still patiently waiting.

'Sorry.' He gestured towards the ambulance. 'That was priority.'

'I'd feel that way too, Superintendent.' The fire officer gave a slight, mirthless grin and his teeth showed white in the darkness. 'Your police surgeon told me about you. I'm Station Officer Rodney – Joe Rodney. Do you want our side of this mess so far?'

'I need it.' Thane saw the first ambulance begin to drive away. The crew of the second were preparing to move Joan Haston's body. Doc Williams was there, standing with Moss and another figure he vaguely recognized as a detective chief inspector based on the north side of the city. He looked at Rodney again. 'Anything you've got.'

'It doesn't amount to anything very clever.' The fire officer shrugged. 'Apart from one variation, this amounts to a standard-enough "welcome home" job. Basic terrorist textbook stuff, but you don't have to be a terrorist to use it. All you need is a pocket knife or maybe a nail-file.' He scowled at the house. 'The woman gets killed – that's a police problem, not mine. But then they do a two-minute rewire job on the doorbell, one that guarantees a nice, fat mains supply spark when anyone uses it. After that, all they had to do was turn on a tap at the gas fire, leave it hissing, and get out.'

'And everything goes bang the first time anyone rings the doorbell?' Thane felt a chill at the thought.

'Very much bang.' Rodney sucked his teeth. 'It would have been an even bigger bang if your girl hadn't visited tonight. By tomorrow you'd have had a major build-up of gas waiting for the first person to ring that bell.'

119

'They wouldn't give a damn,' said Thane softly. 'You said a variation. What kind?'

'The explosion caused some small fires. But there was just one fire that mattered, and it looked as though it had been planned that way.'

'The front room?' guessed Thane. 'Around a computer?'

'Around the melt-down of one,' corrected the fire officer, startled. 'Someone took time to set a bonfire round it, then it looks like they poured a can of paint-stripper over everything to make sure it would ignite. Cassettes, disks, general software – what's left is so much ash and melted plastic.' He paused and considered Thane with interest. 'Why, Superintendent? What's it all about?'

'Not covering up her murder,' said Thane. 'Just winning time for something.'

'Like what?' frowned Rodney.

'I wish I knew,' said Thane bitterly. 'Maybe she found out.'

He turned away. Joan Haston's body was being wheeled towards the second ambulance and he stopped the crewmen then silently, gently, lifted the edge of blanket covering her head. Fire had singed some of that short dark hair, but her face had been spared. Her features looked almost peaceful.

Thane covered the woman's face again and nodded to the ambulancemen. As they approached their vehicle, Doc Williams walked over and gave a tired yawn.

'I'm finished for now,' the police surgeon told Thane. 'I've had a long day, I'm going home. You'll get your autopsy report, priority, tomorrow. But don't expect any surprises – and any time of death estimate you can make will be more accurate than mine. The explosion and fire saw to that.'

'Sleep well, Doc,' said Thane almost automatically.

He watched the police surgeon walk away, briefly wondering how a man with Williams' kind of job could ever harden enough to find sleep easy. Then, for the first time, he walked across to the wrecked little house. It sat like a broken tooth. By some miracle the adjoining houses seemed intact.

A constable on guard at what had been the front door stood aside to let Thane pass. Some tripod-mounted lamps had been erected inside and he made his way into what had been the front room that Robert Haston had used as an office, the front room where Joan Haston had been searching their computer for anything her dead husband had left stored.

It was hard to recognize the mangled, melted carcase of the computer. Its desk had collapsed, the rest was a foul-smelling mix of burned debris. He could see the way items had been piled as the bonfire had been set, his feet crunched on scattered cinders. Then he heard other footsteps and a mild, almost apologetic belch and knew Phil Moss had joined him.

'They did a good job,' said Moss acidly. He sniffed, scowled at the smell, and shrugged. 'I've spoken with the divisional DCI handling the case – Alex Morton, he says he knows you.'

Thane remembered the man he'd seen outside. 'We met somewhere, some time.'

'He's friendly.' Moss shaped a slight grin. Police politics between forces weren't always that way. 'Usual kind of deal – the local division fronts the murder inquiry, keeps clear of any separate Crime Squad investigations, the rest is called mutual cooperation. I can get Strathclyde Headquarters to buy that. Will your people do the same?'

'Yes.' Thane nodded his thanks.

'Good.' His former second-in command gave a fresh,

louder belch and grimaced. 'That's what can still happen when I don't get to eat regularly.' He thumbed out towards the street. 'You'd better go talk with young Dunbar. He's looking for you. I'll stay and poke around.'

Thane went back through the wrecked house and into the street. It was still damp and the steady night drizzle was continuing. He saw the firemen were beginning to roll up their last remaining hoseline, then he saw Francey Dunbar talking with one of the divisional CID men. Catching Dunbar's eye, he beckoned and his sergeant trotted over.

'We've got a witness of sorts, sir,' said Dunbar. His thin young face with its wisp of drooping bandit moustache was hard to read in the diffused glow from the nearest lights. 'The local team were doing door-to-doors and found her that way. I've had a word too.'

'And?'

'She's a neighbour – '

'She?'

'A Mrs Nome, seven houses along, other side of the road. Elderly, lives around her front window, works at noticing things.'

'There's always one somewhere,' said Thane stonily. 'Be glad. We need them.'

'Sir.' Francey Dunbar didn't even try to make it look as if he'd heard a new profound thought. 'She says she saw a visitor arrive at the Haston house – someone on a motorcycle.'

Thane stared. 'When?'

'Mrs Nome reckons that was about an hour before the house blew up. She saw someone open the door and the visitor go in. Her eyesight isn't the greatest, she couldn't identify anyone. Then she stopped watching – her favourite TV game show was starting.' Dunbar wasn't quite finished. 'Another neighbour heard the bike arrive, heard it leave about fifteen minutes later, and thinks there could have been a car too.'

'The rider, Francey?' Thane asked it tightly. 'Man or woman?'

'Mrs Nome couldn't say, we haven't found anyone else who saw anything.' Dunbar shrugged. 'The division team are having another try, their boss said to tell you. You know him?'

'DCI Morton.' Thane nodded. 'Vaguely. Not enough to ask him favours. Where's Jock Dawson?'

'Out door-knocking with the division troops.' Dunbar stuffed his hands into his jacket pockets and scowled. 'If that bike was a Yamaha, or that car was a Volkswagen – '

'Or if we had a magic wand,' snapped Thane. The second ambulance had departed. For the first time he noticed a small Saab coupé lying further down the road, not so much parked as left there. It was Sandra Craig's current choice from the Crime Squad pool. He gestured towards it. 'Make sure someone collects that car.'

'Will do.' Dunbar nodded woodenly. 'What else, sir?'

'With what we've got?' Thane suddenly felt like hitting someone, anyone, except it wouldn't help. 'Keep looking for Gort, keep looking for his woman, keep digging around everyone and hope we get lucky.'

'It would make a change,' said Dunbar sadly.

Thane glared, but couldn't argue.

They were there for another couple of hours, long enough to get word that the hospital check on Sandra Craig had resulted in two cracked ribs showing up on an X-ray examination. She had refused to stay in a casualty bed overnight, and Joe Felix had nursemaided her home.

There was nothing else. Thane said goodnight to the divisional men, sent Francey Dunbar and Jock Dawson on their way, realized that Phil Moss had quietly departed some time earlier, and went back to his own car.

For the second night running it was well after midnight when he got home. Mary had waited up. She looked at him carefully when he came in, then touched his arm.

'Rough?' she asked

Thane nodded. 'The woman was dead.' He saw the question coming. 'Sandra was lucky – she'll be fine.'

Mary poured him a whisky. He drank it, laid down the glass, then they started up to bed.

'Dad – '

It was Kate's voice. Thane went into her darkened room, to find his daughter sitting up in bed. Even in the half-light from the landing, her face was anxious.

'Is Sandra all right, Dad?' she asked.

Thane nodded. Sandra Craig had a star rating as far as Kate was concerned.

'Fine,' he assured her.

'I'm glad,' said his daughter.

She settled back in her bed and he went out, closing the door again. He looked at Mary. She smiled, beckoned, and they went into their room.

He didn't mean it to be that way, but he was asleep within two minutes of his head touching his pillow.

He rose early, left Mary still asleep, and arrived at the Crime Squad headquarters building around seven thirty a.m. There were only a few vehicles in the parking lot at that grey dawn hour but he was surprised to see one of them was Commander Hart's black BMW. When Thane went into the building, Hart was sitting on a corner of the reception desk, talking casually with the man on duty.

'Good.' Jack Hart glanced at his wristwatch and came towards him. 'I expected you about now.' He didn't say what would have happened otherwise. 'Any new word about Sandra Craig?'

124

'Not yet.' Thane shook his head. 'How about your wife?'

'Much better – in what they call a natural sleep. I got thrown out.' Hart's wrinkled, leathery face shaped a pleased grin. He was freshly shaved, and was as bank-manager immaculate as ever. Pausing, the Squad commander allowed the grin to shade back to a scowl. 'So, here I am. I'm here to help, but it stays your case. Understood?'

'Like in "I'm from Head Office and I'm here to help"?' asked Thane.

'Very funny,' snorted Hart. 'I heard a better one from Gloria's nurse.' He cleared his throat carefully. 'Now, there were these two fleas – '

'With a dog, going shopping,' suggested Thane.

'All right, you've heard it.' Hart shrugged and got to business. 'I've read the reports to date. You and your team have plenty to start chasing, so keep them moving. I'll cope with the Spanish police, with Strathclyde – who can be just about as awkward – and do some other mopping up around the edges.' He glanced at his watch again. 'Conference, my room, ten thirty a.m. That gives you three hours. Bring Francey Dunbar if you want. We can always throw him out if he gets too awkward. But you know how I'm going to start? Breakfast – a damned great bacon and egg sandwich, with fried bread.' The grin came back. 'After the last couple of nights, I've earned it!'

Then the Squad commander left, calling loudly for his driver.

Francey Dunbar was next to arrive, on his motorcycle. By eight a.m., a usually deserted time on a Saturday morning, the Squad duty room was busy and noisy and some people were already out chasing possible leads.

Thane was in his office, scoring another of those possible leads off his list – a couple who strongly resembled John Gort and Janey Peters but who were an innocent pair of German tourists who just happened to be driving a Volkswagen hatchback – when the door opened for the fiftieth or so time and Francey Dunbar appeared again. He had a sheet of paper in one hand and his thin young face had enough of a smile to twist his moustache.

'Sandra on the phone,' he said without preliminaries. 'She has this crazy notion about coming in to work.'

Thane raised an eyebrow.

'We spoke. She won't,' assured Dunbar.

'Amicable, was it?' asked Thane.

'She called me a few things.' Dunbar took up his favourite stance, beside Thane's window. 'Nothing to add to what she told you last night.'

Thane nodded in the rough direction of the duty room. 'Anything shaping out there?'

'Not yet. We've had Jack Hart buzzing around like the original blue-tailed what's it.' Dunbar sighed. 'Whose damned case is this anyway?'

'Whose damned case is this anyway – sir,' corrected Thane woodenly. 'We still have it – give or take.' He turned to the small tape player lying on his desk. Sandra Craig had sent in the tape from her answering machine when Joe Felix had taken her back. The tape had been transcribed and copied. He had listened to it a dozen times already. So had Dunbar, but his sergeant's mouth tightened as Thane pressed the 'Play' control and the little tape cassette began turning.

'Detective Constable Craig – Sandra – it's me, Joan Haston.' The dead woman's voice came loud from the little machine. 'You said to call you if I found anything on the computer. 'I – ' she paused, they heard her draw a deep breath '– yes, I think I have. It goes back to his army days, in that Signals regiment. There was a corporal, they were involved in something together. I

126

didn't know, I wouldn't have guessed – ' The tape was only a hiss for another brief moment, then she spoke again, her voice shaky. 'I only found it because I tried one of his old tricks, reversing an entry. But it's there. I've checked – it's true. Come over, Sandra – please. As soon as you can. I think it matters.'

There was a click. The tape had ended. The player switched itself off.

'She checked.' Thane slapped one hand flat on his desk in despair. 'We warned her not to contact anyone.'

'Do we know she did?' asked Dunbar deliberately. 'There are other ways.' He caught Thane's glare. 'We're trying for names of corporals in his old Signals regiment. But army records aren't at their best on a Saturday morning.' Apologetically, he gestured around. 'Who the hell is, sir?'

Thane shrugged. At the same moment his telephone rang.

'Me,' said Phil Moss as soon as he answered. 'Winning?'

'No.'

Moss gave an acid chuckle. 'Keep remembering we're the ones with the white hats. The characters with the black hats always lose. I may have a lead on your Pony woman.'

'That's more than we have,' Thane told him bleakly. 'Pony. What about her?'

'It's not certain. You'll love where it came from,' said Moss sardonically. 'I'll get back to you.'

Moss ended the call and Thane hung up as the line went dead.

'Pony?' asked Dunbar.

'A maybe, for later.' Slowly, deliberately, Thane pushed back his chair and got to his feet. 'Right now, I've had enough. We're going out.'

'Where?'

127

'Computer Cabin. I'm going to stir that pot and see what happens.'

'On a Saturday?' Dunbar was doubtful.

'Would you rather sit on your backside and wait?' asked Thane, heading for the door. 'Then maybe someone else can get killed.'

Looking hurt, Dunbar followed him. But it wasn't that easy. As they went to pass the front reception desk, on their way out, a familiar figure came in through the main glass doors, saw them, and came straight over.

'Nearly missed you, sir.' Inspector Pat Emslie's boyish face managed to be both pleased and slightly apprehensive at the same time. The Transport Police officer gave Dunbar a quick, sideways glance then stopped in front of Thane. There was no way past him. 'Superintendent, you still want Beanbag Slater? I mean, I heard about last night. I – uh – I don't know – '

'I want him.' Thane nodded.

'I could have a lead to him.' Emslie combed a hand through his fair, corn-stubble hair and hesitated. He was wearing an oatmeal-fleck sports coat with leather patches at the elbows. His shirt was bottle green and his trousers dark brown. 'The word is he has a new running mate called Sailor. There's a chance I can get pointed to someone who knows who was hired to help him in something.'

'I see.' Thane looked at the young Transport Police man, reading the rest. 'But there's a problem?'

'A deal.' Emslie nodded. 'We forget we hear a few things at the edges. My contact and his contact don't want problems.'

'What strength is it?' asked Dunbar suspiciously.

'Pretty good.' Emslie kept his eyes on Thane. 'He's reliable, most of the time. Beanbag tried to kick his head in a few years ago. They're not exactly friends.'

128

'Do your deal,' said Thane. 'Then see me again, before you do anything.'

Pat Emslie nodded then glanced past them in the direction of the duty room. He asked, 'Can I use a phone?'

'Help yourself,' agreed Dunbar. 'But avoid the coffee.'

They left him and went out to Thane's car.

It was shaping to be a day of blue skies and light wind, warm enough for most people to look happy and feel happy. Even better, Thane managed to park his Ford in a space almost next to the neon-lit bulk of the Computer Cabin building.

When they went in, Saturday morning seemed a time when computer and electronics fans came shopping in hordes. Every counter and every display stand had its customers, with the sales assistants working hard. Easing through the bustle, Thane led Francey Dunbar across to the rear information desk, where the same middle-aged salesman was on duty and remembered him.

'Back again, Superintendent?' He reached for the internal phone. 'You're lucky. David Mark arrived just minutes ago.'

'What about his brother?'

'On a Saturday?' The man shook his head, smiling at the idea. 'Playing golf, somewhere.'

He used the internal phone, spoke briefly, then raised an eyebrow at whatever was said at the other end. When he replaced the receiver, his smile was slightly forced.

'You've to go up, Superintendent.' He moistened his lips. 'Mr Mark – uh – hopes you won't need much of his time.'

'Except he didn't put it that way?' suggested Dunbar.

The salesman gave a wry nod.

The two Crime Squad men rode the elevator up to the

top floor. When the door slid open the Computer Cabin office area was almost empty of life, some sections unlit, some office equipment covered by its dust hoods. There was no one at the reception desk. Then they heard the quick clicking of heels and the tall blonde woman Thane had been told was Louise Croft came along the corridor towards them.

'David's on the phone.' She greeted them with a quick on-and-off smile, then gestured at the main office. 'Most people up in this area have Saturday off. So I got sent along.' She offered her hand to Thane. 'I'm Louise Croft, in charge of credit control. He told me about you, Superintendent.'

They shook hands. Her grip was firm and cool, then she gave Dunbar a quizzical sideways glance. 'Two of you this time?'

'Sergeant Dunbar,' introduced Thane. His eyes stayed on the woman. That wasn't difficult. Close up, she might look a year or two older – maybe approaching her mid-thirties. Despite her angular build, her face was fine-boned with a wide mouth, green eyes, and what he might have labelled a slightly bored expression. Except for those eyes. They were sharp, they were bright, he had a feeling they would miss very little.

Instead of the business suit of the previous day she was wearing cream-coloured trousers and a fisherman-knit designer sweater. The gold Albert chain at her neck and its matching bracelet had to be real. Her only ring was a solitaire diamond set in a thin gold band.

'Sergeant.' She didn't offer her hand to Dunbar. 'I'll take you along, Superintendent.'

They followed her to the sales manager's door. It was open, and David Mark was just laying down the phone as they went in. He half rose, nodded at Thane, then settled again with a glance through his thick-rimmed spectacles at Louise Croft. She gave a slight shrug.

'Try not to take long about this, Superintendent,' warned the big, shaggy-haired man. David Mark was also in casual weekend clothes – for him, a dark blue shirt and tie and matching cord trousers, a cream-coloured zip-fronted jacket draped over the back of his chair. 'I'm only in to tidy my desk. Then I'm taking the weekend off.'

'Golf?' asked Thane.

'No.' David Mark gave an amused grunt at the idea. 'With my kind of eyesight? If I hit a ball, I never find it again. I'm not like my brother, Superintendent.'

'Where's Jon playing today?' asked Louise Croft casually. She had sat herself in a chair beside Mark's desk, a chair she'd obviously been using earlier.

'Gleneagles, I think.' Mark scowled. 'Hell, I never know for sure until I see his expense sheet. If I know for sure then. Do you have problems with expense sheets, Superintendent?'

'He does,' murmured Francey Dunbar. 'I've heard of your brother, Mr Mark. He's a good player.'

'That's not why you're here.' Mark looked directly at Thane. 'Is it that damned modem again?'

'Mostly.' Thane considered Mark and the woman for a moment. 'A man named Robert Haston, a freelance security-systems installer, was a Computer Cabin customer.'

'Then got himself killed falling out of an express train about a month ago.' The sales manager nodded. 'I spoke to him a few times.' He glanced at Louise Croft. 'Louise would know him too.'

'I did.' She frowned and brushed a stray strand of blonde hair back from her forehead. 'I think I had him come to see me a couple of times – that's part of my job, Superintendent. If people work on credit, I have to keep an eye on how their account stands – that it doesn't get out of hand.'

131

'Did it?' asked Dunbar mildly. 'Get out of hand, I mean?'

'No, Sergeant.' Her words almost brushed him aside. 'Why does it matter, Superintendent?'

'We'd talked with his widow, the way we've talked with other people, about this computer modem puzzle – the way we've talked with you, Mr Mark.' Thane watched David Mark as he spoke. 'She was checking her husband's records. Something happened – and she was found dead last night. Murdered. We think she tried contacting various people. Did either of you hear from her?'

'No.' David Mark blinked and carefully removed his spectacles. 'I'm sorry. I can't help.'

'Nor me.' Louise Croft shook her head. 'I'm sorry too.'

'Could she have tried to contact you last night, Mr Mark?'

'Slow down.' Frowning, the man replaced his spectacles and gave a quick glance at Louise Croft. 'Is that a diplomatic-style police way of asking where I was last night?'

'It could help if we knew.' Thane kept his manner neutral.

'He was with me, Superintendent,' said the blonde woman dryly. 'The way he usually is after office hours – we live together. Some people know, but not here at Computer Cabin. Head office wouldn't approve.'

'All night together?' asked Francey Dunbar bluntly.

'Yes, Sergeant.' She gave a slight, enigmatic smile. 'All night together. Mostly, we watched TV. Then David's brother Jon looked in. I think that was around eight o'clock, when he got back from some damned golf course.'

David Mark nodded agreement. 'Until about midnight – maybe later, I suppose. But – '

'But no one else.' Louise Croft's voice was suddenly

132

colder. 'Any other questions, Superintendent?'

There were. But not for now, decided Thane. Slowly, he shook his head.

'If there's anything later, let me know, Superintendent.' David Mark's sales-manager smile slid back in place. 'Any time.' He glanced at the blonde. 'Louise – '

'I'll see them out,' she nodded.

She did, shepherding them out of Mark's office then firmly leading the way to the elevator. She waited until it arrived then saw them aboard.

'I'm going to ask a favour, Superintendent,' she said. 'You know about David and me. But you don't have to spread it around, do you?'

Then the elevator door closed, shutting her off.

They rode it down, left the busy store and were back in the car before Francey Dunbar said anything. Before he did, he gave a soft curse at the world in general.

'That's what I call being marched out,' he said wryly. He glanced at Thane, who had started the car. 'All night together, only brother Jon for company. Do you buy it, sir?'

'It's convenient.' Thane let the Ford tick over for a moment, rubbing a hand along the steering wheel. 'Convenient – and neat.' And Joan Haston was dead. 'Too damned neat, Francey.'

He didn't like it when things came neatly. His glance strayed to the car's dashboard clock, then he checked in his rear mirror and set the Ford moving.

Jack Hart's conference was due in twenty minutes.

They were back at Crime Squad headquarters, literally leaving Thane's room to go along to Hart's office, when the woman who called herself Pony telephoned again.

'You're the detective superintendent I spoke to last time?' She was suspicious. The other thing in her voice sounded like worry.

'The same one – Thane.' He tried to keep his own manner steady and reassuring. 'Pony, let's stop playing games. Are you Janey Peters?'

'No.' She sounded surprised.

'But you know her?' pressed Thane.

'Yes.' There was a sound which was almost a laugh. 'You could say that. I want to help her, I want to help Johnny Gort.'

'You want to do a deal, Pony,' said Thane bluntly. 'What kind?'

'A promise they're not arrested on any kind of charge. That if you get the people who really matter then you simply chase him back to Spain, that you let Janey go with him.'

'And what about you, Pony?' Thane scowled at Dunbar, who was practically breathing down his neck trying to hear both ends of the conversation. 'What do you get?'

'You wouldn't understand,' she said shortly. 'Janey doesn't know I'm calling you. But I know what she really wants to happen.'

'You care about her,' translated Thane. 'Pony, do you know about last night?'

'Last night?' she was puzzled.

'A woman named Joan Haston was murdered. Her husband died about a month ago. He was almost as good an interface man as Gort – she was asking questions, like why he died.'

He heard a sound like a soft, despairing groan over the line.

'So where are they, Pony?'

'I need that promise – '

'It might be that way.' Thane saw Dunbar's raised eyebrows, but shrugged. 'Right now, that's the best I can do.'

'Do better, Detective Superintendent.' Some resolve

came back into her voice. 'I don't know where they are right now – that's the truth. Janey calls me – they don't know about the calls.'

'They?'

'The people running things. I don't know who they are.' He heard a short, bitter laugh. 'There's a lot I don't know.'

'When did she call you last?'

'About an hour ago.' The woman hesitated. 'She said things have been moved forward twenty-four hours.' Concern tightened her voice. 'That means you've only got till Monday now, not Tuesday. But I need that promise. Then I'll help. You understand?'

'I told you – ' began Thane.

'I'll call back,' said the woman.

The line went dead. She had hung up again. Silently, Thane replaced his receiver.

'You tried,' said Dunbar sadly.

'The next person who tells me that – '

'Gets his head kicked in?' suggested Dunbar mildly.

'Something like it.' Thane looked at his hands, surprised to see they were still steady. If Pony was right they had lost a day. Now they had forty-eight hours left, maybe a little more. Maybe a little less. He picked up the papers he wanted and beckoned Dunbar. 'He's waiting.'

They went through to Jack Hart's office. It was big, fully carpeted, and some etchings of old-time policemen with beards, top hats and frock coats were hung around the walls. The Crime Squad commandant had a commandant-sized desk, with Maggie Fyffe in her secretary's chair to one side. Hart was behind his desk, a pile of telex messages and report sheets in front of him. There were chairs already placed for Thane and Dunbar.

'Sit,' he said almost wearily as they entered. His sad

135

eyes watched as they obeyed, his lined face hard to read. 'I can see something happened. What is it?'

'We've heard again from Pony.'

Briefly, Thane told him what the woman had said. From there, he added what had happened at Computer Cabin.

'That's it?' asked Hart impassively.

'Apart from possibilities.' Thane nodded.

'All right.' For a moment Hart sat with his eyes closed, using both hands to smooth back his thinning grey hair. When he opened his eyes again, he looked at Maggie Fyffe. 'Our turn, Maggie. I gave you the list – you tell them.'

'Sir.' She flicked back a couple of pages of notebook and gave Thane an apologetic glance. 'Army records don't list any soldier – corporal or otherwise – with the names David or Jon Mark as having served with Robert Haston's Signals unit. Criminal Records have no listing for David Mark or Louise Croft. Jon Mark was sentenced to eighteen months' imprisonment eight years ago – he was drunk, attacked someone he didn't like, and nearly killed him. No other convictions.'

'But – ' said Hart gently.

'David Mark is the registered owner of a blue Mercedes coupé.' Maggie Fyffe took the cue. 'He also owns a large bungalow in the Bearsden area, and there's a yacht based at Inverkip marina.'

'He has money,' paraphrased Hart. 'He and Louise Croft have been – uh – co-habiting for about a year. Jon Mark has a yuppie-style apartment not far from where you live, Francey. He drives a Jaguar. They live well. Maybe too well for what they get paid.' He glanced at Thane. 'I think we put a watch on them, as of now.'

'Already done, sir,' said Francey Dunbar cheerfully. 'As soon as we got back – ' He stopped as Thane kicked him under the desk.

136

'Thank you, Sergeant.' Jack Hart made a deliberate, throat-clearing noise. 'Maggie.'

'The Spanish police say several British women visited John Gort's beach bar during the last month. Janey Peters is well known to Gort's staff, shares his bed when she visits. She isn't necessarily the only one.' Maggie Fyffe spoke as if she were discussing the price of butcher meat.

'A different kind of interface.' Hart was indifferent and moved on. 'We now have the initial post-mortem report on Joan Haston. She was killed by two bullets from a Browning thirty-eight automatic – both bullets recovered in excellent condition and it should be an easy ballistics match-up if we ever get a gun. No other real developments, however, and still just that one woman who claims she saw a motorcycle. Remember that it officially stays a Strathclyde case. We keep a low profile out there.' He paused and gave a genuine sigh. 'Well, Haston's widow called someone that evening – that's for sure. Poor damned silly woman.'

'The corporal,' said Thane suddenly, loudly. He drew a deep breath. 'Hell, we could have it wrong. There's another way! We asked army records about the Mark brothers. But there are women soldiers, women corporals.'

'Women dispatch riders, who ride motorcycles!' Francey Dunbar understood first and swallowed hard. 'Maybe like Louise Croft? It could fit!'

'Dear God,' said Jack Hart softly. He sucked his lips for a moment, then nodded. 'Check it, Francey – now. By telephone, direct, and don't let anything in uniform sidetrack you.'

Francey Dunbar was already out of his chair. The office door slammed behind him as he left.

'We'll find out.' Jack Hart moistened his lips and turned to his secretary. 'Maggie, coffee time.'

137

She had a pot steaming gently on a corner table. Going over, she used a china cup and saucer for Hart, added sugar and cream, then brought it over before she repeated the process for Thane and herself. Thane saw he had the cracked cup again.

'You don't appreciate good coffee until you've existed on hospital brew.' Hart took a first taste from his cup and gave an approving grunt. 'All right, Colin. We need some thinking time. How do you see things so far?'

'As one great blur,' said Thane bluntly. At least it made Maggie Fyffe give a faint smile. 'But it centres on the Interface Man, and whoever is running him is ruthless, quite happy to kill as required. We've got something big by the tail.'

'Something very big.' Hart nursed his coffee cup in both hands and sucked his lips. 'Very big, involving a computer. Some kind of thieving – major thieving. I've talked to electronics people, I've had Joe Felix dig around some of his friends. The team behind John Gort have to be into something a whole lot bigger than plain, ordinary computer hacking, stripping for information. They want something that a damned computer is guarding.' He looked across at Maggie Fyffe. 'Maggie, do you follow me?'

She shrugged. 'I think so, sir.'

'I'm glad if anyone does.' Hart stopped and swore mildly as his internal telephone gave a bleep. 'And I said no calls here, didn't I?'

But he lifted the receiver, answered, then his expression changed a little as he listened.

'Send him through,' he ordered. The instrument went down, and he turned to Thane. 'A visitor, mainly looking for you. It's Amos, from the Strathclyde laboratory.'

A moment later there was a cheerful double-tap on Hart's office door, then it opened and Matt Amos ambled

138

in. The forensic scientist was wearing a pink spotted bow tie Thane hadn't seen before and a suede jacket. Grinning a general greeting, he closed the door behind him then dropped into the chair vacated by Francey Dunbar.

'Coffee.' He beamed as he saw the cups. 'No sugar in mine, Maggie.'

'And good morning to you too,' said Hart grimly as she fetched another cup. 'Matt, you told our front desk this was urgent.'

'Urgent enough for me to come over instead of just lifting a telephone.' Matt Amos sat back like a confident, bearded monkey and nodded in Thane's direction. 'Blame him. He even makes me work on a Saturday, which is something I tried hard to avoid – '

'Matt.' Thane saw the gathering scowl on Hart's face. 'Is it the dirt samples from Edinburgh?'

'From the car Janey Peters traded in.' Amos nodded.

'What have we got?' Jack Hart showed immediate, hopeful interest.

'Enough.' Matt Amos looked pleased with himself. 'Commander, how could people like you manage without people like me?'

'One day I'll be tempted to find out,' growled Hart. 'Get to it, Matt. You heard about last night, didn't you?'

'Yes.' The grin vanished from Amos's bearded face. 'Strathclyde are turning the laboratory into a builder's yard with stuff they want examined. How's young Sandra Craig?'

'Doing fine.' Hart showed his impatience.

'Here we go, then.' Amos became suddenly, totally professional. 'We received dust and debris samples from the car, and I knew the general background case. Some of the samples amounted to ordinary road dirt. We found a few human hairs, brunette, long, probably female, with some signs of permanent waving – pre-

139

blonde if they came from Janey Peters. After that, we got into the interesting stuff. You'll get the written report on Monday. Agreed?'

Hart and Thane nodded.

'What we were left with included coastal sand, dried sea salt, a few grass seeds, and some traces of fertilizer chemicals. They've been identified by spectroscopic analysis – meaning we put them into a funny box that gets a spectroscopic signature from each item. We compare that signature, that graph, with standard signatures. Understand me?'

'So far,' agreed Thane softly. 'Keep going.'

'We have two distinct varieties of coastal sand, varieties that shouldn't be together. The sea salt would be from dried spray or seawater. The grass seed is top quality, the kind you'd maybe use on a garden lawn.'

'Or a golf course?' asked Thane.

'Positively a golf course,' murmured Amos. 'The chemical fertilizer clinched it. The head greenkeeper who used the stuff confirmed it. But you were wrong, Colin. You thought about the Old Course at St Andrews. That car spent its time close to the Turnberry championship course in Ayrshire.'

'Where every green is only a chip-shot or so away from the sea,' murmured Jack Hart, staring at him.

'Check it again,' invited Amos. He counted on his fingers. 'Two kinds of coastal sand – one local, the other variety brought in when they built the course bunkers. Sea salt, top-quality grass seed – but the fertilizer is the clincher. The head greenkeeper mixes his own special recipe and he gave the greens an extra feed less than three weeks ago.'

'But you still knew to go straight to Turnberry?' Maggie Fyffe didn't often break in. But she was midway between bewilderment and admiration.

'Well – ' Amos took a long swallow of coffee ' – uh –

there was something else I was going to mention.' He reached into an inside pocket of his suede jacket, brought out a small evidence envelope and handed it to Thane with a wary grin. 'Edinburgh found this jammed in one of the tyre treads.'

Thane looked at the transparent envelope, then at Matt Amos. The envelope held the broken top half of a plastic golf tee. It was red in colour and what remained of the cup-shaped top had been mangled. But a tiny lighthouse emblem was printed in black inside the cup. Round the rim, battered but readable, was the word Turnberry.

'A whisky firm turned them out as part of an advertising gimmick for a pro-am match,' said Amos hastily. 'The lighthouse is the Turnberry club badge and the club pro has been handing them out free. But – well, it wasn't enough on its own. Was it?'

'No, it wasn't.' Jack Hart took the evidence envelope and considered it for several seconds. Then he looked up. 'You've done well, Matt. But do this to me again and I'll tie you over a barbecue.'

'I hear you.' Amos gave a delighted chuckle and stood up. 'We're not doing so good with a different problem – that piece of folded paper Colin brought us from Janey Peters' home. Yes, it was some kind of packet. No, there's no laboratory evidence it was used for drugs. A couple of my people think they've maybe seen folding like it before – they can't remember where or when.'

'Ask them to try, Matt.' Thane said it quietly. 'And thanks for the rest.'

Amos nodded. Then he was on his way, the door opening and closing quietly as he left.

'All change,' said Jack Hart after a moment.

Thane nodded. St Andrews and the Old Course were about eighty miles away, to the north-east. Turnberry, on the Ayrshire coast, was about fifty miles to the south-west.

'Jon Mark is known at every Scottish golf club worth a damn,' he said almost absently. 'He fits in like part of the scenery.'

'Does that give us a half-empty bottle or a half-full bottle?' queried Hart. 'Look on the bright side. A lot of people will recognize him.' He glanced at his wrist-watch. 'I'm going to the hospital to see Gloria. I'll be back.'

'Best wishes to her from me,' said Thane. 'The same from Mary.'

He rose, left the Squad commander's room and went along to his own office. Francey Dunbar was there, standing pensively beside the window.

'Some of this you're going to like, sir,' he said carefully. 'Some of this you're not going to like. That's guaranteed.'

'All right.' Thane sat on the edge of his desk. 'Try the bad first.'

'We've lost David Mark and the Croft woman – '

'Lost them?'

'Lost them,' agreed Dunbar gloomily. He nodded at the telephone. 'The men watching Computer Cabin just called in. They got worried because nothing was happening and checked inside. Mark and Louise Croft had been gone for about twenty minutes by then. Nobody knows anything except that they've gone for the weekend.'

With an effort, Thane fought down his anger. It could happen, it did happen. What good would it do to yell and shout at a couple of cops who had been caught wrong-footed?

'We're still waiting to hear from the army about women corporals.' Dunbar brightened a little. 'Now it starts to get better. Your pal Phil Moss telephoned. It may come late today, but that lead he got about our Pony woman looks like paying off.'

'And we need it,' said Thane grimly. If he had it before the next call came in from Pony, it could make a lot of difference.

'Last thing. The Transport Police relayed a message from Pat Emslie. It says he has a name now – the man who knows about Beanbag Slater. Emslie can't locate him yet, but he knows where he should surface some time this afternoon. When it happens, we'll hear.'

'Good,' said Thane softly. 'Now it's my turn.'

He told his sergeant about Turnberry and saw the glint that it brought to Dunbar's eyes.

They had reached a time that arrived in most cases, sooner or later. Suddenly, unexpectedly, several things could begin happening. It didn't always mean they were winning. But it usually meant they'd stopped losing – and it made all the difference.

Half an hour later a call came in on Colin Thane's telephone. The army records captain on the other end had a public-school drawl and sounded bored. But somebody had been working.

'You guessed it right, Superintendent,' said the Army captain laconically. 'When your man Haston was with his Signals regiment they spent a spell serving in Cyprus. They had an attached section from the Women's Royal Army Corps – that was also when Haston was naughty and was suspected of selling War Department stores on the side. The WRAC section included a Corporal Louise Croft.'

'What was her job?'

'Dispatch rider,' said the army captain. 'She must have been reasonably good, Superintendent. We've a mention that she won the Cyprus command annual motorcycle trials trophy. But she left the army about a year after Haston – nothing here to tell me why.'

Thane thanked him and hung up. Then he threw back his head and allowed himself one triumphant yell at the world outside his window.

He had stopped losing.

It was beginning to come together.

But where had everybody gone?

5

Colin Thane shared a sandwich lunch with some of the day-shift team who were working in the duty room. They were men and women tackling a variety of different problems; it was a good way to remind himself that the Interface Man investigation was just one of the Crime Squad's active caseload.

Eight kilos of cocaine, watched all the way from Hamburg, were currently hidden aboard a truckload of tractor spares queuing at Stranraer harbour for the Irish Sea ferry crossing to Belfast. From there the drug would head for Dublin. Five police forces were co-operating, waiting until the cocaine reached its distribution point. His own Triad case, which he had wanted to stay on ice, was shaping to become active. A Hong Kong Chinese importer living in Edinburgh had been attacked by a stranger armed with a hatchet. Another team were chasing a fire-bomb fanatic who was threatening to torch five churches in five different towns. He had sent the list of towns to a newspaper, one church had already burned down and another had been damaged.

Even Detective Chief Inspector Tina Redder, with her short, jet-black hair and those eye-catching legs, was looking harassed. She had headed a raid on an out-of-town garden centre, hoping to scoop up an embezzling company secretary. Instead, her team had picked up all five members of a gang who had been breaking into mansions and castles in the stately homes league for at least two years.

'Two years, damn them!' She took another bite at the

ham sandwich she was eating and glared indignantly at Thane. 'Two years, Colin!'

'Nice catch, Tina,' mused Thane. 'It'll make a lot of people happy.'

'Have you thought of the damned paperwork – all spread over two years?' She scowled at him. 'There's worse. We brought back a vanload of stolen stuff. Cardboard boxes filled with silver plate, two Meissen china dinner sets, paintings, gold ornaments, would you believe some tapestries?' She had to pause for breath. 'See that army pack behind you?'

Thane turned, saw it, and nodded.

'That damned thing is filled with jewellery. There's more – we're asking for help from some insurance-nominated expert to work out valuations. Yet all I wanted was a nice, ordinary, peaceful embezzlement!'

'There's no justice when you're a cop,' agreed Thane sadly. 'Not on a Saturday.'

He retreated to his own office. It was empty. For the moment most of his team were out or were glued to telephones. The two plain-clothes men who had lost David Mark and Louise Croft at Computer Cabin were trying to salvage their pride by asking questions in the area where the couple lived. They would do the same for Jon Mark. Joe Felix was telephoning sports reporters he knew, asking if Jon Mark was scheduled to play in any golf tournament over the weekend.

Thane had given Francey Dunbar the task of checking where the Mark brothers and Louise Croft might have been on the day Robert Haston had been thrown out of that London–Glasgow express. Dunbar was out, he'd be back when he was ready.

The most important job of all was one that the Crime Squad couldn't tackle – a delicate, probing check of the whole Ayrshire area surrounding Turnberry golf course, then rippling out from there through the general

Ayrshire golfing scene.

It amounted to asking about sightings of people and cars linked to any even faintly unusual activity over the past few weeks. Yet it had to be done without causing any surprise or speculation.

Thane had talked at length to the Ayr-based CID chief whose territory took in Turnberry, dredging up past favours. They had agreed. Any cop located in the area who admitted to playing golf was being sent home to change out of uniform, and then go out to gossip around golf-club locker rooms, professionals' shops and the clubhouse bars.

They were local, they were accepted. They would be thorough. They were being told how close Sandra Craig had come to being dead.

A new thin trickle of telex messages had appeared on his desk. Thane was sorting through them when his telephone rang and he answered. It was Phil Moss.

'About your Pony,' said Moss without preliminaries. 'I've got a name, I've got an address for her. It all checks out. Her name is Elizabeth Lewis. She's a hairdresser, she changed jobs about a month ago – I can't trace where the new job is. But she works on Saturdays and gets home about six. Can you meet me?'

'Yes.' Thane didn't hide the relief in his voice. 'Where and when?'

'Skerry Street, Cathcart, about six p.m. Then we go in together,' suggested Moss.

'At six', agreed Thane. 'Phil – '

'How?' Moss chuckled over the line. 'Thank Wilma, your little problem policewoman out at Williamfield. She'd heard the name, nobody had bothered to ask her.'

'You did,' said Thane thankfully.

'It's the old-fashioned approach,' said Moss balefully. 'They don't teach it any more.' He gave one of his new-style, low-key belches, then Thane heard the line go dead.

147

If they got Pony – Thane moistened his lips at the thought and slowly put down the receiver. He reached for one of the folders in front of him and opened it. Inside were two enlarged prints from Photographic, blow-ups of separate head-and-shoulders pictures they had of John Gort and Janey Peters. Photographic had used an air-brush to alter Janey Peters' hair colouring to blonde and had made an attempt at the styling seen at the airport when she collected Gort.

For a full couple of minutes Thane sat looking at their faces. Sometimes it could help, could give him some small understanding of the person who might be behind a face. So far, in total, he had only seen these two for a matter of seconds under the airport lighting. He had still to talk with either of them.

John Gort, the Interface Man – how was he likely to react to the kind of pressure building around him?

Maybe he had built his own defences over the years. That sharp-featured face with its high cheekbones had done a lot of living. There was a hint of calculating patience about his slightly hooded eyes and thin mouth. When somebody's telephoto lens had caught his picture, Gort had been displeased about something. It showed – but only just – in the twist of those lips.

The Interface Man was a survivor. But what about Janey Peters?

Her photograph was an enlarged detail from someone's snapshot. Even given her altered hair, she was still just a plump, ordinary woman in her mid-thirties. The small scar on the left side of her chin wasn't enough to make any difference one way or another. She had a pleasant face, big, friendly eyes, and small, crinkle-like laughter lines around a heavily lipsticked mouth. An easy-going mouth.

She and Gort might go well together. They probably did. But what were they into, how deep were they in?

How could they get out?

Jack Hart returned from his hospital visit. The Squad commander was cheerful. All was still going well with his wife, and he wanted to be brought up to date. Thane gave him enough of a summary to satisfy him and Hart left, making noises about contacting another of his computer specialists.

The telephone rang again, a call from the Ayrshire CID chief to say his side of the deal was now in full operation. Thane thanked him, hung up, then built a wry steeple with his fingertips and stared at the result, thinking. He knew the area the Ayrshire men had to cover. It wouldn't be quick, it couldn't be easy.

He could picture the long coastal stretch of small towns and smaller fishing villages. It had smooth, sandy beaches punctuated by harsh granite cliffs. It had holiday villages and luxury hotels, as well as places where rich farmland met small industrial estates.

And it had a golf course almost every other mile, with Turnberry as the gem.

Next to football, golf was Scotland's national sport – and Ayrshire's coastal strip could have been made for golf. There were rich courses and poor courses, private courses and municipal courses, two were owned by a Japanese investment company, one was run by a factory works committee. A German industrialist wanted to build two more.

And somewhere out there, somewhere among those trudging golfers thumping little white balls with strange metal sticks, could be the help he needed –

He left the thought there, realizing someone had come into his room.

'Sir?' There was a throat-clearing noise. 'Are you – uh – all right, Superintendent?'

Thane turned, met the worried gaze of Pat Emslie, and gave the Transport Police inspector a reassuring nod.

149

'It's called thinking,' he told Emslie dryly. 'Meaning I was daydreaming – miles away.'

'I've been there, sir.' Emslie grinned, obviously pleased with himself. Then the grin widened, he couldn't wait any longer. 'I know the man who teamed up with Beanbag Slater, sir. He's next-best thing to wrapped up, ready to collect.' Emslie could have been an eager hound, straining at a leash. 'His name is Gerry Waddell – Duck Waddell around his friends. The word is he's been working with Beanbag in some funny-farm robbery deal involving a computer – '

'Slow down!' Out of his chair at a jump, Thane grabbed Emslie by the arm. 'Who said computer?'

'My tout, sir.'

'You didn't use it first?'

'No sir,' Emslie's young face flushed to the roots of his short, corn-straw hair. 'Hell, that's training college stuff!'

'Sorry.' Thane sighed and released his grip on the Transport Police Inspector's arm. 'Does your tout have details?'

'If he does, he didn't tell me.' Emslie shook his head. 'We can collect Waddell any time you want, Super-intendent. You said you always wanted to know first.' The grin wisped back again. 'Anyway, he's working all afternoon.'

'People who work Saturdays are beginning to form a queue,' said Thane softly. He reached for his jacket, which was draped over the back of a chair, and pulled it on. 'You know where he is?'

'For the next half hour.' Emslie was positive. 'He's out as part of a Community Service Order team digging pensioners' gardens – he's on a one-hundred-hours order, Saturday afternoons only. He's a football fan who got into a brawl.'

'Who won't see any more football for a spell.' Thane

150

nodded his understanding. The courts could use Community Service Orders in strange, telling ways as an alternative to prison. Break the Order and the offender drew a lot of wrath. 'You've seen him?'

'He's there, digging away.' Emslie nodded. 'It took time to find his social worker. No one else knew where the garden team was working.'

'What else do you know about him?'

'Waddell?' Emslie frowned. 'He's a second-league burglar, sir. Shops and offices mostly – doesn't make any mess, doesn't get caught too often. We've pulled him in a couple of times for railway thefts.'

'And your tout?'

'Johnny Silver.' Emslie grinned to himself. 'He's a plain little crook, the kind who couldn't go straight if he was fired from a gun. But he owes me.'

'Like the man you mentioned yesterday?' Thane remembered the teenager he'd caught, the father who was useful.

'Like that, but someone else.' Emslie was evasive. 'About Duck Waddell. Give him a chance and he runs. His pals in the Community Service team might try to get in the way.'

'Then we'll take along some help.' Thane beckoned and led the way out of his office.

The Community Service Order team, six men with basic hand tools and a couple of wheelbarrows, were at work around a group of twelve purpose-built cottages for pensioners located next to a school playing field in the Pollok area, about three miles from the Crime Squad's headquarters. It was still a dry day, bright and pleasant, and the gardening team didn't look unhappy.

Colin Thane had parked his car about a hundred yards down the road, at a bend. Emslie was with him. Behind them, hidden from the gardeners' view Jock

Dawson was waiting in his battered Land-Rover dog-van. Joe Felix was with him and Dawson's dogs were snoozing in the rear.

'That one.' Pat Emslie leaned forward in his seat and pointed. 'Second on the left, pushing a barrow.'

'He doesn't look like he'd win prizes.' Thane wasn't impressed. Duck Waddell seemed a typical small-time Glasgow ned: a thin-shouldered man in his late twenties with collar-length brown hair. The man had a narrow face, and even at a distance Thane could see he had a badly bruised, almost closed right eye. He was wearing faded denims with a black rollneck sweater and old, stained training shoes, and his barrow was being trundled with minimal enthusiasm. 'Do they have a supervisor on site?'

'Not officially. Unofficially, about twenty of them.' Emslie nodded towards the cottages. 'Every pensioner watches. Anyone arrives late or leaves early, they report it. The service is free, but they still want their full money's worth.'

Thane watched Duck Waddell push his barrow up a small ramp and empty weeds and rubbish into a small skip. Then the man turned and went back for more. The other members of the gardening team looked equally ordinary as they worked around flowerbeds and shrubs, digging and tidying. A Community Service Order could send a man on his own or with a group, gardening or painting a kitchen, doing a stint helping hospital volunteers, assisting disabled youngsters – any one of a long list of chores. It kept them out of trouble and out of prison. One was as important as the other. Prisons weren't just overcrowded. They were ready to burst at the seams.

Some had. When it happened, it was called a riot. Usually, someone tried to set the prison on fire as almost a routine protest – and things got worse.

152

'They finish at four o'clock, sir.' Emslie glanced at his wristwatch. 'Ten minutes from now.'

'This afternoon they stop early.' Thane reached for his door handle.

They came out of the car together and began walking towards the gardening squad. After only a few steps they'd been seen and every gardener was standing very still, staring in their direction. That lasted only a moment, then Duck Waddell suddenly threw his barrow aside and began running.

'Hold it,' yelled Emslie. 'Police!'

The man didn't look round. Reaching the fence dividing the pensioners' cottages from the school playing field, he vaulted over and kept running. But Colin Thane stopped Emslie as the younger man prepared to head after him.

Behind them, Jock Dawson was out of the Land-Rover, followed by Joe Felix. The Land-Rover's rear door swung open and the two dogs jumped down. The labrador bitch thrashed her tail in delight, the big, black-maned alsatian looked around.

'Take him, you pair.' Jock Dawson pointed towards the fleeing man. 'Goldie, go. Rajah, easy lad.'

The yellow labrador gave one short bark and took off. Streaking past the rest of the motionless gardening team, she hardly broke stride as she cleared the fence into the playing field. Trotting at a more leisurely pace, the alsatian followed her. Hands in his pockets, Dawson glared at the gardeners.

'You lot stay as you are,' he ordered curtly.

Duck Waddell kept sprinting across the playing field. For the two dogs it was a training exercise brought to life. Jock Dawson gave Thane a slight grin, watched his animals, then puckered his lips and gave two sharp whistles.

Goldie accelerated. In a moment she was ahead of

153

Waddell, skidding round in a thrash of legs, facing the man, showing her teeth, barking loudly. Waddell reacted, stumbled and fell. Picking himself up again, he ran off at another angle.

Rajah was there, a slow-trotting baleful menace of a dog with a rumbling noise coming from somewhere deep in his throat. Swinging round, Waddell tried a different direction.

Goldie was already there.

The pair had left one way open, back towards the pensioner cottages and the waiting police. Like a frightened, herded sheep, Waddell tried again. Again, the dogs were ahead of him. Waddell stopped uncertainly and Goldie sat, facing him. Moving at a lope, Rajah's black bulk came nearer. The alsatian showed his teeth in a hopeful, inviting grin.

'Call them off!' Waddell raised his hands in abject surrender. 'Just call the devils off!'

'Walk slowly – towards me,' ordered Jock Dawson. 'Real slowly, friend. Do it, and now.'

Waddell nodded and obeyed, the two dogs trotting behind him with their tails wagging. Once Joe Felix had stepped forward and had handcuffed the man, the two dogs went to Dawson who scratched each of them between the ears.

The gardening squad hadn't moved and were still holding rakes or spades. Interested faces were watching from the cottage windows.

'Excitement over,' Thane told the gardeners. 'You're finished for today, I'll square things with your social worker.' As they scattered he turned to the shaking Duck Waddell. 'You're different. With you, we're just starting. Why did you run?'

Waddell didn't answer. Close up, his black eye was only part of the damage to his face. He had a gash on his nose and one ear was badly swollen. One of the dogs

154

gave a short bark, and he almost jumped.

'Keep that thing away from me,' he pleaded.

'He talks,' grinned Emslie.

'But he doesn't like dogs,' said Thane. He hardened his voice. 'Maybe they don't like you, Waddell. Suppose we heave you into the back of the van with them and find out?'

'You wouldn't.' Waddell stared in horror. 'You couldn't!' He jerked in panic as Joe Felix laid a hand on his shoulder.

'He could,' said Pat Emslie helpfully. 'He's no four-by-two cop, not your usual kind, Duck. He's one of the Scottish Crime Squad bosses. If he wants you buried alive, he just has to approve the overtime.'

'What do you want?' asked Waddell greyly.

'A talk about you and Beanbag Slater,' said Thane grimly. He saw new fear cross the man's face. 'Maybe a talk about murder, maybe double murder.'

The man moaned.

'I'm giving you a chance to get out from under the edges,' said Thane. He considered Waddell's damaged features. 'One chance. Your choice.'

'And we don't like waiting,' said Emslie gently.

Rajah was bored. He gave a great, jaw-stretching yawn. It was enough to decide the man.

'I'll get protection?' he asked.

'The best,' promised Thane.

He had Emslie and Felix take Waddell to the car while he walked over to join Dawson and his dogs. He talked with the dog-handler for a moment or two, and patted the dogs once he was sure they remembered him. Dawson decided to take the dogs for a brief walk around, snapped his fingers, and set off with Rajah and Goldie at his heels. When Thane went back to his car, Pat Emslie was already in the front passenger seat. Joe Felix and their prisoner were in the rear.

155

'We've been talking, sir,' said Emslie dryly as Thane joined them. 'I was asking Duck what happened to his face.' He gave a mock sigh. 'He says his part in the job he was doing with Beanbag finished last night and he was paid off. Then Duck got greedy. He asked for a bonus on top of the agreed rate. That wasn't clever – Duck was bounced off a few walls as a goodbye.'

'By Beanbag?' asked Thane.

Waddell nodded gloomily. 'Beanbag and his pal Sailor Duffy.'

'Martin Duffy,' murmured Joe Felix. 'I know him. The Duffy with sea-time as a cabin steward. He fakes an American accent, but his home town is London.'

'That's him,' agreed Waddell glumly. 'Big an' nasty with it.'

Thane raised an eyebrow at Felix. 'Same league as Beanbag?'

'Maybe a few more brains,' suggested Felix. 'But not too many.'

'So what was the job, Waddell?' Thane reached back from behind the wheel and flicked an imaginary speck of dust from the man's denim jacket. 'That's what I want to know. No great sweat in that for you – not now, when it's over.'

Waddell hesitated. 'That protection – it's guaranteed?'

'If you talk. You still say your part ended last night?'

Waddell nodded.

'Where do we find Beanbag and Sailor?'

'They said they were diving deep for a spell. Very deep – I don't know where.' For a moment Duck Waddell looked down at his feet. 'The money was good. The job was crazy, but the money was good.'

Then out it came. Duck Waddell had worked with Beanbag and Sailor on other jobs. This time, Beanbag Slater had made the approach to him. There was a job

156

coming up. Beanbag and Sailor Duffy were already on the team and they needed a break-in man. They were working for someone who would stay in the background but pay the bills. Waddell didn't need to know anything more.

He agreed.

'Do you know what I had to do?' Waddell glared at the world through his one good eye. 'I mean like for the past couple of weeks, Monday to Friday?' He didn't pause for encouragement. 'The same thing every night. I had to break into the same damned office block in West George Street, right in the centre of town. I had to get Beanbag an' Sailor into an office on the fourth floor, then get them out again when they were ready.'

With no trace ever left that the building might have had visitors, not so much as a paperclip moved. The first visit had taken about three hours. After that, the visits had lasted about ninety minutes each night – always to the same office on the fourth floor. But there was no weekend work.

'What kind of an office?' demanded Thane.

'An insurance agency.' Waddell shrugged. 'I took them in through a basement firedoor, then the rest was easy. There's a night security man, but he just does the usual routine patrol. No problem.'

'So the computer was in the insurance office?' suggested Thane blandly.

'Eh?' Waddell stared at him, puzzled. 'You mean you don't know that bit?' He looked at three impassive faces, shifted uneasily, and the handcuff links jangled. 'There was a computer, yes. But not in that building. Hell, I don't know where it was – they didn't say, I didn't ask.'

Each night, getting there before eleven p.m., staying until after midnight, they had gone to the same office on the fourth floor. Then to the same room and to the same window in that room.

157

Slater and Duffy brought all the equipment they needed in a kitbag, and plugged into one of the insurance office's power points. That was when Sailor Duffy would take charge, Beanbag suddenly reduced to being his assistant, Waddell with nothing to do but wait.

'They had this lash-up contraption of bits an' pieces.' Waddell moistened his lips, still hoping for some sign of approval or even sympathy around him, meeting only stony silence. 'Look, I knew we were listening into somebody's computer working in some other building, not far away – but I don't know how that contraption worked, that's God's truth.'

'Describe it,' said Thane.

There had been what looked like an up-market car radio, with a miniature tape recorder attached. The radio had been fitted with a strange stub of home-made aerial, and wires led from the radio and tape recorder to plug into a thing like a briefcase –

'Did this "thing" have a name?' asked Joe Felix, his face coming alive with interest.

Waddell shrugged. 'A modem, I think. I wasn't allowed to touch it.'

'Did they also use something like a small TV set, as a monitor?' persisted Felix.

'That's right.' Waddell looked surprised.

'Joe.' Thane turned hopefully to Felix. 'Does it make sense?'

'It's heading that way, sir.' The middle-aged detective constable frowned, suddenly and unexpectedly seized Waddell by the sweater, and pulled him nearer. 'This next part matters, you hear me?'

Waddell moistened his lips and nodded.

'Computers use codewords – for access, for identification, so the right terminal gets the right information,' said Felix softly. 'Beanbag and Sailor would wait for that

158

happening. You'd see it. That's when they'd begin recording, right?'

'I – ' Waddell swallowed ' – I don't know anything about computer read-outs.'

'Not your scene,' agreed Felix. 'High-class gibberish, right?'

Waddell nodded.

'But you watched with them. You know the code-words.' With no apparent effort, Joe Felix hauled the man even nearer. 'So tell me. Now.'

'Now is the easy way,' suggested Emslie. 'Later is bad.'

'All right. Now.' Waddell gave in with a miserable air. 'There were two lots of letters – letters, not words. The first set was MIR, the other was UDA. Don't ask me what they meant.'

'Then they recorded,' murmured Felix. 'What about the print-out of whatever they got?'

'Done somewhere else, later.' If there had ever been any fight left in the man, it had gone. 'Someone was always waiting to collect the tape when we left. Beanbag did the hand-over, I was kept away.' He tried to look helpful. 'I saw a car sometimes – a big Mercedes. A couple of other times, there was someone on a motor-cycle. I didn't get near enough to see more than that.'

Joe Felix nodded, released his grip on the man and looked at Thane.

'Maybe we should have a private talk, sir,' he suggested.

They left their handcuffed prisoner in the car and walked a few paces away. The last of the Community Service Order gardeners had gone, the audience at the pensioners' windows had given up. Jock Dawson was putting his dogs back into their van.

'Make sense of it, Joe,' said Thane wearily.

'But keep it basic,' pleaded Emslie.

159

'I'll try,' agreed Felix. 'But I only held on to some of it by my fingertips – and I'll bet a month's pay that even if the Interface Man was still in Spain, he told them how, helped them set it up.'

'Set up what?' snarled Thane.

'Computer terminals are linked by telephone wires,' said Felix patiently. 'But every time a terminal is sending a message or one is coming in, there's – well, a leakage. Like a little VHF radio signal broadcasting from it. What they were doing – ' he shook his head in admiration ' – I've heard it can be done, that's all. You set up a car radio, the kind that tunes itself into the nearest, strongest signal. You tape that signal, once the modem tells you through the VDU screen you're getting what you want.'

'Then they run the tape back later, for a print-out?' Emslie gave a sudden beam of understanding.

'If you've a second modem somewhere to do the translating, and if you've a programmed data-printer unit handy.' Felix saw Thane's expression. 'It's – uh – simple enough. Like with a joke, if you know the bottom line.'

'Suppose we believe Waddell's story. How far from the fourth-floor office window to the place with the computer?'

'Maximum range?' Felix hesitated. 'Normally, maybe a long stone's throw – no more. But with the Interface Man telling them how, maybe a couple of hundred yards.'

In the heart of business Glasgow. Thane had a sick feeling at how many business computer terminals that might involve. How many of them operated at night?

Dawson's Land-Rover horn gave a light hoot behind them. Through his windscreen the dog-handler pointed at Thane then waved his radio handset. Thane nodded. The message was clear enough. Then he glanced at the Ford and their waiting prisoner.

'Not in front of Big-Ears,' he said dryly.

He walked over to the Land-Rover, got in beside a slightly surprised Dawson, and used the radio.

'From Sergeant Dunbar,' said the duty control assistant in her usual detached voice. 'Code Thirteen – he needs a meeting.'

Thane keyed the handset. 'Where?'

'He's parked outside the Computer Cabin warehouse. Will I patch him through sir?'

Thane grimaced at Dawson then used the handset again. 'No. Tell him I'll be with him inside fifteen minutes. Tell him to clean his tail feathers till I get there.'

'Thank you, Superintendent.' The detached voice didn't alter. 'Tail feathers. I'd suggest his cage as well.'

Thane ended the call, and returned the handset to its place on the front parcel-shelf. Leaving the Land-Rover, he went back to Felix and Emslie.

'We're parting.' He gave the Transport Police inspector the Ford's keys. 'I want you and Joe to drive Waddell to this West George Street office block. You let the duty security man know you're there. Then you watch Waddell do his break-in act, all the way to this fourth-floor window. If the story checks, I want a circle on a map. We work inside that circle. How many firms have computers, how many firms work them late through the week.'

Joe Felix looked startled. 'Who do we ask on a Saturday afternoon, for God's sake?'

From Felix, that was close to rebellion. Thane sighed. 'Try, Joe. Before you try, get a full statement out of Waddell, dump him in a cell, and report back to Jack Hart. Ask him to add Sailor Duffy to our Wanted list, tell him I'll be in later.' He glanced at Emslie. 'Can you get away from train-spotting for another couple of days?'

'If you need me.' Emslie was pleased.

161

'We need you,' agreed Thane. 'Sandra's down. Who's left to make the coffee?'

Emslie grinned.

Thane left them. Seconds later, Dawson's dog van was taking him on his way.

Argyle Street was busy when Dawson dropped him near the Computer Cabin showroom-warehouse. As the dog van drove off, Thane saw Francey Dunbar was using the Saab coupé which was also Sandra Craig's current favourite from the Squad vehicle pool. Thane began to walk towards the Saab, then slowed as the front passenger door opened and a girl emerged in a brief, tantalizing display of long legs. She turned to smile at the driver, closed the car door and disappeared into the shopping crowds.

She was the brunette who was Computer Cabin's office receptionist. Thane went over to the Saab and got in at the passenger side. Francey Dunbar sat behind the wheel.

'I saw her,' said Thane.

'She said you'd met.' Dunbar smugly sucked an edge of his moustache. 'That's Danny – for Danielle. She couldn't wait any longer. She has to get ready for an out-of-town date.'

'And you've got a phone number for later,' said Thane stonily. 'How did you find her?'

'She's in Greenpeace.' It was one of his sergeant's typically vague explanations. 'We know the same people.'

'So?' Thane watched the traffic go past outside.

'She's on her day off, but she came in. She couldn't get at anyone's personal diary, but she keeps the main reception appointment book.' Dunbar tapped a pleased little drumbeat tattoo on the steering wheel with his fingertips. It made his silver i.d. bracelet jingle. 'That's the next best thing, sir.'

'How much did you tell her?'

'Not a lot, but Danny is nobody's fool,' said Dunbar. 'She also has Louise Croft high on her personal hate list. I asked her to check the reception book around the Thursday when Robert Haston got chopped by the express train. There are a lot of cancelled appointments in that book, she remembers why. All three of them – David and Jon and Louise – suddenly had to take time off. Louise Croft was away all week, David and Jon had Wednesday and Thursday off then were back Friday morning.'

'Any reasons?' asked Thane, his eyes hard.

'Louise was taking holiday time she had due. David had an urgent business trip. Jon phoned to say he'd been hit by some kind of stomach bug. According to Danny, the result was chaos in Computer Cabin.'

'It would be.' It also meant three of Thane's suspects could have helped in the Intercity killing. 'Did you ask about Beanbag Slater?'

Dunbar nodded. 'And showed her a photograph. She can't remember him. Not up in office territory.'

'Downstairs help.' Thane gave a sour grin. 'Anything else from your Greenpeace girl?'

'Yes.' His sergeant took a moment to frown and tap his fingers on the steering wheel again. 'We were talking about her job. Danny's worked there for almost a year. All she still really knows about Jon Mark is he plays golf and he pats any female bottom that comes within range. Brother David and the Croft woman never mention anything outside of work. Nobody knows anything about what makes them tick.'

'And that's it?' Thane was disappointed.

'No.' Dunbar shook his head. 'Danny heard how we wanted a stock check on that ZB modem. She reckoned that was near to a laugh, a total waste of time. The firm's stock checks are done on computer listings. But all the time there are things that get borrowed or disappear. That's covered by a standard excuse. Anything missing is out on customer test. That's been done ever since she joined.'

'I was told two ZBs were out on loan to an airline.' Thane scowled as Dunbar began his steering wheel tattoo again. 'Stop that, will you Francey? I'm finding it hard enough to think.' He sighed as his sergeant obeyed. 'Now listen. We know what they've been doing. Even if we don't know why.'

Dunbar listened to the story of Duck Waddell and the fourth-floor office raids, surprised then fascinated.

'Let me guess,' he said at the end. 'Now we all get street maps and start hoofing door to door.' He whistled unhappily through his teeth. 'At a weekend?'

'I got the same moan from Joe Felix.' Thane glanced at his wristwatch. He had promised Phil Moss he'd meet him at six. There was half an hour left to get there, and he'd probably need all of it. 'I need a lift over to the South Side. Then you can head back and help the other happy faces.'

Dunbar scowled. But he set the Saab moving.

He had some negative items for Thane on the way. The last he'd heard, there was no report of any significant vehicle sighting or people sighting, there was no particular word back from the probings going on around the Ayrshire golf scene. The two plain-clothes men sent out to check the luxury bungalow in Bearsden where David Mark lived with Louise Croft had found it closed. The two-car garage attached was empty. Neighbours could only describe them as being 'nice' or 'quiet'. In an executive area like Bearsden that was only bettered by being in a Rotary club.

'What about Jon?' asked Thane.

'He likes women, they like him.' Dunbar shrugged. 'He's never too wild, but he gets around. Nine-iron sex-appeal – good in sand bunkers.'

'How about in the rain?' asked Thane sarcastically.

'He probably has a golf umbrella,' suggested Dunbar.

Cathcart is one of the older parts of Glasgow, but with some surprise streets where a developer has managed to discover unused land and build on it. That was the way at Skerry Street, where old houses suddenly gave way to new about halfway along. New meant small, but each house was detached, with its own little garden and a garage at the rear.

Phil Moss's car was parked near the last of the old houses. He got out of it as the Saab arrived and waited while Francey Dunbar dropped Thane then drove away again.

'You're late,' grumbled Moss. He turned up the collar of his grubby coat. There was a faint trace of rain in the air. 'Elizabeth Lewis is home. She arrived five minutes ago.'

'There was traffic.' Thane was immune to Moss's occasional acerbic growls. 'Anyway, give her time to settle in.'

'She's your worry, not mine.' Moss glanced back down the older part of the street to where there was a bright neon sign. 'All right, you can buy me a beer.'

They walked the short distance. The Lighthouse Bar was small, with bull's-eye windows. Inside, a model lighthouse flashed in one corner and the barman was dressed as a lighthouse keeper. But it was early for the Lighthouse Bar's regular trade and they were still his only customers. They ordered a beer each, Thane paid, and then they took the drinks over to a window table which gave them a clear view of the street.

'Elizabeth Lewis.' Thane sipped his drink. 'What do we know about her, Phil?'

'Not a lot.' Moss took a long gulp from his glass then wiped froth from his mouth with his sleeve. 'I tried her

165

name on one or two people who know Janey Peters. They pointed me to Cathcart. Then it wasn't too difficult – I'd been told she was disabled, and she's in the damned telephone book.'

'How close a friend?' Thane watched a car murmur past from the new end of the street. The driver was an elderly man, and alone.

'That's vague. Maybe from schooldays.'

Thane nodded. Somehow, it was the way he had expected.

'How goes it with your side?' Moss nursed what was left of his beer. 'Do I wait for the report sheets?'

'We know more of the questions to ask. The answers are something else.' Thane gave a low-voiced outline which brought Moss up to date. Moss had a new stain on his tie. It looked like soup, but Thane tried to ignore it as he finished. 'Any suggestions?'

'Yes.' Moss set down his empty glass, belched, and gave a lopsided grin. 'Let's go see her.'

The rain was still just a threat as they left the Lighthouse Bar and went down towards the new section of Skerry Street. Moss led the way to a little bungalow which had a tiny but beautifully tended front garden and lace curtains at the windows. A small Renault car was parked outside. The garage at the rear was closed.

Moss rang the doorbell. There were lights inside the house, another came on above their heads after a moment, then the front door opened on a security chain.

'Yes?' asked the woman who looked out through the gap. She was in her late thirties, with short, thinning, mousy-fair hair. She had an attractive mouth, a pert nose, and the bluest eyes Thane had ever seen. They held a strange blend of resolve and resignation.

'Pony?' asked Thane gently.

She sighed, looked at them both again, then nodded.

'I'm Colin Thane. This is Inspector Moss.' Thane waited.

'I know your voice, Superintendent.' She gave a small, wry smile. The door closed enough for her to release the chain, then opened again. 'You'd better come in – unless you like doorstep interviews.'

She stood back to let them in. Elizabeth Lewis was a tall wisp of a woman dressed in tailored dark blue trousers with black shoes and a light blue wool shirt. She walked with a stick. Limping heavily on her right leg, she closed the front door again then beckoned and led the way into her front room. It had wallpaper peppered with tiny roses. There were some small china ornaments on a shelf above an electric fire, and a couch and armchairs were upholstered in a deep cream fabric.

'So you found me.' She leaned heavily on her stick for a moment, considering them both again. 'I didn't think you would.'

'It wasn't easy,' said Thane.

'Maybe I'm glad you did.' The mousy-haired woman sighed. 'Do I ask if you have any new offer to give that could help them?'

'Gort and Janey Peters?' Thane shook his head. 'No promises, Pony. I'm sorry.'

'You say that like you almost mean it. What about you, Inspector – ah – ?'

'Moss.' Phil Moss gave a small shrug. 'I just got caught up at the edges.'

'That makes two of us.' Elizabeth Lewis used the stick to settle into one of the chairs then considered the stick with a jaundiced frown. 'I don't always need this thing. There are good days and bad days.' Then she waved them towards the couch. 'Sit down. You both make the room look untidy.'

They sat side by side on the couch. Thane noticed the telephone on a small table beside a TV set. There was a portable typewriter on another table in the far corner.

'How long have you known Janey?' It was Moss who spoke first.

'As long as I can properly remember.' Elizabeth switched from the frown to a faint smile, thinking about it. 'We were fostered together, brought in from separate family disasters. Janey's parents were raving drunks. My mother did the proverbial vanishing and left me behind, then I'm told my father used me as a football against a wall.' One hand touched her crippled leg. 'That's how I got this, Inspector. But after that we got lucky.'

'Lucky?' Thane raised an eyebrow.

'Lucky.' She nodded. 'Like I said, we were fostered together. It stayed that way – we could have been sisters.'

'And it's still that way?'

'We've built our own lives. That's all.' She nodded.

'Why call yourself Pony?'

'Just a nickname from when Janey and I were kids. I was Pony, she was Tiger.' Her eyes strayed towards the telephone.

'She should have phoned by now?' guessed Moss. 'If she could?'

Elizabeth Lewis's mouth tightened. She nodded.

'But you still don't know where she is?'

'No.' She gave an angry movement with her hand that knocked her stick to the carpet. 'She wouldn't tell me. That's the way it's been from the start of this.'

Silently, Phil Moss retrieved the stick, handed it back to her, and returned to sit beside Thane.

'When did you see her last?' asked Thane.

'Thursday night.' The tall frail woman looked at them with a bitter amusement. 'She and Johnny Gort spent the night here. If you don't believe me, look in the garage. Her new car is lying in there, just the way I've got suitcases of her stuff in my spare room.'

168

Thane swore. Moss stared at her open-mouthed.

And the telephone rang. Elizabeth Lewis lurched over and grabbed the receiver before they could even think of stopping her. She answered, then her shoulders sagged. She looked at Thane and let him take the receiver.

'Wrong number,' she said bitterly.

A man at the other end of the line made puzzled noises about wanting to talk to his Aunt Flo, then hung up. Thane replaced the receiver and Elizabeth Lewis went back to her chair, close to tears.

'Where are the garage keys?' asked Moss.

'In the kitchen, hanging up.' She answered almost mechanically.

Moss left them. Waiting, Thane could hear him moving around, taking a glance into the other rooms, then going outside. If Elizabeth Lewis heard, she said nothing. Then, at last, Moss returned. He nodded.

'The way she said. Including the Volkswagen in the garage.'

'Damn you,' said Elizabeth Lewis unexpectedly. 'Damn all of you.'

Then she was on her feet, taking a swing at a totally startled Moss with her stick. She missed, and before she could try again Thane had grabbed her arm. She might be disabled, she might appear frail, but she was still strong and he had to force her arm down. But finally she dropped the stick and collapsed into her chair again.

'We'll say that didn't happen.' Thane stood over her until those blue eyes looked up at him. 'Janey could still call you – I don't know. A lot of things are happening. You're Pony, she's Tiger? Well, right now, the best you can do to help Tiger is tell us what all this is about.'

Elizabeth Lewis looked at Moss. His thin, lined face shaped a surprise hint of a smile of encouragement and he nodded. That seemed to decide her.

'They didn't want this,' she said suddenly. 'Johnny

169

Gort just wanted people to forget about the Interface Man. He'd had enough.'

'And he never did break up with Janey?'

'Never.' Elizabeth Lewis shook her head. 'That was to protect them both.'

'But they've been together in Spain a few times?'

'More than a few.' The mousy-haired woman almost chuckled.

'There are a lot of things we don't know.' Thane went over to the typewriter on its table. 'What about the tip-off letter that we got from Spain?'

'I wrote it. Here.' She shrugged. 'By that time Janey had told me what was happening. I'd telephoned Johnny, I couldn't make him change his mind. He said that was more than his life was worth. I believed him – and they knew about Janey, they were using her as a go-between. She was at risk too.'

'But how did you get it posted in Spain?' demanded Phil Moss.

'I took it out there,' said Elizabeth Lewis simply. 'I had a Monday off.' She seemed embarrassed. 'I thought people would pay more attention if it arrived from Spain.'

'People did,' said Thane grimly. He drew a deep breath. 'You mean you flew out – '

'Out in the morning, back in the evening. I was due back at work on the Tuesday.' She paused. Almost apologetically, she added, 'It wasn't too expensive. I got those cheap, last-minute seats. You know about them?'

Then Elizabeth Lewis told them the rest. It didn't take long. From the start, Janey Peters had confided in her and trusted her, but without giving names or places. It had even stayed that way when her friend brought several suitcases of possessions over from Williamfield then announced she was going away for two weeks. That when she reappeared, John Gort would be getting ready to fly in from Spain.

170

'But she shut you out,' suggested Thane.

'She was protecting me,' said the tall woman quietly. 'She always has.'

He nodded, knowing he couldn't argue.

'Did Janey know you'd be at the airport on Thursday, when Gort flew in?'

'No.'

'But she brought Gort back here afterwards?'

The woman nodded calmly. 'We'd arranged that. These people – the people they're with – had agreed it was safest if they didn't travel far. Anyway, after what happened at the airport, they had to hide the Volkswagen. It couldn't be used.'

'You didn't see these people?' asked Moss.

She shook her head.

'Gort didn't talk about them?'

'Janey wouldn't have allowed him.' Elizabeth Lewis shook her head again. 'He was tired, he had a drink, he went to bed. Janey stayed up with me for a spell, and said she'd keep in touch. In the morning they telephoned and ordered a taxi. It came, they left. That's all I know.'

'Except for Janey's phone calls,' reminded Thane dryly. 'How does she manage them?'

'She says there's a phone she can use, one that is safe – '

'Seemed safe?' suggested Thane brutally.

Elizabeth Lewis nodded silently.

Unusually, Moss made the encouraging noises. 'There are plenty of different reasons why she could be late tonight.' He kept talking. 'You can't think of anything that might even hint where they are?' When the woman shook her head, he tried again. 'Does Janey play golf?'

'Golf?' She saw he meant it. 'No.' Suddenly, Elizabeth Lewis surprised them by getting to her feet. She leaned on her stick. 'Are you going to wait?'

'For now,' said Thane. 'She could still phone.' He took a moment looking at the row of porcelain ornaments on their shelf. They were all small Lladro figures from Spain. 'If you're going to stay here, I'll get a police-woman over for later.'

'I haven't eaten.' She frowned at them. 'I'll make bacon and eggs and coffee for three – it'll give me something to do. There's one condition.'

'Name it,' said Thane.

'Your friend.' She pointed at Moss. 'That's half a plate of chicken soup on his tie. If he takes it off, I'll sponge it.'

'Something else to do?' said Thane softly.

Her mouth tightened and she nodded.

Moss took off his tie.

She sponged the tie, she made the food, and they ate. Moss helped with the washing up.

It was more than an hour past the time when Janey Peters should have called. The waiting was having its effect on Elizabeth Lewis, who had gone back to sitting near her telephone as if that might help to make it ring.

Instead, the doorbell rang.

'Expecting anyone?' asked Thane.

'No.' She shook her head. 'It might be a neighbour.'

'I'll go.' Thane went through to the front door.

The bell rang again and he unlocked the door, switched on the porch light, then began to open the door. He saw the shape of a man on the other side, then the whole door seemed to be flying in at him on its hinges as whoever was out there shouldered it hard and viciously. He took some of the force on his left arm, the rest of it on his chest, and was thrown back.

'Bloody hell!' gulped Beanbag Slater, already halfway in.

Then the fat man had turned and was running out again.

172

There was a car waiting outside. It had no lights and there was only a soft murmur from its engine. Beanbag reached it and tumbled in on the passenger side as Thane appeared from the house.

The driver's window was down. Thane saw a startled face, then a gun. He threw himself sideways, into one of Elizabeth Lewis's flowerbeds, as the weapon fired twice. One bullet whined off the brickwork behind him, the other smacked into the door frame.

Still without lights, the car accelerated away. It vanished down Skerry Street as Moss helped Thane to his feet. White-faced, Elizabeth Lewis was standing under the porch light.

'All right?' asked Moss.

Thane nodded.

But the car had come to collect Elizabeth Lewis – one way or another. He remembered the 'wrong number' telephone call she had answered. If they wanted her, what had happened to Janey Peters?

He had seen the driver: Jon Mark. There was no chance of doubt with that thin face, long broken nose and short fair hair. The car was a Jaguar.

Thane's arm was still numb. He rubbed it as he walked back to Elizabeth Lewis.

'We'll need to move you,' he told her. 'Till it's safer.'

'I understand.' She touched the scarred wood where the bullet had hit the door frame. Her face was still pale, but her voice was steady. 'And Janey – Janey and Johnny Gort?'

Colin Thane shook his head. He didn't want to even try to guess at an answer.

6

What was left was for other people to take over. That meant a general radio alert for the Jaguar and its two occupants, with no particular hope of success. It meant local divisional CID and their Scenes of Crime team, with Phil Moss soothing around the fact that it still all belonged to the Scottish Crime Squad. It meant discovering that a well-meaning neighbour, early on the scene, had trampled across the one set of footprints Beanbag Slater had left on the edge of a flower border, that the bullet which had hit the door frame had flattened on brick behind the wood, leaving ballistics a useless slug of metal – they'd need to find the other bullet which had ricocheted off into the night.

Phil Moss had arranged for Elizabeth Lewis to spend the night in a hotel. A policewoman had helped her to pack and would stay with her.

'Then we keep her until whenever,' suggested Moss.

Thane nodded. They were standing outside the woman's house. Several police cars were parked around, the garden had been taped off and was under guard. Limping on her stick, Elizabeth Lewis had just been guided out to one of the cars. Her overnight case was already loaded aboard.

'Thanks for finding her, Phil,' he said softly. 'Finding her soon enough.'

'They'll be proud of me at Headquarters,' said Moss cynically. He belched at the cloudy moon overhead. 'There's probably a form I should have filled in first.'

Thane left him and went over to Elizabeth Lewis as she settled into the rear of the police car.

'About Gort and Janey,' he told her. 'As soon as we've any firm news, we'll let you know.'

She reached out a hand and touched his arm. 'Whatever it is?'

'Whatever it is,' he promised. 'If you remember anything more, get word to me.' A thought struck him. 'Did either of them tell you how much Gort would be paid for this one?'

'One hundred thousand pounds and expenses,' said Elizabeth Lewis calmly. 'Janey told me. If it happened – and if they were paid, Superintendent.'

'If.' Thane didn't allow his expression to change. But if one hundred thousand was the Interface Man's consultancy fee, how big was the total amount involved?

He said goodnight. She gave a slight, wry smile as he closed the car door.

Thane waited until she had been driven away, heading for the hotel. It was safe, it was managed by a retired chief inspector. Then he went over to the Crime Squad pool car which had been sent out to collect him. The driver was one of the night-shift team, content to stay silent and drive.

Thane was glad. He had more than enough to think about.

That same hint of rain was back in the air by the time they reached the Crime Squad headquarters building. The parking lot was unusually busy for a Saturday night and the building itself was a blaze of lights.

When Thane went in, almost the first person he saw was Jack Hart. The Squad's commander looked tired and had earned the right to be after spending most of two nights at his wife's bedside. But his lined face could still shape a resigned, moderately cheerful welcome while he loafed against the reception desk.

'If you'd any sense, you'd have stayed away,' he told

Thane. 'Anything more on the Pony thing?'

Thane shook his head. He'd already radioed in a basic report.

'Only the size of what's on offer to Gort. They'll pay one hundred thousand and expenses.'

'But he has to stay alive to spend it.' Hart came off the desk and watched a couple of night-shift men go past them, heading out. 'Well, we've plenty of people working here, we're just not getting much as a bottom line. We've no sightings of any kind – that includes the Turnberry golf scene. The Jaguar that Jon Mark was driving hasn't been seen anywhere since he tried to shoot you.' The Squad commander paused and brightened. 'The good news is I'm getting Gloria home tomorrow. The latest hospital tests are fine. It's the way I've always told her – she has a cast-iron head, her real danger is rust.'

Thane chuckled. Beneath the comedy, Hart was both pleased and relieved. 'Mary says if you could use any help – '

'Thank her. But we'll be fine.' Hart shook his head. 'They're all the same. It's like when a woman marries a cop she joins a mafia.' His expression changed, his mind switching again. 'I've given your troops my office for anything that says Interface Man. Tina Redder has taken over the duty room with that treasure trove of stuff she uncovered. There's more stuff still coming in – it's getting like an Aladdin's cave. I gave your office to someone else. It's musical chairs all round.'

They went along the corridor to the Squad commander's large, usually showcase-neat office. Opening the door, Hart grimaced and waved him in. Extra tables and telephones had been installed. Large-scale maps had been pinned to one wall. Thane counted eight people working in the room. Francey Dunbar had installed himself behind Hart's desk and was using Hart's telephone.

Most of the telephones were in use. The result was noisy but apparently methodical. As Thane watched he saw Pat Emslie finish a call on one of the lines. The Transport Police inspector saw Thane and gave a quick grin before he ticked a list then lifted his receiver again.

'I've got Emslie as a volunteer.' Hart appointed himself Thane's guide. 'He's coordinating, Francey is heading up on this damned computer caper. I put Joe Felix in charge of the survey around that office in West George Street.'

Thane studied the nearest map. It had a felt-tip-inked circle centred round the office block which Duck Waddell claimed to have visited so regularly.

'Does the story stand up?' he asked.

'The fourth-floor office, the room, the window.' Hart nodded. 'But that area is wall-to-wall business territory – everything from banks and insurance to foreign consulates and stock-control centres. All deserted for the weekend, Colin.'

But with computer terminals?'

'Like they breed around there.' Hart gestured his disgust, then glanced at Francey Dunbar, who had come over. 'Tell him, Sergeant.'

'It gets worse,' agreed Dunbar sadly. 'We locate someone who runs an office in the magic circle, even an office with only just one computer terminal – and maybe it shuts down when the office closes, but maybe it's rented out after hours to someone else who has hired main computer time. Maybe several someone elses.'

'So then we have to find those someone elses, to know about any regular late-night computer traffic,' growled Hart.

'I've never liked computers much,' admitted Francey Dunbar. He needed a shave and was beginning to look tired. 'All they do for me is screw up my income tax.'

'How far have you got?' asked Thane.

Dunbar shook his head. 'Maybe halfway. Not every-body we're contacting feels happy about helping. We're probably stirring a few skeletons they don't want people knowing about.'

They let him go back to another ringing telephone. For a moment Jack Hart continued to consider the map and its circled area.

'The way Joe Felix put things together for you is correct – but maybe over-simplified,' he told Thane. 'I've spoken to our tame experts. Yes, you can do it with a budget package of electronics and a TV set. Things get complicated when you increase the distance between you and the signal source – a lot worse when you could have a choice of signals coming in. But if you've someone like the Interface Man supplying bolt-on filters or other goodies – ' Hart shrugged and left it there.

Thane said nothing. But it also had to help if you knew where the computer was located and where to pick up those signals with the password signatures MIR and UDA. They had to mean something to someone.

'Suppose you want to be safe when you're using a computer?' asked Hart. 'Forget tapping lines, I mean radiation-access safe. You need what they call a secure room at each end. That means everything – the walls, the ceiling, even the damned floor – lined with metal foil. But suppose you don't, suppose you catch someone at it?' He gave a derisive grunt. 'I'd hand everything to the lawyers and hide!'

Thane knew what he meant. Scottish law was grey around the whole area of stealing computer data. The Scottish courts, like those in some other countries, had never regarded information on its own as property. So if information wasn't property how could it be stolen? The courts were catching up. But the courts would take their own sweet time about it.

'You're going to be around?' asked Hart.

178

'For a spell,' agreed Thane.

'Good.' Hart eased them out of his commandeered office and back into the corridor. 'I nearly forgot. You say you know Superintendent Gallon, the man running the Ayrshire checks?'

'Andy Gallon – yes, pretty well.' Thane smiled a little. 'He usually goes fishing at the weekends.'

'Not this weekend,' said Hart. 'I want you and Gallon to meet tomorrow for a general up-date session – time and place to be arranged tomorrow morning.' He beckoned. 'I'm going to stick my nose in at the duty room. You'd better come too, so that you know what's happening.'

Thane went with him.

The duty room had been transformed into what could have been a cross between an antiques warehouse and a jewellery store. Desks and shelves had vanished under Chinese vases and ornate clocks, gold and silverware glinted under the lights, paintings were stacked along one wall. Some of Detective Chief Inspector Tina Redder's team were unpacking two boxes of bronze figurines.

'Commander.' Tina Redder came towards them. The man she brought with her, a grey-haired, middle-aged stranger, wore an open-necked sports shirt and a lovat-check suit. She nudged him forward. 'Sir, you wanted to meet Mr Hodge, sent to help us by the insurance companies' association.'

'Peter Hodge, Commander.' The man gave a cheerful grin. 'I'm paid to look at things then try a wild guess at what they're worth.'

Tina Redder completed the introductions, then Hodge gestured at the display of treasures around them.

'There's a lot of good stuff here.' A twinkle showed in his eyes. 'Good stuff – but it will cause a lot of problems for a lot of people.'

'Tracing some of it back where it belongs?' presumed Hart.

'There's that,' admitted Hodge. He gave Tina Redder a deliberately innocent glance. 'But the real trouble will be getting people to admit they recognize things – if they've already had an insurance pay-out. Will they want to give the cash back?' He gave a mock sigh. 'It won't be easy.'

Tina Redder gave him a glare. Thane saw she was carrying her coat.

'Have you finished here?' asked Hart mildly.

'We're finished for tonight – at least, I am,' said Hodge. 'I've catalogued the gold and silver, I'll come back in the morning to complete the jewellery. What's left is mostly broken pieces. They'd separated a lot of stones from settings, then probably sold the loose gold or whatever as scrap.' He glanced at his watch. 'Ten o'clock. Chief Inspector, I still can't persuade you about that drink?'

'Another time,' said Tina Redder firmly. 'I've had a long day, Mr Hodge. I'm going home, I'm going to have a bath, I'm going to bed. What time do you want to start tomorrow?'

'Eight a.m.,' suggested Hodge. 'Finish by mid-day. Then we could think about that drink again – '

'I'll see you to your car, Mr Hodge,' said Tina Redder grimly.

She looked at Jack Hart and Thane in a way that dared them to say anything. Then she marched the openly admiring insurance valuator on his way.

'That's a good-looking woman,' murmured Hart once they'd gone. 'But she'd take some handling.' He sighed. 'Hodge doesn't know he's lucky being turned down. One wrong move, and my guess is that Tina would chop him up for firewood.'

Jack Hart left for home soon after that. Then,

180

gradually, even the Interface Man operation began to wind down a little.

It revived for a hopeful half hour when a blue Mercedes was chased after an accident on the Glasgow–Edinburgh motorway. But the registration plates were wrong. The occupants, two teenage car thieves, were suitably awed at the amount of attention they received. Then they were locked up for one of Monday's court sittings.

Monday. According to Elizabeth Lewis, the Interface Man deadline was Monday. But still there was nothing from the Turnberry area, still there was no reported sighting from anywhere else.

Thane went back yet again to the team in Jack Hart's office, still working under those large-scale maps with the circled office-block area. There were still plenty of blanks within the circle but he could see people were tiring. When Joe Felix and his survey team came in, he sent them home. Pat Emslie and some of the others were next.

When he looked round for Francey Dunbar he found his sergeant taking an incoming telephone call along in the otherwise deserted duty room. Dunbar saw him, looked vaguely embarrassed, and mumbled something to whoever was on the other end of the line. He winced at the reply, then hung up.

'Just Sandra, sir,' he said warily, joining Thane.

'Is she all right?' asked Thane.

'She – uh – sounds that way.' Dunbar sighed to himself and shook his head. 'She says she's fine.'

'I don't want her trying to sneak back on duty tomorrow,' warned Thane.

'She knows,' agreed his sergeant.

His voice made it clear that, as far as Detective Constable Sandra Craig was concerned, it wouldn't make a blind bit of difference.

181

He talked with Dunbar about the list of computer terminals that now existed within the West George Street circle. Some were already being eliminated because they didn't work at night. Some handled traffic so dull that they could also be ruled out. No one, so far, admitted to knowing anything about those password signature letters MIR and UDA.

'Tomorrow, maybe,' suggested Dunbar, fighting down a yawn.

Thane gave a reluctant nod. It was already tomorrow. The clock had just clicked past midnight.

'Home,' he said. 'In the morning, we start here. Then there's a conference being set up in Ayrshire.'

'Great,' declared Dunbar sarcastically. 'Do I play, or do I carry the golf bags?'

They handed over to a skeleton detail from the night-shift team and went their separate ways.

It was the third day in a row that Thane had had an early start, the third in a row he'd arrived home well after midnight. When he went into the house the dog wakened enough to give a complaining growl. Everyone else was asleep. Mary had dropped off with her bedlight on and a book still in her hand.

Thane removed the book, switched off the bedlight, undressed in the dark, and crawled into bed.

'God,' said a complaining mumble. 'Your feet are cold.'

He retreated to his own side of the bed. He didn't so much drift into sleep as crash into a vague nightmare. He was trapped in some kind of a sandglass run by a computer. Then someone tapped out MIR followed by UDA and everything fused.

He wakened again a few minutes after seven a.m. Bright sunlight was filtering in through the closed bedroom curtains and he could hear birds chirping. Beside him,

182

Mary muttered a protest and burrowed deeper under the blankets as he got up. But by the time Thane had showered and shaved she was in her dressing gown and moving around downstairs.

He chose a light blue shirt, a dark blue tie thinly striped with red, and his grey suit. His shoes needed polishing, but he gave them a quick rub with some toilet tissues and decided they'd get by. Clyde had arrived and was already snoring across the foot of the bed. There still wasn't a sound from either Tommy's room or Kate's. The Thane children had a rule that Sunday began late.

Mary had orange juice, toast and coffee ready for him when he went downstairs. She tried not to yawn as she kissed him.

'Someone like you used to live here.' She stood back and inspected him. 'You'll do. What's it going to be? Another day like yesterday?'

'It looks that way,' admitted Thane. 'But once this is over – '

'You'll take some time off,' Mary finished it for him. 'And, of course, this time you mean it.'

'You and me,' he promised. 'A hotel up north, in the Highlands. For a long weekend. No dog, no kids.'

'Can I have that in writing?' She gave a resigned chuckle which took the sting from the words, then thumbed him towards the table. 'Eat some breakfast.'

Something thudded outside their front door then a hurricane of barking dog came down the stairs. Mary Thane gave up.

'Think of the bright side, woman,' she told herself aloud. 'You'll have the Sunday papers to yourself.'

When Colin Thane left their house and started his car, nothing else was stirring in their street. But at least the day was still bright, the sky was a clear blue, and the drive across the city was pleasant and on almost deserted roads. Two girls out jogging gave him a wave as he went

183

past, which made him grin. Further on, a fox streaked across the road and disappeared into a lane. Foxes were beginning to invade the city. People called them Urban Foxes and let them get on with it.

It was only minutes after eight when he reached the Scottish Crime Squad headquarters, but the parking lot was already beginning to fill. He saw Jack Hart's black BMW in its place, and Francey Dunbar's motorcycle. Thane left his Ford near Dunbar's machine and went into the building.

Jack Hart's driver, looking as newly laundered as ever, was temporarily manning the reception desk. But even though it was Sunday, Maggie Fyffe was also in. When the Squad commander asked her to work at a weekend, he was worried.

'Where is he anyway?' asked Thane after they'd made good-morning noises.

'In his own office,' said Maggie Fyffe. 'Your Interface team have found themselves a corner in the duty room.' She shook her head. 'That's after he found your pet sergeant having breakfast at his desk and threw him out.'

Thane winced, but went through. Hart's office curtains had been opened. So had a window. The same circled maps were still on the walls. But the Squad commander was back at his desk. The Interface inquiry team – Pat Emslie and Joe Felix among them – were still moving their stuff out and there was no sign of Francey Dunbar.

'Good morning.' Jack Hart gave him a surprising beam. 'Another couple of hours, and they throw Gloria out of that hospital. I've got a Welcome Home bottle laid in.' He chuckled like a schoolboy. 'Hell, I even put clean straw on the floor.'

'She'll like clean straw,' agreed Thane mildly.

'So back to work.' Hart gestured at the thin handful of

184

telex messages in front of him. 'Nothing that matters from overnight. No sightings, no nothing. Elizabeth Lewis is tucked up safe in her hotel, Duck Waddell is quite happy to stay in his cell. There's a final post-mortem report on Joan Haston that doesn't tell us anything we didn't know already.'

'No more on the Mark brothers, or Louise Croft?'

'Background? A line or two – nothing vital.' Hart made to stir the telex messages with a forefinger. 'It's here – ' he broke off, looking up, as Francey Dunbar came into his office at a near trot. Hart scowled. 'Something wrong, Sergeant?'

'No, sir – not wrong.' Dunbar ignored him, his attention on Thane, his thin moustache almost quivering. 'There's something in the duty room. Something you'd better see right now.'

'If it's that important – ' Thane gave Hart an apologetic glance.

'Can you take two of us, Sergeant?' asked Hart with a dangerous interest.

Dunbar nodded. He set a crisp pace as they followed him through.

The main duty room looked much the same as it had the previous night, apart from the small space that had been won back by the Interface team. Tina Redder was prowling around a display of paintings near the back, where some of her team were beginning to re-pack items. Nearer, the tweed-suited figure of Peter Hodge was hunched over a bench. The insurance valuator held something in one hand, examining it through an eye-glass under a bright light.

Wordlessly, Francey Dunbar led them over behind Hodge then pointed. Thane looked, understood, and moistened his lips.

'Mr Hodge.'

'Huh?' The insurance valuator removed the eyeglass,

185

looked up, and gave a resigned smile of recognition. 'Hello, Superintendent. You here too, Commander?'

'Mr Hodge.' Thane reached past the man and touched a carefully folded piece of paper lying on the bench. It had the same folds, the same shape, as the mysterious piece of paper they'd found at Janey Peters' home in Williamfield. 'Did you make that?'

'Yes.' Hodge was puzzled. 'Why?'

'What's it for?' Thane saw the man's growing bewilderment. 'It matters.'

'I'll show you, Superintendent.' Hodge picked up the folded paper, letting it open into its little package shape. With his other hand he reached four tiny green gemstones lying with some other loose jewellery. 'These are emeralds.' Expertly, he poured the four stones into the folded paper, turned two edges, and placed the closed result on the bench. 'That's all it's for – carrying gemstones around. Mainly for diamond parcels.'

'Diamond parcels?' Jack Hart leaned forward, emphasizing the last word. 'What the hell is a diamond parcel?'

'Just what it says – a parcel with diamonds,' said Hodge patiently. 'If you're a jeweller or a diamond merchant, it's the traditional way to carry them. I served my apprenticeship as a jeweller and that's when I learned it. First-year jewellery apprentices still learn it. Of course – ' he frowned at the folded paper ' – some top dealers maybe use a square of lint inside the paper, or give it a tissue lining. But that's mainly for show.'

Thane swallowed. Tina Redder had come over, but he ignored her.

'And this special kind of folding is only for carrying diamonds?'

'It should be – by custom and tradition.' Hodge sat back and combed a hand over his grey hair, looking almost apologetic. 'I meant to bring some envelopes with me this morning for the other loose stones, but I forgot.'

'This diamond parcel thing,' said Jack Hart curtly. 'Show me. Make one.'

'No problem.' Hodge found a sheet of scrap paper. His fingers flew as he measured and folded with a skill that was close to automatic, and he kept up a running commentary. 'Any more or less square-shaped piece of paper will do. Make a quarter width fold-in down the length of each of the two vertical sides. Make a firm crease, then flatten them out again. Now the horizontal sides, right? Fold across into five equal strips, then crease. You've one narrow shape, and the inside is the pocket of your diamond parcel. Then back to your original vertical creases. Fold them over the main strip. That closes the sides – and that's it.'

The little paper shape mocked at them.

'Too damned right it is,' said Francey Dunbar softly.

Hart looked at him for a moment through half-hooded eyes, then turned to Thane.

'Well?'

'Now we know,' agreed Thane bitterly. 'That's the same folding we found at Williamfield.'

'Diamonds.' Hart sucked his teeth and scowled. 'Mr Hodge, you said a diamond parcel. How many diamonds to a parcel?'

'It varies. You can be talking top stones or samples.' Hodge shrugged, still puzzled but amiable. 'Ten, twenty, fifty – somebody could be carrying one parcel or half a dozen parcels.' He looked at all three of them, then at Tina Redder in the background. 'Why?'

'Wait.' Jack Hart wasn't finished. He sucked his teeth as if making up his mind about something. 'You know diamonds, you know the jewellery trade. Agreed?'

The insurance valuator nodded.

'Then think diamonds, think jewellery. Do the letters

187

MIR or UDA have any special meaning? Firms, a dealer, an organization, or any kind of professional shorthand?'

'No. Sorry.' Peter Hodge laid the package with the emeralds beside the other loose stones he'd been examining. Reaching into the top pocket of his suit, he took out a small cheroot. He unwrapped the cheroot, lit it with a small gold cigarette lighter, took a first deep draw, then gave a sudden frown. 'MIR and UDA. Do they have to be initials?'

Thane answered first. 'They can be any damned thing. They came off a computer.'

'Maybe – ' Hodge hesitated. 'It could be, I suppose.'

'Try it.' Jack Hart made it close to a snarl.

'Maybe you're talking place-name words.' Hodge took a new, small draw on his cheroot and let the smoke out slowly. 'Not letters, not initials, Commander. Mir as one name. Uda – Uda as in Udachnaya. Mir and Udachnaya, meaning Peace and Success. That's the translation into English.'

They stared at him.

'I don't understand,' said Tina Redder, still part of the background.

'Shut up, Tina.' Hart made it a plea. He swung back to Hodge again. 'Mir and Whatever. What are they, where are they?'

'The names of the two largest Soviet diamond mines,' said Peter Hodge warily.

'Soviet as in Russia?' asked Francey Dunbar.

'Soviet as in Siberia,' corrected Hodge. He smiled, back on sure ground. 'The Russians have a diamond mining industry almost as big as South Africa. Some people say bigger. Mir and Udachnaya are like South Africa's Kimberley and Jagersfontein.'

Softly, systematically, Jack Hart cursed very quietly under his breath. Then he glanced at Tina Redder.

188

'We're going to borrow your Mr Hodge,' he said wearily. 'You'll get him back.' His eyes switched to Thane and Dunbar. 'My office. Now.'

They went through. Then they settled in chairs while Jack Hart sat in glowering silence for almost a full minute. At last he drew a deep breath and looked across his desk towards Peter Hodge.

'Mir and Udach – '

'Udachnaya.' Hodge gave a slightly wary nod.

'You're sure about them?' Hart's voice was grey and unhappy.

'That they exist?' Hodge nodded. 'I know they exist, that they're part of the Soviet diamond industry. They're both up in the permafrost regions – they had to build a town and a nuclear power station before they could work Mir. All I know about Udachnaya is it is another three hundred miles north, in the Arctic Circle.' He saw disbelief on the other faces. 'Look, the Russians only found their first diamond diggings after World War Two. They don't shout about it, because they've got to sell their stones to the capitalist West. But geologists reckon they're into the same kind of diamondiferous platform as the South African mines.'

'A lot of diamonds?'

Hodge nodded. 'The trade reckon about twelve million carats a year – maybe twenty per cent of it gem quality, the rest industrial. That's good by anybody's standards.'

Francey Dunbar cleared his throat gently. 'Who sells them? Do they have agents, dealers?'

'Not the way you mean, Sergeant.' The grey-haired insurance valuator shook his head. 'They keep in step with the international Central Selling Organization – it works out of London, Amsterdam and Switzerland. Just about every diamond-producing country in the world sells directly to CSO or goes along with its rules. CSO

189

buys in diamonds, keeps the market stable for everyone. Have you ever bought a diamond ring for anyone?'

Dunbar gave a slight grin. 'Not so far.'

'When you do, any diamonds in that ring for your girl will have passed through the CSO system or have been influenced by it,' said Hodge dryly. 'You don't want a lecture, I'm not qualified to give one. But if there's a good year for diamond production then Central Selling can buy in all those diamonds. Then maybe it puts a few sackfuls in a safe, keeps them back from the market until there's a year when production isn't so good.'

'Supply and demand?' frowned Dunbar.

'Balanced supply and demand, steady prices,' agreed Hodge. He shrugged. 'Nobody wants to see diamond prices jump around too much. Too many governments would get caught up in the financial backlash.'

'Suppose we get back to what we have,' suggested Colin Thane with a deliberate calm. He glanced at Hart, who gave a grateful nod. 'There's no direct Scottish trade in Russian diamonds?'

'None.' Hodge shook his head.

'Yet we've the names of two Soviet diamond mines turning up in the middle of an expected major robbery – but we're still not sure where, we're not sure when.' Thane saw Hodge blink. 'That's how it is, Mr Hodge. If you've any ideas, let's hear them.'

'We could use them,' muttered Hart.

Hodge bit his lip, sighed, and shook his head.

'I could try phoning some people in the trade,' he suggested half-heartedly.

'We could maybe do better,' said Thane softly. He looked directly at Hart. 'We could ask the Russians.'

'We could also start World War Three,' said Hart icily. He saw Francey Dunbar stir. 'Sergeant, if you even try to say *glasnost* you'll regret it. Understand?'

'Sir.' Dunbar had sense enough to just nod.

190

'The Russians.' Hart chewed his lip for a moment and seemed to have second thoughts. He frowned at Thane. 'You mean some kind of trade mission could be here, maybe working in the Glasgow area?'

'Some kind of anything Russian would do,' said Thane flatly. 'What about those computer terminals the Interface team have been locating?'

'Nothing Russian there.' Francey Dunbar shook his head 'Not yet, at any rate.'

'Damn and damn.' Jack Hart got up, prowled the length of his office, then came back to them again. A faint hope showed on his lined face. 'If there's any kind of Russian trade delegation involved, our Government people should know. They'd have to keep an eye on things, right? Either way, nobody will thank us if we do nothing. So what the hell? I'll try them.' He turned to Peter Hodge. 'And you can give me a list of the people you think you could call. I want to check it first.'

His telephone rang. Hart scooped up the receiver, answered with a growl, listened, and they saw his expression change.

'Say that again?' he asked.

The voice at the other end obliged.

'Good,' said Hart grimly. 'He's with me now, he'll be there. Thank you.'

He hung up, a new glint in his eyes, and faced Thane.

'Ayrshire say they know where Janey Peters spent some of her time during the last couple of weeks. It's confirmed, both Mark brothers are placed with her.'

'Turnberry?' asked Thane.

'No.' Hart shook his head. 'But not too far away, and still in golf land. At Troon.'

'Troon?' Thane gave a startled glance at Francey Dunbar. Troon was also on the Ayrshire coast, but more than twenty miles to the north of Turnberry. It had its own separate cluster of championship golf courses. None

191

of Matt Amos's scientific evidence pointed that way. 'Who says?'

'The message was from your friendly Superintendent Gallon.' Hart pressed the buzzer on his desk to summon Maggie Fyffe. 'He wants to meet you where it happened, at the Marine Hotel. He's heading up from Turnberry, where things are still a blank. He'll be at Troon by ten a.m.' As Maggie Fyffe came in, Hart gestured towards Hodge. 'Maggie, take Mr Hodge somewhere quiet. He wants to write a list of names for me.'

'Tina Redder wants him back, sir,' reminded his secretary.

'Tina can take her place in the queue.' Hart sent the insurance valuator on his way with a quick twitch of a smile, then waited until Maggie Fyffe and Hodge had gone out. As the door closed behind them, he switched his attention back to Thane and Dunbar. 'Russians or Martians, I'll run things this end. Colin, I want you to take your full team into Ayrshire. Then be ready to follow through at that end.'

'They're down there somewhere.' Thane gave a slight nod of agreement.

'They have to be. Plus Gort and Janey Peters – dead or alive,' said Hart. Then he paused and a look of glazed horror came over his face. 'How the hell do I find time to get Gloria out of hospital with this going on?'

'You'll manage something, sir.' Francey Dunbar knew him well enough.

'I suppose.' Hart watched the two men rise and start to leave. 'Maybe she's got bus-fare money with her.' Then, as they reached the door, his manner changed. 'Be lucky in Ayrshire. I don't want any more of our people on any casualty list – not if we can avoid it.'

Thane and Francey Dunbar left about fifteen minutes later. They used Thane's car, with Dunbar driving.

192

Jock Dawson and his dogs would follow them down in the Land-Rover. It would have another Squad car in convoy, bringing Joe Felix and Pat Emslie. Dawson would have company, a large and hairy detective constable known as The Animal and borrowed from Tina Redder's team. The Animal would make up for Sandra Craig's absence. His size and fearsome appearance always made him useful to have around – and Dawson's dogs liked him.

Every man was armed. The time had passed when that was unusual in any British force. Weapons were issued to qualified officers as a matter of course whenever the opposition were likely to be armed. Each weapon and its ammunition had to be signed out, each weapon and each round had to be accounted for once the operation ended. They had .38 Smith and Wessons, the standard Squad issue. Two Savage pump-action shotguns and a Heckler and Koch automatic rifle were stowed in Dawson's dog-van.

The Heckler and Koch was for The Animal. He was the Squad's top marksman.

Colin Thane's mind was on other things as the dust-covered Ford made its way out of the city.

An outsider might have said that what they had amounted to a madness of a notion – a notion based on nothing more than a piece of folded paper and the way the names of two Siberian diamond mines were said to have turned up on some computer crosstalk. Except that it was a notion which could point to a major, coldly calculated robbery – big enough to justify bringing in the Interface Man, big enough to have already brought about two murders.

'I was thinking,' said Francey Dunbar suddenly. He kept his eyes on the road, weaving the Ford through heavy coast-bound traffic as if it didn't exist. 'Do you know any Russian, sir?'

'No.' Thane froze as a bus swung out to overtake something ahead of them, but fled back in again as Dunbar blasted his horn. 'Why?'

'It could be awkward if we find any of them. How do we explain things to them?' Dunbar sighed and answered his own question. 'Grab them first, then sort it out later?'

'Let someone else sort it out later,' corrected Thane. He grinned to himself. It was a Jack Hart type reply.

The morning stayed dry and bright and they reached their destination almost on time. Troon was a modest seaside town, one like plenty of others on the Firth of Clyde. It had been a holiday town before the age of big jets and package holidays. Now it was one of the outer commuter satellites for Glasgow.

Royal Troon championship golf course sat next to the shore on one side of town. It dated back to the 1870s, and it was a hundred years later before any woman had ever been allowed into the Royal Troon clubhouse – which had almost taken a war. Compared with it, Turnberry to the south was a brash newcomer, not built until the 1920s. The Marine Hotel matched that mood. A large, turreted Victorian building with carved stonework, it had been modernized enough to have its swimming pool, sauna and solarium – and to hold its four-star rating. The guest cars parked outside were mostly luxury limousines.

Two were different. They were police cars. The man Thane had come to meet was standing at the top of the hotel's entrance steps, looking out towards the green of the golf course and, behind it, the white-flecked sea.

'How's life in the big city?' asked Detective Super-intendent Andy Gallon as Thane reached him. He was a big, bald man who wore rimless half-moon spectacles on a large beak of a nose. He was wearing an old sports jacket which had leather patches at the cuffs and elbows,

194

'plus-two' corduroy trousers and a grey sweater. 'Still catching the occasional thief, Colin?'

'Still trying.' Thane shook hands with the Ayrshire CID man. Andy Gallon had a hoarse voice, caused by a brick hitting him in the throat when he was a young cop. The way he dressed made him look like an eccentric millionaire, but even the thought of being questioned by Andy Gallon made some criminals plead guilty. 'We need this one, Andy.'

'I heard.' Gallon glanced at Francey Dunbar. 'Does that one belong to you?'

Thane introduced them. Gallon grinned at Dunbar, shook his hand, and thumbed towards a tall, thin man lurking not far behind him. 'That's mine, Detective Sergeant Rice. Looks like an undertaker, moves like one.'

Detective Sergeant Bernie Rice nodded cheerfully. He wore a dark blue blazer with grey trousers, a white shirt and a blue tie patterned with tiny anchors.

'Any more coming, sir?' he asked Thane.

'Later.' Thane left Francey Dunbar to attach himself to the Ayrshire sergeant and faced Andy Gallon. 'We're going critical on this, Andy. You say they were here. No room for doubt?'

'They were here.' Gallon turned to lead the way into the hotel. 'I've organized us a corner. Let's use it.'

They went in, past the lobby reception desk and a showcase display of women's fashion golfwear. The lobby area was busy with guests arriving and departing, a talkative, noisy mix of nationalities. Everyone's luggage seemed to include a golf bag.

'Along here.' Andy Gallon guided a way through it all then up a short stairway and along a corridor to his 'organized corner'. It was a first-floor private lounge, with coffee, biscuits and soft drinks waiting on a table. There was a telephone, and the view from the balcony was out towards the inevitable blend of sea and golfing fairway. Closing the door, Gallon went over to the coffee table. 'This is on the house.'

He wasn't going to be hurried. They helped themselves to coffee, Detective Sergeant Rice blandly shoved some extra biscuits into his pocket, then they stood in a group near the window.

'This goes back to last weekend,' said Gallon without warning. He nodded towards his sergeant. 'Bernie knows some of the staff here. One of them contacted him this morning, Bernie checked and contacted me. Right?'

Thane nodded. Francey Dunbar pulled his attention back from a tall, slim blonde who had just appeared on the Royal Troon fairway.

'Last weekend,' repeated Gallon. 'It was damned nearly a clan gathering. David Mark and Louise Croft were here, and stayed two nights. Another woman who signed the hotel register as Jane Croft also stayed both nights – she said she was Louise Croft's cousin, but we've shown a photograph of Janey Peters to our witnesses, and she matches.' He hadn't finished. 'Add Jon Mark – he was here the second night only. He arrived with another man, a stranger. The story was they'd been golfing, and they both joined brother David and the two women for a meal. Then the stranger left. Next day, David Mark paid the bill for everything.'

'And the stranger?' asked Thane.

Gallon shrugged. 'He may have been here a couple of times before with Jon.' He glanced at his sergeant. 'Bernie?'

'He's described as middle-aged, thinning dark hair, expensive clothes and a nice expensive tan,' said Detective Sergeant Rice dryly. 'Speaks with a slight foreign accent – could be French, might be Italian.' He grimaced. 'That's the best we can get. It's from the waiter who was on their table that night.'

196

'One foreign stranger,' said Detective Superintendent Gallon sardonically. He glanced at Thane. 'Do you want to run your o   questioning?'

'No.' Thane shook his head. 'Anything more?'

'Not much. Jon Mark is a regular here. His brother and Louise Croft have been guests, but don't golf. Louise's "Cousin Janey" – your Janey Peters – is in the hotel register as spending an overnight twice before with them, but over a month ago.' Gallon paused and scowled over his half-moon spectacles. 'It seems that Jon told the reception desk he might be back this weekend. But he didn't make a reservation, and he didn't show.'

Francey Dunbar took a gulp of coffee, sucked a wet end of his thin moustache, and shaped a suspicious frown. 'Everyone seems to find it easy to remember Jon Mark.'

'Around here?' Andy Gallon gave Thane a sideways grin. 'Jon Mark is a golfer – a good-enough amateur to play in any pro-am he wants. That's enough. Do you play golf, son?'

Dunbar blinked and shook his head. 'No, sir.'

'That's sensible. Why spend hours being cruel to a poor wee defenceless ball? Try fishing if you want real sport.' Gallon abandoned his coffee and stuck his hands in the pockets of his leather-patched jacket. 'You tell him about Ayrshire and golf, Colin. He's yours.'

'Later,' said Thane.

But he had once brought Mary to this hotel for a weekend break. The first afternoon, while she'd gone shopping in Troon, he'd discovered the small brass plaques on doors in the hotel corridors and had followed them along. Each brass plaque bore the name of a world-class golfer. Each marked the door of the bedroom where that golfer had slept when he won a British Open championship held at Troon.

Some of the names were from the past, some from the

present. Bobby Locke's name was there near to Walter Havers'. There was Arnold Palmer and Tom Weiskopf, Walter Hagen and Jack Nicklaus, and a long list more.

'Later, like you say.' Gallon was amused. Then his eyes hardened as he watched Thane over the half-moon spectacles. 'I telephoned your Commander Hart before you got here, brought him up to date. Your turn, Colin. What's going on – apart from a general panic?'

'A few extra problems,' said Thane woodenly.

'Like?' asked Gallon.

He gave the Ayrshire man a brief outline. By the time he'd finished, even Andy Gallon was open-mouthed, Gallon's sergeant looked close to stunned.

'Bloody hell,' said Gallon softly. 'Keep stirring the pot, and what happens next?' He shook his head. 'I don't like people who shoot at cops. Not when I'm anywhere around. What about Gort and Janey Peters?'

Thane shook his head. 'We don't know. The same with this whole diamond story.'

'Maybe Red diamonds.' Gallon scowled out of the window. 'I'm with you. They've maybe used this place for meetings, but the sharp end still has to be around Turnberry.'

Turnberry, those miles south along the coast, wasn't a town. It was basically two intertwined golf courses beside an even bigger luxury hotel, all fringed by a scatter of tiny fishing ports and equally small farming villages. Detective Superintendent Andy Gallon's men had acted exactly as Thane had asked. Without fuss, they had checked the area around. They had found nothing.

'Maybe it would have been different if we'd gone in heavy,' suggested Sergeant Rice. He enjoyed the thought. 'Maybe if we'd kicked in a few doors – '

'We'd all be in an even bigger mess,' grunted Gallon. 'Be quiet, Bernie. Sergeants should be seen and not heard.' He gave Thane an apologetic shrug. 'Still, what do we do for our next trick?'

'We're talking of some kind of meeting, some kind of rendezvous. That could mean a hotel or a house – near that golf course, probably right on its edge.' Thane was looking out of the window, watching a small yacht with tan sails which was heading out from land. 'But who says they'll do the obvious?' He glanced round at Dunbar. 'Francey, we did check out that story that the Mark brothers owned a yacht?'

'We did.' Dunbar nodded. 'David is the yachtsman, he has a six-berth motor sailer called *The Lora*, but we know where she is. She's berthed in a marina north of here. There's been no sign of life aboard and – ' he looked at Thane, understood, and gave a low groan to himself ' – and there's a whole damned line of other boats lying there beside her. So if they could borrow another boat from a friendly owner – '

'That's not unusual. It happens often enough.' Sergeant Rice nodded wisely, then flushed as Thane frowned at him. 'It's my scene, sir.' He touched his anchor-patterned necktie. 'I crewed for – '

'He doesn't care if you crewed for flaming Noah in his flaming Ark,' said Andy Gallon with a husky intensity. 'All right, get on with it.'

'Which marina?' asked Rice.

'Inverkip,' answered Dunbar.

'And don't use that damned telephone – find another,' snarled Gallon as Rice made for the telephone in the corner. 'I want that one kept clear.'

Rice nodded and left them.

'Francey.' Thane was still at the window. He pointed down at the hotel driveway. A grubby Land-Rover and a Ford coupé had just arrived outside. The rest of the Crime Squad team had joined them.

They left Gallon on his own and went out to meet the

vehicles. Jock Dawson grinned out from the Land-Rover, and The Animal was with him. Joe Felix and Pat Emslie got out of the Ford. But their driver, last to emerge, made Thane give a soft curse of surprise.

'What the hell are you doing here?' he asked.

Sandra Craig had done a good job with make-up. But a cut on her face was still covered by a small, flesh-coloured adhesive strip and she couldn't mask all the bruising and swelling around it – or the careful way she walked. It was still only thirty-six hours since an ambulance had taken her to hospital.

'I – uh – sort of arrived at Headquarters as they were leaving, sir.' The redhead eyed Thane cautiously. She was wearing her denim jacket and trousers, teamed with a cream mohair sweater. 'I suppose I talked them into it.'

'And?'

She looked down at her feet. 'I'll just keep in the background, sir.'

'You'll do what?' asked Francey Dunbar in cynical disbelief.

Sandra Craig treated him to a glare. 'And I'll keep my nose out of where it doesn't belong.'

Thane saw Dunbar wince. But the redhead was still waiting, the others were watching.

'In the background,' he agreed. 'All right, you can stay.'

She grinned her thanks and turned away. He beckoned Dunbar nearer.

'So what did you do to rattle Sandra's cage?' he asked.

'It was Friday night, after that house blew up,' muttered Dunbar. 'When I got home, I sent a cable to her pet naval officer – '

'The one who dropped her?'

'He didn't drop her. They had a small mutual war about something,' scowled Dunbar. 'He's on a fleet

200

minesweeper on patrol in the Persian Gulf, he telephoned her, ship to shore, the moment he got the cable. Hell, I thought she'd be glad.'

'Rule number nine hundred and ninety,' said Thane dryly. 'Don't try to understand women.'

He went back into the hotel with Dunbar.

'Sir.' Sandra Craig and the others were making ready to follow. She looked at Thane hopefully. 'Do we get to eat here?'

He shrugged. 'Probably not.'

But even Thane didn't know the storm of trouble that was about to break over them. Soon, no one was going to have time to think about eating – or anything else.

7

It was another forty minutes before things really started happening again. The telephone rang several times in the room they'd taken over, but each time the report was routine. Using another telephone location in one of the hotel bedrooms, Detective Sergeant Bernie Rice continued to work on checking out what had happened around David Mark's yacht at her marina berth. He appeared now and then, to shake his head and vanish again.

The weather can change quickly on the west coast of Scotland. In those same forty minutes a surprise wind came gusting in from the north-west. Sunday, which had started off with blue skies and sparkling waves, became totally different. A blanket of cloud appeared overhead and the sea became a dull iron-grey. The little marker flags began flapping on the Royal Troon greens. Blowing in from the beach, fine sand began to sting at golfers' eyes and lips. A well-targeted ball could be caught by any of those gusts and curve off into deep rough.

The Crime Squad team were past masters of the art of making themselves comfortable anywhere. It wasn't difficult in four-star hotel surroundings.

Then the telephone rang again. Sandra Craig answered it, looked across at Thane, and put her hand over the mouthpiece.

'Commander Hart, sir.'

Thane took the call, conscious that Andy Gallon had eased over beside him. The Ayrshire detective superintendent didn't want to be left out of anything.

'Every damned thing we've imagined might just be

right,' said Jack Hart, his voice a carefully controlled monotone over the line. 'I said might – don't ask me to guarantee it. I'm not going to bog you down with details, Colin. But I've bounced my way through our own Government people and from there I've been getting some fast-shuffle treatment from the Russians direct – first their Consular people in Edinburgh, now the Soviet Embassy in London.'

Thane gave a genuine whistle of surprise. 'No objections coming from our side?'

'Not so far,' said Hart dryly. 'Special Branch are rumbling about maybe being in their territory. But the diplomats think we're probably mad. They're sitting waiting. So far, the Russians are admitting nothing, denying nothing. But every time I say the word diamonds, I can almost hear them quiver.'

It could all be real. That took a moment to digest, then Thane frowned at the telephone's mouthpiece.

'Do they have any special Trade Mission visit up here?'

'I got the standard public relations answer. There are always Soviet Trade Mission teams moving around.' Hart said it with disgust, but added a triumphant snarl. 'That's where we've got them. We've got that computer terminal located – or it looks that way. It's a Bank of Central Scotland branch office. Our computer people say it would be within the receiving range of the Interface Man gadget, and the bank agrees it rents out spare late-night computer time.'

'Do I win a prize for guessing?' asked Thane softly.

'Monday to Friday, eleven p.m. until midnight, there's a long-term contract hire to the Glasgow branch of the North British and Soviet Trade Agency.' Hart's voice was back to the previous controlled monotone. 'That's just a rented back-room outfit, one man and some part-time staff. They use the computer link to feed occasional trade data down to the Soviet people in London – exciting things like fish prices and production figures.'

Andy Gallon nudged Thane and mouthed a silent, puzzled question. Thane shook his head. He could sense there was more coming.

'Do the bank keep any kind of check?' he asked.

'No. Privacy is part of the deal,' Hart told him. 'But what we've got is – is – ' there was a pause, then a sudden, violent sneeze. 'Hang on.' The next noise on the line was the Squad commander blowing his nose, then Hart was back on the line. 'Now I've a blasted cold coming on. That's what happens when you have to hang around damned hospitals. Where the hell was I?'

'Privacy,' prompted Thane.

'Right. But what we've got is a bank night-security man who says someone new has been turning up from the North British and Soviet Trade Agency for the last few weeks, to use the computer time. He has the right identification, that's all that matters to the bank, but he's been linking with their London embassy almost every week-night.'

'Do we know him?' Thane shrugged at another scowl from Andy Gallon. The Ayrshire detective would have to wait. 'If he isn't their regular man – '

'He isn't, and their regular man has taken a beautifully timed few days' leave,' said Jack Hart sarcastically. 'Will I surprise you? Nobody knows where.'

'What's going on?' asked Thane wearily. 'Do they know?'

'Our little Russian friends?' Hart sneezed again and swore again. 'Hell, yes. Some of them – I'd bet money on it. They're doing exactly what our people would do if it was happening to us. They're playing for time until they find someone high enough up to make a decision. Then we'll hear – but not before, not from the Ivans.'

Andy Gallon was whispering. Thane caught enough of it to understand, and nodded.

'Superintendent Gallon sent a description of a stranger seen with Jon Mark – '

'And now he's breathing down your neck about it,' surmised Jack Hart. 'Nothing yet – a possibility, yes, but nothing more. There's an outside chance it could tie in with something odd that Hodge, our tame insurance valuator, thinks he may have discovered. It's too early yet.' The Squad commander paused, giving Thane time to shake his head at Andy Gallon and be rewarded with a grimace. Then Hart switched it round. 'What about your end of things? Is anything more happening?'

'You'll be the first to know,' promised Thane.

'I'd damned well better be,' said Hart stonily. 'And Colin – '

'Sir?'

'I'm not going to ask how Detective Constable Craig gets herself back on duty, answering telephones,' said Hart grimly. 'Not now. But someone had better have a good answer when I do. Keep in touch.'

The line went dead. He had hung up.

'Well?' asked Andy Gallon impatiently as Thane replaced his own receiver. 'What's the story now?'

Thane told him, all of them. When he finished, Gallon scowled at him over those half-moon spectacles.

'So we're supposed to twiddle our fingers while some Soviet boss makes up his mind?'

'Be patient, Comrade Superintendent,' said Francey Dunbar in a stage whisper.

Gallon heard him, reddened, but restrained himself.

'Where the hell is Bernie Rice?' he demanded huskily. 'What's he doing – having a snooze somewhere?'

No one answered. If one detective sergeant might escape Andy Gallon's rage, it looked as if the other, nearer home, might be less lucky. Jock Dawson and The Animal faded away with the excuse that Dawson's dogs needed a chance to stretch their legs. Sandra Craig decided to locate more sandwiches and another cup of coffee, and Francey Dunbar had sense enough to make a diplomatic exit with her.

That left Thane and Gallon with only Pat Emslie for company, and the stubble-haired Transport Police inspector looked ready to escape by the window. Instead, the door clicked open and a wary but pleased Sergeant Rice walked in. He looked at Gallon, then at Thane and gave a twist of a grin.

'I think we've got them,' he said simply. 'David Mark's yacht is still lying at Inverkip marina. But he had an arrangement to borrow a boat from another owner. She's another motor sailer, *Corbie Three* – about the same size, black hull, white deckwork. She sailed early on Friday evening.'

'Friday evening?' Thane exchanged a glance with Pat Emslie and saw the same doubt. Friday evening began reaching into the time when Joan Haston had been murdered, when other things had been happening. 'Do we know who was aboard?'

'Yes, sir. I spoke to another skipper who saw *Corbie Three* leaving and – ' Rice saw Andy Gallon's baleful impatience and shortened it ' – David Mark took her out. There was someone else he says he has seen crew with David Mark before, and two strangers. One was a plump blonde woman, the other was a man – maybe late forties, thin, tanned face, short fair hair.'

'Did he speak with them?' demanded Gallon.

'No, sir.' Rice shook his head.

Thane took a deep breath and let it out slowly. He was satisfied. They had the first firm, totally independent sighting of John Gort and Janey Peters since Glasgow Airport. It was the first sighting of any kind to place the

Interface Man with any of the people who had brought him over from Spain.

'Did anyone see them go aboard?' asked Emslie.

'No.' Rice shook his head. 'Any marina is quiet around this time of year. But I don't think they sailed very far that evening – they could idle around until dusk, then anchor.'

'Maybe even come ashore?' suggested Thane.

'*Corbie Three* has a rubber dinghy.' Rice gave Superintendent Andy Gallon a cautious sideways glance. 'She had it on deck when we saw her yesterday.'

Gallon's eyes narrowed behind his spectacles. 'We were together all yesterday, Sergeant.'

'Yes, sir.' Rice nodded. 'A black hull, white deckwork – remember the yacht going in at Port Brannan? No sails, using her engine?'

'That one.' Andy Gallon swore hoarsely and viciously. 'You're sure?'

'No, sir,' said his sergeant. 'But the next best thing. She matches what I was told about her. If I wanted to park a boat that size where she wouldn't attract much attention – '

'You'd try Port Brannan.' Andy Gallon finished it for his sergeant then gave a slow, scowling nod. 'Who checked down there? The local man?'

Rice shook his head. 'We needed him at Turnberry. It was one of the cops drafted in from outside.'

'Whoever he is, I may just kill him if this is right,' said Gallon in a matter-of-fact way.

'Port Brannan.' Thane had to grab Andy Gallon's arm to break in on the exchange. 'Would one of you tell me where it is and what it is?'

'Sorry.' Gallon gave a wry nod of understanding. 'It's just beyond the south end of Turnberry, a pocket-sized old fishing village – or what's left of it. There's the old quay where an occasional fishing boat still ties up.

There's the Cleek Inn, as small as they come and next to the quay. It picks up some trade from golfers, maybe a few fishermen. A married couple ran it last time I went there.'

'Still do,' said Rice. 'There's nothing else. The old fishing cottages were abandoned years ago. Then most of them were demolished.'

'Suppose you tried telephoning?' suggested Pat Emslie who had been totally ignored. 'You could say you were a golfer, looking for a room – '

'I tried before I came through, Inspector,' said Rice. He gave a sad gesture with his hands. 'Their phone line is out of action. I checked with the exchange – they say it has been that way since late yesterday, that it's on a repair linesman's list for Monday.'

'Give me a moment,' pleaded Andy Gallon, his hoarse voice struggling to stay calm. He used some of his frustration to punch the side of a chair. 'Somebody did check there yesterday, spoke to a woman at the Cleek the way I was told?'

Rice gave a silent nod. Behind them, Thane saw Pat Emslie was ready to open his mouth. He kept the Transport Police inspector silent with a quick scowl. This was one for the two local men to sort out.

'I think I can maybe put some of it together for you, Thane,' said Superintendent Andy Gallon wearily. 'We're into October, right? That's end-of-season for a lot of places. Take Turnberry Hotel – it's closed down for redecorating, it opens again for Christmas. Turnberry is big, the Cleek is like a garden shed beside it. But we were told that the Cleek had shut down for a spell.'

'Being replumbed,' murmured Rice. 'They've put up Closed signs.'

'But the owners are still there, we were told it was checked, that there were no problems.' Gallon sucked his lips. 'That's it. Sorry. Apologies.'

'None asked,' said Thane. There were any number of possibilities for what had happened, including the chance that whoever had answered the door at the Cleek Inn had spoken with a gun close to her back. He glanced at his wristwatch. 'How long to get down there?'

'Half an hour,' said Gallon grimly. 'Give me a little longer if you want the local cop handy.'

'We need him,' agreed Thane. 'And we do it back-door style if we can, Andy. We don't charge in blowing bugles.'

'That's a pity.' Gallon made an effort to recover some of his humour. 'I was a Boy Scout the last time anyone gave me the chance to blow a bugle.' He raised a questioning eyebrow. 'Do we tell your boss?'

The telephone on the corner table began ringing before Thane could say anything. Pat Emslie, nearest, lifted the receiver and answered. Then he put his hand over the mouthpiece and grimaced at Thane.

'Commander Hart again, sir. For you, and he says it's urgent.'

'He's a commander,' muttered Rice under his breath. 'When you're a commander, everything is urgent.'

Thane grinned, went over and took the receiver from Emslie. Hart greeted him with a growl.

'We've got things starting to happen,' Thane told him. 'We may have them located.'

'Where?' demanded Hart.

'South of Turnberry. At what's left of a fishing village, Port Brannan.'

'What the hell could they do there?' Hart sounded surprised.

Briefly, factually, Thane told the Crime Squad commander what they knew. He didn't mention the failed police check. It wouldn't have helped anyone.

'I'm hoping you're right.' Hart's voice held a trace of tension as it came over the line. 'I've some news for you.

We thought this was big – it is, and it happens to be getting bigger!'

'The Soviet end?' asked Thane.

'Yes.' Hart managed to make the one word an agreement and a curse. 'Part of it from them – though that's like dragging out teeth. The rest is from Tina's insurance valuator pal. Peter Hodge has hit on some jewellery trade gossip that ties in.' The Squad commander broke off to sneeze and blow his nose. 'I'll give you the Soviet part first. Ready for a name?'

'Ready.' Thane saw Andy Gallon trying to overhear, and eased the phone a little way from his ear to make it easier for the Ayrshire man.

'Aleksey Novikov,' said Hart bitterly. 'He's a senior trade official attached to their London Embassy – our people say that part is genuine. He's no kind of secret agent. Novikov has been handling something special for several weeks, working out of the North British and Soviet Trade Agency in Scotland.'

'What do they mean by something special?'

'If you wait, you'll hear,' said Hart heavily. 'Just damned listen, will you?'

'Sorry.' Thane waited.

'Right.' Hart sneezed again. 'They're admitting it involved diamonds. They're admitting that Novikov was MIR, the Glasgow end of that computer traffic. UDA is the London Embassy. Basically, Novikov was running the operation, making most of the arrangements. No one else knew the final details – and now they can't find him, they're beginning to panic.'

'We're talking a lot of diamonds?'

'We're talking a hell of a lot,' snarled Hart. 'That's all they'll tell me – except that three so-called couriers took them north by road last week. The stones probably came into London by diplomatic bag.' He growled to himself.

210

'A lot of people are beginning to gather around, wanting to ask a lot of questions.'

'What's Peter Hodge's angle?' asked Thane, his lips feeling dry, his mind trying to cope with what he was being told.

'Your dark-haired golfing stranger, the one seen with the Mark brothers,' said Hart. 'Somebody else saw him, one of Hodge's jewellery contacts who plays golf. Your man is Thomas Brundell, he's Swiss based, and a big-league diamond merchant – but there's talk he's in major financial trouble.'

'Which could make him useful to the Marks.'

'There's more.' Hart said it with a grim satisfaction. 'Hodge decides to check the story. He tries another couple of jewellery trade contacts who are golfers. They haven't seen Brundell. But they've seen some people just as interesting – even spoken to some of them. Right now there are at least five of the world's top diamond buyers all just by chance in Scotland at the same time, all golfers, all staying more or less together, playing their way around the top Scottish courses. Ask why.'

It came together after a moment. Everything came together, from the very beginning.

'An auction?'

'A diamonds auction, a damned big one, and it has to run into a hell of a lot of millions.' Hart's voice was flat, holding his feelings down. 'That's how it stands, as of now. Whatever you've got already, stir in some Russians, maybe some diamond merchants, and a hell of a lot of diamonds.' He sighed. 'You know something? If things are the way we think, then Gort and the Peters woman have just become the world's worst life-insurance risks.'

It sounded that way.

'At least I know,' said Thane.

211

He said goodbye and hung up. A gust of wind outside made the glass of the hotel window shiver. The sky looked greyer than ever.

One hour later Colin Thane was crouching in the shelter of a patch of dark green gorse bush and scrub. Beside him Francey Dunbar used a pair of borrowed binoculars and peered ahead. Detective Superintendent Gallon was with them. So was a middle-aged mild-faced police constable whose strip of coastal beat included Port Brannan.

Everyone else and their vehicles were further back, behind a strip of woodland. Port Brannan was about five hundred yards ahead, dark and bleak under the grey sky, the wind sending waves crashing in along the rocks which formed the shore and lashing curtains of spray across its tiny harbour.

Inland, there were green fields and cattle were grazing. South along the shore, a few houses marked a road junction. North, the boundary edge of Turnberry golf course showed long fairways and fierce bunkers. A few golfers were still playing their way round, battling against the wind. In the far distance a white lighthouse tower marked a line of shoal rocks – and the course's tenth green. Nearer, the long outline of Turnberry Hotel lay like a luxury barracks block, the kind of barracks expected by vacationing millionaires.

Those five hundred yards ahead of the hidden four men, the Cleek Inn and Port Brannan were part of a different world.

The old fishing village lay at the end of a pot-holed track which ran close to the left of where they were hiding. It snaked down a gradual slope of scrub and trees, rough grass and weathered rock, coming from the nearest pretence of a main road near where the police vehicles were hiding. As it reached Port Brannan a

212

Closed sign nailed to a fence post was duplicated by another Closed sign slightly further down.

Thane eased on to his elbows and beckoned the constable over. The man wriggled across the ground with the ease of someone who knew the fields and hills as well as any poacher. Country cops usually saw nothing wrong with having an illegal deer carcase hanging in their garage, or a mysterious salmon lying in the family deep-freeze.

His name was Donny MacLean. He wore an old grey raincoat to hide his uniform, they'd collected him near Turnberry, and Thane was relying on him as guide.

'Study the place, take your time,' Thane told him. 'I want to know about anything different from usual – anything at all.'

MacLean nodded, eased a branch of bush a fraction to one side to give a better view, and began a slow, careful study.

'Francey.' Thane crawled a couple of yards and dropped down beside his sergeant, who still had the binoculars. 'Stay with the boat. Watch for any change there.' He glanced back at Andy Gallon, but the Ayrshire CID man was placidly chewing a strand of grass, content to wait.

From the moment they'd had their first glimpse of Port Brannan, it had taken an extra quarter of an hour to reach their present positions and avoid being seen from the old fishing village. Now, looking down that last gentle slope towards the place, Thane realized it was even smaller than he had expected.

The original fishing families who built Port Brannan had taken advantage of a narrow break in a low black outcrop of coastal rock. The original break, like a narrow channel, had run in from the sea then had broadened out in a mix of sand and shallow water behind the rocks. The result had been the foundation for a small breakwater and quay shaped like an inverted letter L.

Corbie Three was berthed against the section of quay formed by the inner edge of the breakwater arm. The breakwater's stonework, like the stonework around the rest of the harbour, was cracked and neglected. Any metal equipment left was rusted and broken, a snapped toy-sized crane lay toppled – and the black-hulled yacht almost had the harbour to herself. The only other craft were a few shabby open-decked fishing boats and an ancient ship's lifeboat, all lying deserted and beached along the inner shallows.

A man wrapped in a heavy duffel coat slouched down beside the *Corbie Three*'s deckwork, sheltering from the wind. They had already identified him as Beanbag Slater and the city thug looked miserable, his hands stuffed deep into the duffel coat's pockets. But from where he sheltered he had an all-round view of anything that might approach from sea or land – and the yacht was only a long stone's throw away from the Cleek Inn.

Narrow, grey and single-storey, the Cleek Inn was located a short distance back from the inner quay. Port Brannan's only remaining habitable building, it had a slate roof and the kind of narrow windows meant to keep out winter storms. The heavy front door was closed and most of the windows were shuttered. But the Cleek Inn was occupied. A tell-tale curl of smoke was rising from one of its chimneys, rising then being whipped away by the wind. A small van and an elderly car were parked outside, near where some fishing nets had been draped out along the quay to dry or be repaired.

To the rear there was a separate large building like a windowless barn. It had the look of a garage and storehouse, it had no windows, and the corrugated iron roof showed several patches. Further back, Thane could see traces of what had once been the foundations of cottage walls. Now the nearest seemed to be used as a rubbish tip. Another was littered with what looked like parts of an abandoned boat engine.

'Sir – ' hissed the local constable.

Thane nodded. 'Francey?'

'On him,' said Dunbar, tightening his grip on the binoculars.

A man had just slipped out of the Cleek Inn by a partly hidden side door. He was carrying a lightweight machine-pistol. For a moment he stood in the open and waved towards *Corbie Three* and Beanbag gave a grouchy wave back. Then the man turned and went over to the building with the corrugated roof. He dragged open the wide main door and left it open as he went inside.

'I can see cars.' Dunbar kept the binoculars steady, sucking an edge of moustache as he concentrated. 'Several of them. One is a damned Rolls-Royce, another two we know – David's Mercedes, brother Jon's Jaguar. There's another thing like a small truck.' He stopped. The man had emerged again and was pulling the door shut. He still had the machine-pistol but was carrying what looked like a small metal toolkit. He went back to the Cleek Inn and in by the same side door. It closed behind him. With a grunt of relief, Francey Dunbar lowered the binoculars. 'I've only seen Sailor Duffy as a Records photograph, sir. But the face matches.'

Thane nodded. They had identified two hired thugs, they had located where the Mark team had assorted transport hidden. But they needed more.

'I'll presume you saw that weapon,' said Andy Gallon huskily. He had abandoned the stalk of grass and eased nearer. 'That was a damned nine-mil Uzi – you didn't mention that kind of thing, did you?'

'I always forget to mention something,' admitted Thane sadly.

He looked down the low slope at the little harbour, a faint possibility beginning to shape in his mind. It was a

215

long-shot risk, but it might work. It amounted to balancing alternatives.

Down there, that old stone fishing inn could now be holding several captives. He could choose from a list – and they could all be there, from the Soviet diamond auction team to the group of diamond-dealer golfers, to any other innocents caught up in it like the Cleek Inn's staff – and he had to add two more, John Gort and Janey Peters.

What happened to all or any of them depended on what he decided next. If he waited, it might only be worse.

'Donny.' He beckoned, and Constable MacLean wriggled over. The local man seemed to be enjoying himself. Thane pointed towards the Cleek Inn. 'How well do you know that place?'

'I've been a few times, sir.' MacLean was wary. 'It's run by a young English couple, the Hamiltons. They've a live-in widow woman as a general help.'

'You know her too?' asked Gallon mildly.

'Not that way, sir.' MacLean shook his head. He faced Thane again. 'You wanted to know if I noticed anything different about the place, sir.'

Thane nodded. A new gust of wind was rustling and whistling through the scrub. Somehow, despite that sky, it still hadn't rained.

'Security,' said the local constable simply. 'Those Hamiltons were putting in all kinds of extra devices, like they were guarding the Crown Jewels. Tradesmen coming down from Glasgow to do the work too.' He shrugged. 'They've put in more. They've added outside floodlights.'

'Binoculars, Sergeant,' said Gallon curtly. He took the binoculars from a surprised Dunbar, used them briefly, then returned them. 'Floodlights, yes. But the expensive variety, with passive infra-red back-up. You can see the sensor units.' He grunted. 'We've just talked a couple of local high-risk drug warehouses into installing that kind of system, and it costs.'

Thane nodded. Invisible infra-red beams could be placed to act like a total barrier fence. Anything intruding into any of the beams at up to a hundred feet could cause floodlights to come on, could start sirens yelping, could even result in an automatic alarm being telephoned to the police. But he had a feeling the Interface Man would have coped without too much worry.

'That side door,' he said to the local constable. 'Where does it lead?'

'The back kitchen, sir.'

'Any better way in?'

MacLean thought. 'What about their security system, sir?'

'Forget it,' advised Thane.

'There's a built-on deep-freeze room at the rear,' said MacLean slowly. 'They knocked a door through to it from the main inn. There's a stupid wee window, sir – a thing any half-grown man could haul out with his hands.' He paused hopefully. 'It might be the way, sir.'

'We'll make it,' said Thane softly. 'Won't we, Francey?'

His sergeant grinned. 'No problem.' But then he thumbed towards *Corbie Three*. 'What about him? He'd see us.'

Thane nodded. Beanbag came first. He turned to Andy Gallon. 'We're going to need some help. Risky help.'

'You've got it,' said Gallon. 'When do we start?'

It took another fifteen minutes. The watchers beside the patch of scrub had changed and one was The Animal with the Heckler and Koch rifle. Another was Sandra

217

Craig, with the binoculars and using a hand-held radio. Twice during that fifteen minutes she used the radio and her voice murmured a warning of movement as someone appeared outside the inn. First it was Louise Croft, who was wearing her motorcycling leathers. She walked over to the yacht, went aboard for a moment, spoke to Beanbag, then returned to the inn. A little later, a dark-haired man emerged, nervously lit a cigarette, looked around, then tossed the cigarette away and went in again.

But by the end of these fifteen minutes several other things had happened – and three crouching, darting figures had covered a wide half-circle which took them down to the shore on the far side of the black rocks.

Colin Thane led the way as they tackled the rocks, cursing under his breath as he scrambled close above the pounding waves. Within moments he was being drenched in spray and there was a salt taste on his lips. Behind him Sergeant Francey Dunbar was making it all look easy. Last in their little line, the distinctive corn-stubble hair of Pat Emslie disappeared briefly as the Transport Police inspector stumbled on an edge of rock, went down, and struggled up again with a newly acquired limp.

Then they had made it. They were lying flat on the outer lip of the Port Brannan breakwater, the bare, pole-like mast of *Corbie Three* swaying gently only feet away in the sheltered harbour water.

Any noise they had made coming over the rocks would have been drowned by the sea and the wind. They still formed a steady background as Thane spoke into the hand-held radio he was carrying.

'Anything, Sandra?' he asked softly.

'Nothing, sir.' Her voice was a murmur from the tiny speaker.

He tucked the radio away, glanced at Dunbar and

218

Emslie, and nodded. Francey Dunbar drew his .38 Smith and Wesson, hefted it by the squat metal barrel, then edged over the top of the breakwater. Thane made a mental count of three, beckoned, and he followed with Emslie.

They dropped on to the quayside in time to see Francey Dunbar make a quick, cat-like leap across to the yacht's deck. Suddenly, he vanished behind the deck-house. There was the beginning of a startled cry, then the clear sound of the .38's butt connecting with Beanbag Slater's skull. Another moment and Dunbar reappeared dragging the limp figure of the fat man. With him came a sawn-off shotgun, attached to Beanbag's wrist by a short rope lanyard.

By then, Thane and Emslie were also aboard. They took the unconscious thug from Dunbar, and Emslie removed the man's duffel coat. Quickly the young Transport Police inspector pulled it on, took the sawn-off shotgun, then went round to the other side of the deckhouse to take over the same lookout position.

From the Cleek Inn, it should seem as if nothing had changed.

'Get this one below,' ordered Thane.

He helped Dunbar to drag their prisoner over to the yacht's cockpit. From there they bumped him down into the main cabin, which was a minor chaos of dirty crockery, half-eaten food and empty beer cans, signs that the last occupants had spent some time there. Looking around, Dunbar finally handcuffed the captive to the handle of a heavy metal locker.

By then the man was already making moaning noises and beginning to come round again. Francey Dunbar was always economical when it came to using force.

Thane used his radio. 'On schedule, Sandra. We'll give you a Go.'

'We'll wait for a Go,' her voice was a metallic whisper.

Francey Dunbar tapped a fist twice on the deckhouse bulkhead and an immediate, reassuring double-tap reply came from outside. Emslie had no problems. At their feet Beanbag Slater's eyes were open and he was looking up at them, dazed, just discovering the handcuffs. He started to moisten his lips, but they ignored him. Someone else had begun a slow, regular tapping aboard the *Corbie Three*, someone else who was somewhere near. Their prisoner heard it too. Suddenly, there was a new fear in his eyes.

'Where?' Thane prodded him with a foot.

The fat man looked past him, towards the closed door of the forepeak cabin. It was bolted shut on their side – and still the slow, regular tapping went on. Dunbar produced his .38 again and held it ready as Thane slid the bolt and pushed the door open.

They stared. They had found Janey Peters.

She was lying fully dressed on top of one of the bunks. She had been tied hand and foot, she was gagged, and she had been badly beaten. Both eyes were bruised and swollen, her face was cut, and earlier bleeding had dried around her split lips and damaged mouth. She made the same tapping noise once more, knocking her head against the side of the yacht, then those swollen slits of eyes stared at the two detectives with a flaring, desperate hope.

They removed the gag and cut her loose. While Thane helped her to sit upright, Dunbar cursed his way past Beanbag Slater then returned with some water in a cup. Thane held it to her lips as she took a first painful swallow, then another. She was suffering from cramp and showed it, but they couldn't wait.

'Where's Johnny?' asked Thane. 'At the inn?'

She nodded.

'Who did this?'

'David Mark.' Her voice wasn't much more than a whisper. 'We'd gone ashore – '

220

'And you tried to phone Pony?' Thane made a quick, soothing noise as she nodded again. 'She's safe.'

'They stopped me before I could make the call.' The woman took another painful sip at the water then gave Francey Dunbar a grateful nod as he tried to massage her wrists. 'They – they knew about Pony.'

So she had been beaten, while she denied making any previous calls. They had gone to collect Pony – and she had been beaten again when they returned after finding the police already there. John Gort, a gun against his spine, couldn't interfere. But she had still stuck to her story, and at last they had given up.

'They kept me alive because they needed Johnny,' she said simply. 'But they were still nervous – that's why they went in early.' Pausing, she tried to sit up, managed it, swung her legs over the edge of the bunk, and let Thane support her. 'You know about the diamonds?'

'Most of it.'

'They were going to go in after dusk tonight. The diamond buyers were to lunch here today, view the diamonds, then come back bid-and-buy style to-morrow.' She gave a noise which was meant to be a laugh. It hurt her. 'But Louise Croft persuaded them to go in this morning, at dawn – that was their mistake.'

'Why?' Thane stopped and cursed as the little personal radio came to life.

'We're ready for your Go,' reminded Sandra's voice unemotionally.

'Soon,' he answered shortly. 'Wait.'

There were things they had to know, things Janey Peters could tell them.

'You said a mistake,' prompted Francey Dunbar. 'What kind?'

'They got in.' She took another sip of water. 'The four Russians arrived yesterday, there were the hotel couple and their live-in woman, they thought they had enough security – '

But Aleksey Novikov and his three minders hadn't reckoned on anyone like the Interface Man. All the Cleek Inn's elaborate security systems had been knocked out. One Russian had been shot and wounded in a brief scuffle, then the invaders from *Corbie Three* were in control.

'They thought they knew everything,' said Janey Peters, almost enjoying it. 'All the systems, even all about the special strongbox safe Novikov had installed. But then they found an extra – there's a timelock on the safe door, it can't be opened before three this afternoon.'

'Johnny's working on it?' asked Thane.

She nodded.

'Where is this strongroom?'

'In the private function room off the cocktail bar.' Her voice was becoming more of a mumble, her mouth was obviously hurting. But those swollen slits of eyes were desperate in their intensity. 'If anything goes wrong, they'll kill Johnny – ' She stopped. 'You think they will anyway?'

'Yes.' said Thane. He gave her a moment. 'How well do you know the layout over there, Janey?'

She shrugged. 'I lived there the best part of the last two weeks and pretended to play golf on that stupid damned course – I was supposed to see all that was going on.'

'What about people?' asked Dunbar. 'The ones they're holding?'

'I don't know.' She shook her head. 'I heard the five diamond buyers arrive in two cars about an hour or so ago. They locked them up.' This time, she tried to stand and managed to stay up. 'You know that's how it all started – another diamond buyer knows Jon Mark, gave him the idea?'

'Brundell.' Thane nodded. 'We know about him.' He helped her to the door, where she could see Beanbag Slater lying handcuffed in the main cabin. 'Can you cope if we leave you with him?'

'That one?' Janey Peters glared at the fat man, who shrank back. 'Yes. It'll be nice . . . won't it, Beanbag?' Then she touched Thane's arm. 'About Johnny – '

'We'll try,' promised Thane. He used the little two-way radio again. 'Sandra. Go – repeat, Go.'

They were out on the yacht's deck, waiting behind the shelter of the deckhouse, as it began to happen. The car that came slowly but noisily down the track towards Port Brannan and the Cleek Inn certainly didn't look like a police car. It was one of the Crime Squad vehicles. It stopped on the quayside outside the Cleek Inn, the passenger door swung open, and Andy Gallon made a leisurely business of climbing out.

With his patched jacket and those half-moon spectacles, the Ayrshire detective superintendent looked as far removed as ever from any kind of policeman. Sergeant Rice, in his shirt sleeves, his tie hanging loose, got out from behind the wheel. Gallon ambled over to the Cleek Inn's door, made a show of finding it locked, and began banging on it with his fist.

'Now,' said Thane, and nudged Dunbar.

'Good luck,' murmured Pat Emslie, still hunched in the open wearing Beanbag's duffel coat, still on apparent lookout duty.

Andy Gallon could give them two, maybe three minutes of distraction. They could hear his loud, hoarse complaints that he and his friend were customers and wanted a drink – and by then Thane and Dunbar were darting along the short length of breakwater from one rusting piece of cover to the next.

They had almost reached the side of the old inn

building when they heard the front door click open and another voice answer Andy Gallon's continued protests. Gallon was out of sight now, but still noisily keeping it going. Then, hugging the shelter of the stonework, they had made the rear of the building and in another moment were crouching beside the freezer-room extension.

The little window was there, just as the local constable had described. The wooden frame looked more than insecure. Francey Dunbar grinned, reached inside his jacket and brought out the short metal tyre lever he'd borrowed from Jock Dawson's Land-Rover. But Thane stopped him, pointing. Below the window, almost at ground level, a small services hatch was equally inviting.

It yielded at Dunbar's first try. There was a short protesting splintering of wood, then it came away from the wall as Dunbar tried again.

From round the front of the building they heard the main door slam shut and Andy Gallon make a slow withdrawal towards his car, still loudly complaining to the world at large. Then his car started up.

As it began to drive away, Thane and Dunbar were wriggling in through the gap where the services hatch had been. Inside the freezer room several big chest-freezer units were quietly humming. The door into the main hotel faced them.

Drawing his .38, glancing at Dunbar to see he had done the same, Thane tiptoed over and tried the door handle. It turned, the door opened a crack, and he looked into the Cleek Inn's deserted dining room. They went through into it, then heard voices. Cautiously, pausing every other step, they went towards the voices and entered the cocktail bar.

The function room was ahead, exactly as Janey Peters had described it – but with the overhead lights blazing down on a group of people gathered around the big, glinting strongbox safe lying in the middle of the floor. It was as big as a desk, its metal had a strange, almost space-age sheen, and a panel of winking lights flashed above the door at the front.

'Now get on with it,' ordered David Mark. The tall, lanky Computer Cabin sales manager stood scowling over John Gort, who was making a delicate adjustment to a meter-like device he'd attached above the winking lights. Mark turned. 'Has that idiot gone?'

'They've driven back up the track,' confirmed Jon Mark, standing by the room's shuttered window.

They were all there. Sailor Duffy lounged in a corner, the Uzi machine-pistol propped beside him. Louise Croft stood nearby, her hands in the pockets of her motorcycle jacket, her face impassive, ignoring the dark-haired stranger beside her. They had found Thomas Brundell, the man who had first launched the whole scheme.

'Well?' demanded David Mark.

'I'm trying,' said John Gort wearily. He rose from his crouch beside the strongbox safe. He turned to face David Mark. For an instant he was looking straight out at Thane. He stiffened, then forced a grin at Mark. 'Everything takes time – '

David Mark cuffed him hard across the face.

'Go, Francey,' said Colin Thane.

Three steps forward took them into the function room, then Louise Croft screamed a warning.

'Armed police,' yelled Francey Dunbar, his .38 coming up in the Squad's two-handed firing grip. 'Freeze – everybody.'

'Go, Sandra! Go, go, go,' shouted Thane into the handset radio, his own .38 ready.

The woman was still screaming. Brundell had dived for cover behind the safe – and David Mark came round snarling, drawing a revolver from a shoulder holster.

Francey Dunbar fired twice, and as David Mark crumpled, it was his brother's turn. Jon Mark charged across the room as if he'd gone berserk, hands clawing for Thane. Stepping back, Thane clubbed him on the side of the head with the barrel of the .38 and Jon went down.

'For God's sake, look out,' bellowed John Gort.

An instant later, Francey Dunbar shoved Thane down and dropped with him. Sailor Duffy had grabbed the machine-pistol. His first wild burst ripped over their heads. There was another, then Duffy was running – and Louise Croft had already gone.

Thane scrambled up. Francey Dunbar was clutching one arm where a bullet had grazed him. He gestured Thane on his way.

The front door lay open. As Thane reached it he heard vehicles racing down the track towards the inn – and saw Sailor Duffy standing only twenty feet away, the machine-pistol pointing again.

A single shot from a high-powered rifle sounded from the patch of scrub on the slope. Sailor Duffy straightened, his mouth dropped open in surprise, and then he fell dead. The Animal and the Heckler and Koch rifle seldom missed.

Thane heard footsteps behind him and swung round. It was John Gort, still looking dazed, uncertain about all that was happening.

'Janey – ' began Gort.

'She's safe.' Thane looked around again. They still hadn't seen Louise Croft.

A moment later, he understood why. A motorcycle engine snarled into life, then a slim leather-clad figure on a Yamaha trail bike came racing out from the barn-like shed.

Louise Croft handled the machine beautifully. The wind catching her hair, she brought the Yamaha skidding round the corner of the shed, on to the track. At the same moment Jock Dawson's big, battered Land-Rover dog-van came storming down towards the quay.

They collided hard. The Land-Rover skidded to a halt, Rajah and Goldie barking furiously in the rear. The Yamaha was hurled a clear fifteen feet by the impact, scraping along the quayside stones.

Louise Croft was thrown almost twice as far. She lay with her head twisted at the obscene angle that meant a broken neck. But there was no way a white-faced Dawson could have avoided her.

Other people were arriving – Pat Emslie from the yacht, the others from the hill, including Andy Gallon. Wordlessly, Thane went back into the room where the strongbox safe lay glinting. Francey Dunbar was there. David Mark had two bullets in his chest, but would live. His brother was already trying to sit up, Brundell had reappeared from cover.

'We'll need an ambulance,' said Francey wryly.

'And you go along with it,' said Thane. He saw John Gort had come back in and was standing beside the safe. He smiled at the Interface Man. 'This one beat you.'

'Forty million dollars' worth,' said Gort softly.

He shrugged, reached forward, and spun a dial. The safe quietly clicked open. For a couple of seconds Thane saw a great mass of glinting stones. Then Gort pushed the door shut again.

'I just thought something might turn up,' mused Gort. 'So I waited. Where's Janey?'

They sent him on his way to the yacht.

Then confusion took over. Ambulances arrived. They found the hotel people locked in one bedroom, five frightened diamond merchants in another. The four Russians, one of them with a bullet in his shoulder, had been bound hand and foot and incarcerated in their own security van.

227

Sailor Duffy was dead, Louise Croft was dead. But that left the Mark brothers, Beanbag and Brundell. There was a lot of work remaining. There had to be other people on the sidelines, people to be found and dealt with.

It was another Thursday, almost a month later and coming up to Christmas, when Colin Thane next drove out to Glasgow Airport. It was mid-afternoon, and the public-address system was giving a last call for passengers on the outward British Airways flight to Malaga.

He used his warrant card to get through security into the international departure area. He saw them straight away among the passengers and went over.

'Superintendent.' John Gort gave him a twisted half-smile. 'I thought you might be along.'

'Somebody had to make sure you went,' said Thane.

He looked past the Interface Man. Janey Peters' face had mended well, though she would always have at least two new scars. Elizabeth Lewis was with her, leaning on her stick, smiling. Pony and Tiger were back together.

'They need each other,' said Gort softly. 'I've plenty of room.' He looked at Thane. 'It's over?'

'For you,' said Thane.

It had to be. Officially, most of it hadn't happened – not the Interface Man's role, not any mention of diamonds or a proposed diamond auction. The Russians wanted it that way, wanted it very badly. They were busy enough trying to hush up the fact that they'd planned a sneaky test-attempt to abolish the middleman in their diamond sales. A few officials had planned it on their own, and now they were learning that over-enthusiastic capitalism had its own risks.

So officially, there had been an attempted hold-up of some distinguished members of the international jewellery trade, who had been visiting Scotland on a golf outing.

228

The rest, the way both Hastons had been murdered, the deaths at the Cleek Inn, would be for the courts. Tidied.

'I won't be back,' said John Gort.

'Good,' said Thane.

They shook hands and he turned away.

He stayed in his car until he saw the Boeing jet take off for Spain and sunshine. The Ford's radio had been muttering about an armed hold-up north of the river. The gunman had been wearing a Santa Claus rubber face mask.

He'd been caught. By two dogs from a passing dog-van.

'Ho-ho-jinglebells-ho,' said Colin Thane to the muttering set. 'Don't forget the holly in the handcuffs.'

He called Control, advised the operator he was off watch and off duty, then switched off the radio.

It was time he went home.